Crackshot

CRACK SHOT

Roger Busby

G.K. Hall &Co. • **Chivers Press**
Thorndike, Maine USA **Bath, Avon, England**

This Large Print edition is published by G.K. Hall & Co., USA
and by Chivers Press, England.

Published in 1996 in the U.S. by arrangement with Watson, Little
Ltd.

Published in 1996 in the U.K. by arrangement with the author.

U.S. Softcover	0-7838-1868-8	(Paperback Collection Edition)
U.K. Hardcover	0-7451-4966-9	(Chivers Large Print)
U.K. Softcover	0-7451-4967-7	(Camden Large Print)

The text of this Large Print edition is unabridged.
Other aspects of the book may vary from the original edition.

Set in 16 pt. Century Schoolbook.

Printed in the United States on permanent paper.

British Library Cataloguing in Publication Data available

Library of Congress Cataloging in Publication Data

Busby, Roger.
    Crackshot / Roger Busby.
        p.   cm.
    ISBN 0-7838-1868-8 (lg. print : sc)
    1. Large type books. I. Title.
[PR6052.U76C73 1996]
823'.914—dc20   96-20627

For Maureen

CHAPTER 1

The Brown Bag Bandit was feeding OO Buck into a Sage Sidewinder. Five fat magnum shells, each containing twelve copper-jacketed pellets instead of the standard nine. On fully automatic the stubby shotgun could put sixty chunks of lead into the air with devastating firepower.

It was Thanksgiving Eve in New York City and the Bandit was sitting on a studio couch in a fifth-floor apartment at the Hotel Martinique, a gloomy Empire-style monstrosity at West 32nd Street and Broadway. He was naked but for a towel wrapped around his waist, his thick black hair wet from the shower.

The Bandit held the shotgun vertical, the pistol grip braced against his knee as he picked up each of the cartridges laid out beside him and slid them carefully into the pump magazine slung beneath the short barrel. The action could be racked for single shot or with the trigger held depressed each new shell would spring into the breech as the spent cartridge ejected. The shotgun was just 24 inches long, ideal for concealment.

'I sure as hell don't know what's happening to this town,' the girl continued her one-sided conversation as the Bandit remained absorbed in the ritual of loading the weapon. 'I mean, I came out of the Firefly, what was it, two — two-thirty — this morning and this kid grabs me, couldn't have been more than nine, ten years old and he's doing rock. Little hustler, I was his momma I'd've torn his heart out.' The girl was wearing a sheer silk blouse and a black leather miniskirt. She sat beside the Bandit, her dancer's legs drawn up under her and tossed her tawny mane in disgust. 'I mean, kids like that running around the streets that time of night pushing crack.' She tossed her hair again. 'You used to know where you were around Manhattan. The gangsters were all guineas and street kids were jiving around like *West Side Story* with weird names on the backs of their jackets, taking swipes at each other with switch blades. Now all you've got is babies messing with your life. I ought to write to the goddamn Mayor.'

The Bandit continued his silent communion. The shotgun had always been his favorite weapon. It commanded instant respect, and if things went wrong it did not demand great skills of marksmanship to get the job done. Yes, the shotgun always delivered.

'I've been meaning to ask you,' the girl said, watching him with growing fascination. 'You doing something with Marco?' Briefly she thought about her boss, the Colombian who owned the Firefly Club on 42nd Street where she performed as an erotic dancer. He had introduced them a month ago and right away the Bandit had moved in with her, taken her to bed without preamble, sweet and tender as a long-time lover. Made her tingle. 'Not that I'm prying, you understand,' she hastened on. 'Only I ought to warn you that Marco's a bad, bad dude, if you rub him the wrong way. You're doing something with Marco, you just watch yourself, that's all I'm saying.'

The Bandit ran his fingers lovingly down the length of the weapon and continued his meditation.

'Oh, and something else,' the girl said. 'I've been thinking about what you were saying about blood and all that born again thing. OK, I'll buy it, so maybe the Sundance Kid didn't die at — where was it? — San Vicente, only how can you tell you're his kin? I mean, how do you know for sure?'

The Bandit finished loading the Sidewinder and turned his face to her, still holding the shotgun erect. 'Hey,' the girl said, entranced by the phallic appeal of the stubby weapon, 'maybe I could use that thing in the act, sort of Annie Oakley routine, what d'you think?'

She looked into his eyes then and saw something so dangerous that she felt herself shudder as she leaned forward and shimmied against the shotgun. The feel of the silk against the cold gunmetal as her breasts brushed the gun brought her nipples up hard. Her lips parted in a soft sigh as she reached along his thigh murmuring: 'Baby . . . are you turning me on.' Her eyes glazed and with the shotgun pressed between them she drew the Bandit down on to the couch and began to work the tight miniskirt up over her hips. 'You do this with anybody else,' she whispered, 'I swear I'll kill you.'

Ten blocks north at the corner of West 42nd Street and 6th Avenue Byrne and Hennessy were setting up their hot dog stand. It was mid-morning and traffic was already heavy at the intersection under a hanging sign from which a radiator grille ensnared in a barred red circle snarled the legend: *Gridlock busters — don't block the box!* Across the street the First Federal Bank rose in a stark black and white tower, etched against the surrounding high rise.

'You ought to see this guy, this brother-in-law of mine, he was driving trucks all his life. Macs, eighteen-wheelers, and all the time he's to hell and gone, up to Canada, down to Florida, barrelling down the highway, what a life. Free as a breeze, so what's he do, this bozo, he throws it all away. Just like that. He came back from Orlando or somewhere where he's been getting a healthy tan, and he walks right into the office and he throws his keys down on the boss's desk and says, "I quit." So what's he do? Goes into the fast food business and right away he's making a fortune, everything he touches turns to gold. Now I'll tell you, this guy, he looks like Paul Newman, crinkly blue eyes and all the charm, and he's got the girls drooling all over him only he's giving them the freeze, he's so busy making bucks. Which brings me to my point, we've got to be doing something wrong here.'

Michael Byrne kept the monologue going as he man-handled the box cart into position and Patricia Hennessy put up the gaudy red and yellow parasol emblazoned with the Frank-furter legend.

'You're smothering the goddamn things with ketchup is what's wrong here. How many times have I got to tell you, Mike, you don't do what you're doing, which is murdering the whole thing with the lousy ketchup. Who d'you think's going to want to eat a hot dog looks like its throat's been cut, for Christ's sake?'

Hennessy stood back, hands on hips, and watched Byrne crouch down, getting the gas burners started. She was wearing jeans and a blue jacket with her hair tucked under a woollen watch cap.

'I happen to like ketchup,' Byrne said, get-ting to his feet now the burners were alight and setting a jumbo sauce container in the shape of a giant tomato on the front of the

11

narrow counter. With a grin and a flourish he said: 'What I aim to do is go down in history as the hot dog man who turned New York into the Big Tomato.' He hitched his jerkin over his workshirt, wiped his hands on his cords and tugged a baseball cap over his eyes.

'I ought to call that brother-in-law of yours,' Hennessy said. 'Get him to come down here and give you a few pointers.'

Byrne ripped open a packet of Frankfurters and deposited the pink sausages into the pan as the heat came up. 'You know what would happen if you did that? All you'd do is fall in love with the guy in ten seconds flat and then he'd break your little heart.' He danced around the stand and before she could dodge him, reached out and playfully pinched her cheek.

Looking sleek, the Brown Bag Bandit came out of the lobby of the Martinique and paused under the canopy, pockmarked with sockets from which light bulbs had long since disappeared. The first two letters of the once illuminated hotel sign which ran across the front of the building were also missing and trash now littered the entrance where a liveried doorman had once stood sentinel.

The Bandit had dressed carefully in a conservative grey business suit, blue button-down Brooks Brothers shirt, a striped club tie and tasselled loafers. His tan trenchcoat was unbuttoned and tinted Ray-bans added the final touch to the image of a Wall Street yuppie. Under the coat he carried the Sidewinder in a quick-release holster slung below his left shoulder, the butt facing forward just above his waist.

As he turned towards Broadway and began to walk, the Bandit felt the pulse of the city quicken. He began to stroll leisurely uptown, reflecting that he had not always regarded himself in such flowery terms, not until some whimsical hack on the *Daily News* had coined the phrase when comparing him to a latter-day Robin Hood, pulling down fat cats to help the needy — all because he'd cannoned into a waddling tub of lard on a fast heist and she'd grabbed a roll of greenbacks as packets of bills skittered across the sidewalk and squawked to the press about a heaven-sent windfall. Maybe the reputation had been worth that five grand because it was after that that he began to think himself into the romantic image of a born again Sundance Kid and his inclination to pit his wits against New York's Finest blossomed into a compulsion. Armed robbery, he concluded, was an art form, a hitherto unexplored tributary of show business, and he determined to become its finest exponent, relishing each thirty-second performance on the security videos like a Hollywood première.

Strolling up Broadway on the swelling

13

throng of sightseers, he savoured his pride in the majesty of Manhattan, the kid from Jersey who had stood in the weeds of the derelict docks and stared across the Hudson at the spiky skyline dreaming of fame and fortune in that magic place across the river. The pride of an adopted son.

It was a crisp morning. The steam rising from the ornate manhole covers and billowing from the chimneys positioned over the road-works cast a veil over the street scene. Tomorrow it would all burst into colour as Macy's parade heralded the start of the Christmas season and he would maybe take a stroll up to Central Park to see the start of the procession, but right now the adrenalin was flowing as he neared the junction of West 42nd Street and 6th Avenue and began to psych himself up for his performance. Everything suddenly clicked into sharp focus.

Across the street from the First Federal Bank a noisy argument was taking place. A beefy Con Ed repairman, his AMC pickup angled in to the kerb, was haranguing a pair of hot dog sellers.

'What happened to Barney?' the repairman demanded querulously, beer belly bulging out the front of his overalls, a fur cap with ear flaps perched on his head.

'I told you, buddy, I don't know any Barney,' Byrne replied.

'You stole his spot, right?'

'Whose spot?' Hennessy asked.

'Barney . . . Barney . . . had a gimpy leg. This was always his spot.'

'Look, we don't know any Barney, you got that, fella?' Byrne said.

'Steal a cripple's spot. Jesus!' the repairman said, 'I ought to report you.'

'You want a hot dog, mister?' Hennessy said.

'You kidding?' The repairman was outraged. 'Sure I wanted a hot dog. I wanted one of Barney's hot dogs. I've been getting myself ready all morning, one of Barney's Franks, melt in your mouth. So I pull over and what do I find? A couple of chiselers swiped Barney's spot.'

A brown uniformed traffic supervisor gave up trying to unscramble the snarl-up at the intersection and ambled across. She was a stocky woman with gold-rimmed spectacles and a malevolent gleam in her eye.

'Your truck, mister?' she asked the repairman.

'Well, it ain't Santa's sleigh,' the Con Ed stalwart retorted sarcastically.

'Move it!' The brown suit jerked her thumb. 'That's a traffic violation. No standing on this street.'

'In case it's escaped your notice,' the repairman said, squinting down at her, 'that says "Emergency Service" on the side of that truck there. Con Ed emergency. I can stick that baby wherever I like.'

The traffic supervisor's expression hardened as she reached for her pad.

'You write me up, you're going to have to eat it.'

'Friend, you want a hot dog or not?' Byrne said.

'I don't buy hot dogs off cripple-robbers. Give me a juice.'

'For another thing, you're in the fire lane, that's another misdemeanour.'

'What flavour?'

'I'll take pineapple.'

'You'll take a ticket, you don't move that truck, and I mean right now.'

'We don't have pineapple.'

'What do you have?'

Byrne said: 'We have hot dogs.'

'I tell you where you can stick your hot dogs!' the repairman exploded, and the rest of the exchange was lost as the Bandit judged his moment and stepped off the street and into the bank.

Just inside the smoked glass armoured door an overweight guard leaned against a pillar and stifled a yawn. Without hesitating, the Bandit walked across the business area to the nearest teller's position behind which sat a black girl with a tight afro and a welcoming expression on her face. As he approached her the Bandit glanced up and saw the eye of the security camera give him the once-over and then move on. As the video lens tracked away he stood in front of the girl.

'May I help you?' she asked brightly and returning her smile the Bandit reached inside his trenchcoat with his right hand and with one smooth movement produced the Sidewinder, laying the fore-stock on the desk as he used his body to shield the gun from sight. Her eyes popped.

With his left hand the Bandit proffered a folded brown paper grocery bag. Very calmly he told the girl: 'You sure can. Just take the money out of your cash drawer there, just the bills. Leave the last few in so the spring clip doesn't set off the alarm, put the money in the brown bag here and nobody's going to get hurt.'

The girl's eyes widened into saucers as she stared at the shotgun and the Bandit prompted her. 'Honey, you're looking at the Brown Bag Bandit. You're going to be famous, you're going to be on Eye Witness News.'

He grinned. 'Now just hand over the money like company policy.'

His eyes flicked upwards as she obeyed him, scooping packs of banknotes into the paper bag, and when he saw the lens of the camera stop suddenly and snap back towards him, he moved his position to make sure they'd get his best profile.

In the street outside the bank the Con Ed

repairman continued to rail against the injustice of the world. 'Jesus, a working guy takes a minute to pull over for a bite, what's he find? A couple of cheapies have stifled his old pal. This has got to be Sick City.'

Byrne grinned as the man stomped back to his pickup. 'Have a nice day!' he called after him.

Patti Hennessy had turned and was looking across at the bank, a puzzled frown forming on her face. 'Mick!' she exclaimed. 'Over there, look . . . the bank over there . . . something funny's going on.'

The Bandit came out of the bank holding the bulging brown bag in the crook of his arm. He was crossing the street, walking diagonally towards the hot dog stand when Patti saw his face clearly. It was the face she had seen a hundred times before; a face about to be swallowed up by the crowd thronging the sidewalk. She felt her stomach knot. Inside the fringe of the hot dog parasol where a selection of mug shots were taped out of sight, she saw the very same staring back at her from a photograph. 'Mike!'

Byrne reacted, unzipping his body warmer to reveal the NYPD patrolman's shield pinned to the lining as he went for the four-inch Smith and Wesson hidden in his waistband.

'Hey, you!' he challenged the Bandit who was almost abreast of them, walking briskly. 'Police, hold it!'

The instant he saw the flash of the tin, the Bandit dropped his bag, his right hand snaked inside his coat and snatched out the Sidewinder, his left hand grasping the slider. Very fast.

Byrne was still tugging his revolver from its holster when he saw the trenchcoat flap open and the weapon swing around towards him.

Instinctively he shoved his partner aside with a yell: 'Shotgun! Get down!' Knowing it was already too late.

The Bandit's lips twisted into a sneer as he opened fire. On automatic the Sidewinder delivered all five shells in rapid succession, the ripple recoil jerking the Bandit into a marionette jig as his fusillade raked the hot dog stand with buckshot, shredding its flimsy panels.

Thrown off balance, the Bandit stumbled over his booty lying where he had dropped it at his feet. The bag ruptured, scattering packs of high denomination dollar bills across the pavement. Like with the fat lady, the Bandit clicked off a flash of *déjà vu,* his feet, already running, flying from under him, and as he went down, he began to laugh.

In the same split second Patti Hennessy recovered from Byrne's shove and found that her police issue .38 Smith was somehow in her hands, held out in front of her in a two-handed shooter's grip, her knees bent, body crouched forward and a voice rising above the

19

keening in her ears was shouting: 'Police! Freeze or I'll shoot!' The man in the trench-coat, sprawled in the pile of greenbacks, looked up at her, laughing.

Her head threatened to burst from the howling inside her skull and her heart hammered against her ribs. 'Face down, spread your arms and legs! Don't look at me!' In astonishment as she fought down her panic, she recognized the voice as her own and discovered in equal amazement that she had unconsciously pulled the trigger through the first movement of the double action and another hairsbreadth would discharge the revolver she held steady on the man's head.

The Bandit lay still and as fright subsided she willed herself to ease off the trigger. Reality was returning and with it a new nightmare. 'Mike!' she called out to her partner not daring to glance away from the Bandit. 'Mike? Mike!' Out of the corner of her eye she caught a glimpse of Byrne's body sprawled beside the toppled hot dog stand, unmoving, the face and chest a mass of blood. Blood everywhere! Splashed across the pavement, flecking her own clothing. Thick, red blood. She almost gagged at the horror of it, her legs threatening to buckle under her. The street swam in and out of focus.

People . . . scattering, running . . . 'Mike! Mike!' An edge of panic sharpened her voice. There was no response from her fallen partner and she felt an overwhelming vengeful rage well up within her, silently urging the man under her gun to try to make a break for it, give her the excuse to finish it right there and then.

Carefully, not fully trusting herself, Patti took one hand off the pistol, reached out the radio from under her jacket and pressed the talk button. 'Nine Eddy portable,' she repeated their call sign trying to keep her voice from shaking, 'Ten-thirteen . . . ten-thirteen . . . shots fired West 42nd Street and 6th. Officer down . . . officer down . . .' Knowing that this most dreaded of all radio codes would bring the bluesuits falling out of the sky to help her.

With his cheek against the flagstones the Brown Bag Bandit was still chuckling at the irony of the moment. 'Shut up!' Patti Hennessy screamed at him as she edged around and kicked the shotgun away. A crowd was gathering, a circle of staring eyes keeping their distance, yet fascinated, watching her like a freak at a peepshow. In desperation she took another glance at Michael Byrne, saw that he was on his back, his face and upper body drenched red. His poor face! Less than half a minute ago they had been kidding round, and now in an instant he was dead. It was just too cruel. The chuckling Bandit drove her crazy. 'Just goddamn SHUT UP!' she yelled at the prostrate figure. In the distance she could hear the whoops of the sirens as units responded to her 10.13. Soon they would be at her side. Soon it would over. Hurry . . . please hurry! Her arm holding the gun was aching terribly and she feared she might faint now that the shock was setting in. Her peripheral vision caught movement and she stole a glance back at Byrne and immediately her heart leaped into her throat as she believed she saw him begin to sit up. Sweet Jesus, hurry, she pleaded silently, I'm hallucinating! Before her disbelieving eyes the dead Michael Byrne slowly rose up and began to explore the sticky mess of his face. The sirens were growing louder.

On the point of swooning, Patti heard her own voice croak, 'Mike?'

His face split into a grin as he licked a finger. 'Ketchup,' he said.

CHAPTER 2

Balancing two cartons of coffee on top of a flat pizza box, a uinformed cop came out of the Pizza Hut on West 35th street and ambled towards a newish brick and cement four-storey building outside which blue and white radio patrol cars were echelon parked against the kerb. Across a beige concrete canopy jutting out over the sidewalk bronzed lettering spelled out *Midtown Precinct South.*

Three shallow steps led up to an entrance flanked by green wall lamps bearing the precinct designation. The cop shouldered open one of the mesh-protected swing doors which bore the emblem of the New York Police Department and stepped into the gritty artificial light inside the lobby.

Drabness pervaded the scene as the predators and their victims mingled with the bluesuits who tried to keep some semblance of order in this slice of highrise Manhattan. Underfoot the concrete floor had long since blackened into glassy smoothness by the constant tramp of the thick-soled, heavy-duty footwear favoured by generations of street cops. Behind the rail of a chest-high desk which divided off the left-hand side of the room the shirtsleeved station shift was preoccupied with the routine of running the house. A radio base station chattered incessantly. Overhead, flying above the mayhem, a blue and gold banner proclaimed: *Busiest in the World.*

Still balancing the pizza and coffee in one hand, the new arrival hitched the belt around his waist, sagging under the weight of assorted law enforcement paraphernalia, nodded amiably to the nearby desk man, who wore bright new sergeant's chevrons on his collar and a string of merit bars above the dull badge on his chest, and swung left down the corridor which led to the captain's office.

There were two men in the room, which held a pair of steel desks cluttered with paperwork and a selection of mismatched chairs. One wall exhibited a display of weekly crime graphs below a street map, across which swarmed a rash of pin markers. Diffused by the grille protecting the dust-caked windows, the thin November daylight fought a losing battle with the gloom.

'With all due respect —' Vince Walker was laying on the sarcasm — 'Chief Hanson don't know nothing about what's going on out there on the streets.' He broke off when the pizza cop walked in.

'Oh, thanks, Roy.' Captain Ted Kietel sitting behind the far desk brushed aside a lick of hair which had fallen across his forehead and took two inches of cigar out of his mouth. The uniform set his delivery down on the edge of the desk and grinned. 'Sure, boss, any time.'

'Do I owe you?'

'Nah, it's OK.'

He turned and went out, closing the door behind him.

'Chief Hanson.' Walker returned to the attack, pronouncing the name scathingly. 'Since when did Chief Hanson have the first idea what's going on out there? He's sitting pretty down at Police Plaza, playing politics while we're cleaning up the open sewers of this town. You and me, Ted.' He tapped his chest. 'You and me!'

'Now take it easy, Vince,' Keitel retorted, rolling the soggy end of the White Owl around in his mouth and blowing smoke rings. 'I'm not saying he's right. Right's got nothing to do with it. All I'm saying is Hanson's Chief of Patrol and you're a precinct detective —'

'First grade,' Walker interjected, and Kietel waved a hand in a weary gesture. He took the butt out of his mouth and jabbed it across the desk to emphasize the point. 'First grade, captain, deputy inspector, whatever, don't make one iota of difference. If the Chief of Patrol says he don't want your Street Narcotics Unit in plain clothes, then that's all there is to it. Chain of command. Now tell me you've got that through your thick skull?'

They stared at each other for a moment,

neither giving ground. Two men, both in their forties, classmates from the Academy and now twenty-five-year veterans whose paths through the labyrinthine structure of the New York Police Department had taken markedly different routes.

Ted Keitel, slim, trim and dapper in blazer and tan slacks, had been the youngest captain on the force, the highest rank achievable by competitive civil service test. That had been four years ago and now the captain was hungry for his next promotion, to deputy inspector and maybe right on up to Chief of Department. But only now that those dizzy heights seemed attainable did he fully appreciate the painful fact that all ranks above his own were within the gift of the Police Commissioner and so at this critical stage in his career it certainly wouldn't do to buck the Chief of Patrol. This he hoped his bleak expression would convey to the ornery critter across the desk.

Vince Walker read the message in the captain's eyes, but backing down was not in his nature. By contrast, Walker was taller, lanky and rawboned, the long planes of his face deeply lined, accentuating a wide mouth on which hovered a sardonic smile.

Twice commended for outstanding valour in his early years on the streets of East Harlem, three times *Daily News* hero-of-the-month, Walker had been a natural for the detective division in a time when field promotions to the brotherhood of the gold shield were the order of the day. But for all their carefully cultivated mystique, the detectives, who had their own order of seniority, rising from third to second and ultimately first grade, were in truth just patrolmen assigned to plain clothes duty and outranked by the newest uniformed sergeant.

Yet some measure of the legendary gold shield could be gained from the fact that Vince Walker, looking like a throwback to the 'sixties in his cheap grey sateen-sheened suit, an unfashionably narrow electric blue tie stencilled with a flower power pattern blazing from the front of his yellow shirt and lovingly preserved elastic-sided brown leather cordovans, could lounge effortlessly in his captain's office and challenge a dictate from the highest echelons of the Department.

'Look, Ted,' he began again, 'you know the score as well as I do.' His bony wrists protruded several inches from his shirt cuffs. 'We've got dealers down in Bryant Park right outside the library pushing crack like they're sodajerks. So what happens? The uniforms pull 'em in on some nickel and dime thing, possession of a prohibited substance, some shit like that, and what do they do, they go to court and right away they're let off by the judge who's running through his caseload like he's checking off the grocery list and in an hour they're back in the park with the bleepers on swarming like locusts, pushing the product. And why? I'll tell you, Ted: because these dudes are more scared of the whole-salers across the river in Brooklyn, who're going to come over that bridge with baseball bats the minute they don't meet their quo-tas, than they ever are of the majesty of the law.

'So the only impression we ever make on the goddamn epidemic which is turning our young people into space cadets is by hitting 'em where it hurts. And in case it's escaped your notice, that's exactly what my SNU under-covers have been doing, breaking up the party. We already got 'em fragmented all over mid-town, on the run and so jumpy they're even dealing right out the back of the house here, they're getting so desperate. Now we're not through yet. Pretty soon those schmucks across the river are going to get the message that this is no longer such a good proposition and they're going to go over to Jersey, which is not in our jurisdiction and therefore not our problem.'

Without pausing for breath, Walker said: 'What we've got out there is a war of attrition and the minute we look like we might just be winning, the brass wants to pull the rug out from under my SNU operation. You see any sense in that, Ted?'

'Call me Ted all you like here in the office,' Keitel rebuked him mildly, 'only outside of

28

these four walls, while we're on the city's time, it's Captain, OK?'

Keitel prised open the cardboard box and folded the lid back. Inside was a plain pizza, dripping cheese, already sliced into segments.

'You want brunch?'

Walker was reluctant to give ground. 'I've got Chief Hanson buttoned down. He's on the make. I had my fill of that when I was on the squads, task force, major cases, safe loft and truck. I've seen what the world looks like from Police Plaza, some hotshot gets a bee in his bonnet, and all of a sudden we have to drop everything else. Yeah, I've got Chief Hanson, the kiddyporn king. Six months back he was apeshit about kiddyporn and nobody could figure out why until a guy on the DA's squad found some blue rinse Deputy in the Mayor's office had had a fit on a swing through the combat zone and Hanson had traded a favour, get the guys who like to see little kids get molested in their skinflicks. So we hit 'em, remember, and the *Times* carried a couple of how-we-cleaned-up-the-city features and the Deputy Mayor got a pat on the head and Hanson got Chief of Patrol. Only it was just baloney because all the while the thing that's really screwing up this city is crack, so while we're chasing the porno freaks the product is coming down like a blizzard and the dudes have got nothing to worry about except maybe dying of Aids and that's a one in fifteen shot right now.'

'You detectives —' Keitel shook his head in disbelief as he folded a slice of pizza, raised it to his mouth, chewed and swallowed, then took a gulp of coffee — 'you see things black and white. The world's not like that any more. What it is, is many shades of grey. You've got to learn to roll with the punches or the system's going to bulldoze you. Right now Hanson calls the shots, but he won't be there forever. You don't just have to be a good cop these days, you have to be a politician, that's the other side of the real world.'

Walker took a piece of pizza and flipped the plastic top from his coffee container. 'You want to put that on a placard and walk around Times Square?' he responded sourly. 'You want to preach that to the kids who're so spaced out they've got carpentry knives up their sleeves slitting pockets to steal enough bucks to feed their habit. That's what I'm talking about.'

'Vincent, let's cut the bullshit,' Keitel said wearily, licking his fingers. 'You had the Street Narcotics Unit as an experiment and I can understand why you don't want to let it go, only that's how it's got to be. Hanson just cancelled your ticket, no more undercover. It's come down on the tablet of stone.'

The captain pointed a finger at Walker's chest. 'Disband the SNU and get all your people back into uniform before Hanson starts roasting nuts. You got that?'

Walker took a bite of pizza. 'Pulling rank now, Ted?' But there was no rancour in the remark.

'Vincent . . . Vince,' Keitel groaned. 'Tomorrow's Thanksgiving. Do this for me and I'll owe you one. What more can I say?'

'For you, Captain,' Walker conceded, 'but not for Hanson.'

Keitel nodded, satisfied with the bargain. With any of the other gold shields in the precinct's detective unit it would have been a straight order, for as the executive officer Ted Keitel cultivated a ramrod image, brooking no argument from subordinates. But he knew his men and Vince Walker was a special case. A waltz around the issue would pay dividends in the long run even if he did have to miss a decent lunch to play one of the boys. Keitel eased himself back in his chair. 'So tell me something.' He changed the subject. 'How's our British cousin coming along?'

'There's another victim of the system,' Walker observed drily as he considered the detective-sergeant from London he had been assigned to assist. 'Oh, I've got him in the Madison Towers, nothing but the best for our friend from Scotland Yard. He's going down to The Tombs this afternoon to see his bail jumper, see if he can get rolling on extradition.' A quizzical expression formed on his

31

face: 'You got any idea how we got ourselves saddled with this one?'

Keitel shrugged, content that Walker had dropped his antagonism to the SNU directive. 'Came through channels to the boss.' He referred to the Deputy Inspector in command of Midtown South. 'Special request from the First Dep, so as this was a glamour job our leader naturally picked the best talent on his squad. That's the price you pay for being a celebrity, Vince.'

Walker snorted at the backhanded compliment. 'Buckpassing, more like. Downtown they're all too busy flying a tight holding pattern, burnishing their reputations. Nobody wants to do police work any more.'

'So what's his story, the Brit?'

'Like I said, victim of the system,' Walker said, relaxing as the conversation moved into a breeze-shooting session. 'There was a bullion robbery in London, bonded warehouse at Heathrow Airport. Sergeant Rowley caught the job and he and his partner got the collars, only the dudes walked when their star witness evaporated.'

Walker recalled the outline of Rowley's story. 'The perps were identical twins and bad news by all accounts. In court they threatened to off our man.'

'Where have I heard that before?' Keitel observed wryly.

'Oh sure, only this pair really meant business,' Walker said. 'Rowley's partner was the prime mover in the arrests, tough guy, only he had a heart attack, and when the case folded it was the Sarge took the flak and got booted back into a blue suit for his trouble. It was then these jokers proved they meant business; they blew up his patrol car.'

Keitel gave a low whistle. 'Car bomb? That's heavy action.'

'Oh, it gets heavier,' Walker said. 'You remember the Snow Man bust?'

'I read about it. Wasn't that the one where they shipped the coke in a cadaver?'

'That's the one,' Walker confirmed. 'Well, the yellow bars were collateral for the coke shipment and it was Sergeant Rowley we pulled off the bust.'

'He's a busy guy.'

'Isn't he,' Walker agreed. 'Only here's the kicker. They nab the body-snatchers in the act, Mafia types, take 'em to court where the prosecutor screws it up and the capo gets bail. Before Scotland Yard can bat an eyelid he'd flown the coop on a forged passport and where does he get picked up? JFK Immigration.'

'Don't they all,' Keitel said. 'Uncle Sam's real choosy about who gets to set foot in the Land of the Free.'

'So right now he's cooling his heels in The Tombs and who comes winging over to see what can be salvaged? Sergeant Tony Rowley.'

'Nice,' Keitel said. 'Some mob lawyer's going

to be making a pile of dough out of that little fiasco. Extradition brings 'em out like bees to honey. A guy who knows his way around the law could string something like that out forever.'

'New York, New York,' Walker said. 'It's a hell of a town.'

'So this Brit, this Sergeant Rowley, he's OK?'

'Seems basically a regular guy,' Walker said. 'A little wide-eyed, a little unfamiliar with the way we do things around here, but basically a street cop all the same.'

'You two should get on like a house on fire.'

Walker grinned. 'Sure, I'll show him the sights, take him to see the parade tomorrow, lighten him up a little before he gets buried in the red tape.'

The phone on the captain's desk buzzed. Keitel licked his fingers, reached out and picked it up. Then he jerked upright in his chair as if electrified. 'Hey . . . hey . . . hold it!' There was alarm in his voice. 'Give me that again!' He listened for a moment and his expression grew pained. 'OK,' he said into the phone, 'just roll the procedures. No . . . no . . . I'll take care of downtown myself . . . yeah, the Chief too.'

Keitel put the phone down, his face grim. 'Couple of cops just got burned. Shoot-out at 42nd and 6th.'

Walker winced.

'Looks like it was our friend the Brown Bag

Bandit,' Keitel said. 'Came out of the First National blazing away. They say we've got him . . . but there's an officer down.'

Walker was already out of his chair. 'Who're the cops?'

'Hey, wait a minute,' Keitel said, 'you're not going anywhere. Sit down again and take a deep breath.' The captain slumped, his shoulders sagging. 'We're going to get fried on the griddle when this gets to Hanson. They just told me the cops were your SNU undercovers.'

As Keitel spoke a motorcade was cutting a swathe through the traffic, heading for Midtown South. In the back of the police van sandwiched between two RMP cars Patti Hennessy sat with the cops escorting her prisoner and tried desperately to calm her nerves. Her partner had stayed behind to describe the sequence of events to the investigators at the scene, events which, replayed with dazzling clarity, threatened to burst Patti's head as officers manning the intersections held up the tide of cars and waved the speeding convoy through.

Unperturbed, the Bandit sat with his handcuffed hands between his knees and watched the streets flash past as the girl beside him fought down her emotions, the most compelling of which was an overwhelming desire to smack the smirk off the man's face.

At the precinct they bundled the prisoner

through the back entrance of the station house, recorded his arrest at the booking desk and then lodged him in the wire mesh holding cage. At her first chance to slip away, Patti Hennessy went to the restroom and alone at last, finally surrendered to her emotions.

Booked and documented on charges of armed robbery and assaulting police officers with a deadly weapon, the Brown Bag Bandit's details were wired to the various police units with particular interest in such crimes. The Criminal Identification Unit ran him through city, state and FBI crime computers. No known record, no prior convictions, came the reply. Only the Career Criminal Unit downtown offered an opinion.

'Will you look at this stuff.' Walker ripped the profile from the printer. 'You'd have thought those geniuses on the CCU could have come up with something solid.'

'Hoboken, New Jersey,' Keitel read from the text. 'Let's hope he can sing like Frank Sinatra.'

The captain finished reading the profile. 'Came from nowhere right into the major league.' Keitel fished out a fresh cigar and rolled the tip in his mouth. 'You know what you've got to do, Vince?'

Walker said, 'You don't have to draw me a picture. Quick confessions impress the DA like all hell, and when he gets to court we put on a nice show for the TV cameras.'

Keitel struck a match and held the flame to the stogie. Then in a loud voice he said, 'I'm telling you as a friend, Vince, you'd better beat Hanson to the punch, or you're going to be walking a footbeat out at Breezy Point. That's how he brings insubordinate detectives to heel.'

'Not after the six o'clock news says we captured the Brown Bag Bandit and the Manhattan DA gets his photo opportunity. The Mayor's going to want me in the parade tomorrow and Chief Hanson's going to be eating crow instead of turkey for Thanksgiving.'

'You'd better be right,' Keitel replied, unconvinced.

'Want to come along and watch the old magic work?' Walker suggested, but the captain shook his head. 'I've got a rearguard action of my own to fight,' he said. 'Like why the SNU operation was still running after Hanson cancelled your ticket.'

'Say I disobeyed your order, Captain,' Walker said. 'My shoulders are broad enough.'

Keitel scowled. 'Get your smart ass out of here before I change my mind.'

The Bandit's disarming manner and amused detachment began to rattle the lock-up shift.

'Busiest in the world, eh?' the Bandit observed, leaning against the back of the cage. 'My, oh my, that must be busy!'

'Don't get smart,' the desk sergeant growled.

'You're in deep shit.'

But still the Bandit's cheerful acceptance of his capture unnerved them, and the word went around that they had a psycho on their hands. The desk men were relieved when the call came to take their prisoner upstairs to the detective squad room.

With the Bandit between them, two gaolers followed the white footprints painted on the dull red composition floor and went up a flight of stairs to a vacant interrogation room. They marched the Bandit inside and gladly handed him over to the gangling detective catching the case, their eyes reflecting their superstitions. The hero robber of the tabloids had turned out to be the worst kind of wierdo, the kind who'd kill a cop without turning a hair, and it was that thought which forcibly reminded them of their own fragile mortality.

The interrogation room was lit by the glare of an overhead light, the bare cement walls a dirty yellow. The purely functional furniture consisted of a table and two chairs.

Vince Walker sat at one side of the table, at ease in the spartan simplicity of the confessional. The detective had a tape-recorder set up on the table in front of him and when he told the Bandit to sit down he began the patient process of gaining the prisoner's confidence.

'My old man —' the Bandit offered a conversational nonsequitur. 'Forty years on the railways, got his handshake from Amtrak and the privilege to sit by the rails and watch the trains go by, drooling into his beard. Now my ma was a Longabough, good New Jersey family, that name ring any bells?'

'Run it by me,' Walker offered, content to let the interrogation find its own pace.

'The Sundance Kid.' The Bandit launched into his fantasy, 'My grand-daddy, Harry Longabough.' His eyes grew bright as he leaned his elbows on the table. 'I mean, I'm telling you this for a reason, so you'll see how it is, family tradition.'

Walker left the tape-recorder switched off for the time being. 'Look,' he said pleasantly, 'we can do this the easy way, my friend, or we can do this the hard way. I've got all the time in the world. Now d'you want to tell me about the things you've been doing and we'll see what we can work out, or am I going to have to do a job on you, because as of now you belong to me.'

The Bandit said, 'You know. Sundance didn't die at San Vicente like everybody says. He was too smart for those hicks.'

'Oh, I believe you,' Walker humoured him.

'Sure.' The Bandit nodded. 'Like when the Pinkertons pushed Butch and Sundance into the muzzles of the Bolivian army. When it comes to it we've all got to jump, right?' His face broke into a grin.

'Right,' Walker agreed, playing along with

39

his prisoner. 'So let's you and me talk about bank robbery, huh, Sundance?'

'Wrong.' The Bandit straightened up. 'You want to shoot the breeze, fine. You want to get down to cases, then I've got to make my phone call.'

'You mind telling me who you're going to call, cowboy?'

The Bandit smiled. 'Uncle,' he said.

CHAPTER 3

A tide of yellow cabs streamed downtown on Broadway. It was still afternoon, but soon the light would be gone. The ribbon of sky visible down the canyons of Manhattan already blushed dusty pink.

In the flare of brake lights a battered Plymouth hack, long since stripped of chrome and hubcaps, swung left on to 34th Street, picked up speed and, hood flapping, raced for the access ramp to the FDR Drive. Behind the wheel the cabbie steered one-handed, cradling the mike of his CB in the other as he harangued his dispatcher in a litany of whining Spanish.

On the sagging blue vinyl of the back seat, a stranger in town, gaunt, with a distinctive badger stripe running through his dark hair, watched the highrise give way to compacted urban sprawl as the cab bounced over vast metal plates which served as temporary road repairs, caroomed on to the Drive and was swept along in the fast current of moving metal streaking down towards the lower East Side.

Detective-Sergeant Tony Rowley considered

himself streetwise, but his streets were on the other side of the Atlantic. He was familiar with the nuances of London's underworld, from the frenetic pace of the West End to the dockland maze which was his own stamping ground south of the river. Yet to his astonishment he found himself entranced by New York, smitten by the bold brash beat of Manhattan, just another tourist bedazzled by the sights.

Lulled into a reflective mood as the cab carried him downtown for his appointment at The Tombs, Rowley had to concentrate to bring events of his recent past back into focus. With an effort he recalled his mentor, Dad Garratt, felt himself begin to smile at the thought that Dad would have loved Manhattan with its constant undercurrent of low-life criminal intrigue.

Dad had been a Squad DI and Rowley his skipper when they lifted The Twins for the Heathrow bullion job, and that was when Rowley's troubles had begun. The prosecution case hinged on the word of a supergrass Dad had salted away in Cornwall, but when the wily old DI's heart gave out and their informant took the rap for a double murder, suddenly the evidence evaporated. The Twins walked free and Rowley felt the blistering heat of his superiors' wrath as, overnight, he became the scapegoat to protect the reputations of the Metropolitan CID hierarchy. With an underworld contract out on his life, and then the car bombing to prove the point, in desperation Rowley had struck a bargain with SO 11, the Crime Intelligence Section of the Yard's Specialist Operations Branch, the misfits of the force who were not averse to employing unorthodox methods of their own when it came to snaring villains on their target list. One of their own, a disgraced DS as a stalking-horse, had appealed to SO 11's penchant for the bizarre. Then when the bullion robbery had been linked to an organized crime conspiracy, down payment on a shipment of cocaine, Rowley had been drafted into NEL, Narcotics Enforcement Liaison, a multinational task force drawing together the cream of Europe's drug investigation agencies.

The next part of the story Rowley had told to Detective Vincent Walker as a means of establishing his credentials when he arrived in New York.

They sat in the Whaler Bar of the Madison Towers Hotel at 38th and Madison.

'I was on the Snow Man bust . . .' Rowley began the exchange of anecdotes by which the two detectives would judge each other's calibre.

'I heard about that one,' Walker said.

'I was chaperoning one of your people, a narc with Drug Enforcement Administration.'

'Don't talk to me about the DEA,' Walker

growled with such venom that Rowley made a mental note.

'We went over to Munich, me and him,' Rowley said. 'Working with the Kriminal Polizei. We leaned on a guy who was wired to The Enterprise.'

'Yeah, I heard that too,' Walker replied deadpan. 'The Enterprise is major league, running product all over the place.'

'Bigger than The French Connection?'

Walker smiled. 'That was 'sixties hype. We didn't call it that, in the job it was always the Tuminaro case after the Mafia family Grosso and Egan broke up.' He shook his head. 'The Enterprise is smarter now, it runs like a multinational, only instead of pumping oil, it's pumping product.'

Rowley resumed the story. 'We squeezed our man over in Germany until he gave us enough to go on, but it backfired in the end because the Polizei just couldn't bear to let the shipment fly out from under their noses.'

Walker chuckled, tasting his drink. 'The Enterprise shipped the product anyway,' Rowley said. 'Twenty million sterling pure Colombian cocaine. Worth a hundred mill on the street.'

'Who's the guy in The Tombs?'

'The capo,' Rowley explained. 'We nabbed 'em at a funeral parlour. The old man's Frank Spinelli, the undertaker, only he's also a kingpin in the London branch of the family. *Capo di tutti capi.*'

Walker nodded. The mob angle interested him. 'So how'd he slip through your fingers?'

'Went up for remand at Bow Street,' Rowley said. 'Only the prosecutor was having an off day, and before we could do anything about it, the court gave him bail. You know how his brief —'

'Brief?'

'Lawyer,' Rowley explained. 'Put up a song and dance routine. Respectable businessman, pillar of the community, strenuously denies the charge, complete answer, etc., etc. It was an Oscar performance which completely outclassed our man and got Spinelli bail on condition he surrendered his passport and produced two solid sureties. One hour after he walked out of the court, even before we could get an all-ports on the wire, the capo was aboard a Jumbo with a forged passport in his pocket at 40,000 feet heading for the USA. At least your Immigration was on the ball. They held him at JFK on the strength of the Interpol telex.'

'So you're the catcher?'

'They needed someone familiar with the case to be the messenger boy. I'm just here to talk to your people about possibilities of getting Spinelli back before we send an extradition team over with the warrants.'

Walker finished his drink. 'Well, you couldn't have picked a better time. This town lights up for Thanksgiving. Drink up, have

45

another before we eat.'

Reflecting on this conversation piece, Rowley found himself staring out of the window of the taxi. He blinked and checked his bearings. They were on the East River Drive now, the elevated section, sweeping past the revamped sea port. In the front seat the cabbie shifted position on the beaded massage mat draped over his seat and unleashed a further torrent of abuse into his radio as he swung on to an exit ramp and plunged down into the municipal quarter of the city. On Canal Street the taxi rattled to a stop outside the forbidding fortress of the Manhattan House of Detention for Men, known more familiarly as The Tombs.

Rowley found Vince Walker waiting for him in the shadow of the looming blockhouse of the prison, his long face solemn.

'I'm going to have to take a rain check,' he apologized. 'They want me over at Police Plaza and I don't think it would be in my best interests to turn down the invitation.'

'Trouble?' Rowley asked, reading the other's face.

'Right here in River City,' Walker replied. He told Rowley what had happened and then said, 'Let me explain something about police organization. Any police organization eventually becomes a self-serving bureaucracy, it doesn't matter what it is, NYPD, Scotland Yard, the Keystone

Cops. It's a carnvore gnawing at its own flesh. You step off the line, it just gets up and bites you.'

'Don't I know it,' Rowley sympathized.

'Let me put it another way,' Walker said. 'All the pressures coming down are to get the job done, only to get the job done you have to bend the rules. It's like walking around in a mine-field. No matter how careful you are, even-tually something's going to blow up in your face. Forget results now, that was yesterday's song, now the power brokers have to purge the system with a little blood.'

'I've had some experience of that, Vince. It's the same the world over.'

'You'd better believe it,' Walker said. They began to walk towards the lofty entrance to the prison. 'Look —' he returned to the busi-ness in hand — 'I'll square it with the man here. You get done and then come over to headquarters and we'll compare notes.'

'Can you fix for me to see Spinelli alone?' Rowley asked. 'No guard, no tape, no video?'

'Sure, why not? This guy's your fugitive, he's nothing to us. The most we're ever going to do is kick him out of the country as an undesirable alien. You want to have a picnic with the guy, Tony, you've got it. Consider it done.'

Rowley nodded as Walker pushed open the massive bronze-trimmed door and the anti-septic odour of the institution hit him.

'Thanks,' he said, 'I appreciate it.'

'Any time,' Walker said. 'Grab it while you can. It's Thanksgiving and I've got a feeling I'm going to end up the turkey.'

Four men were around the highly polished table in the conference room on the Chief of Department's floor at the red brick cube squatting in the in the middle of Police Plaza. The conference room occupied a corner of the headquarters building with windows overlooking the Brooklyn Bridge.

If the location had been chosen to intimidate Vince Walker, then it hadn't succeeded. Dragging him downtown just to ream him out for disobeying orders was typical of the slavish rituals the brass loved to act out just to reassure themselves of their power.

At the top of the table there was the portly figure of Eric Hanson, the Chief of Patrol, whose criteria for success was the daily body count of blue suits on the streets. Beside him there was Quentin Rooney, a pallid Deputy Inspector who had wheedled his way into a position of power as aide to the Chief of Department, the highest line rank below the appointees, the Police Commissioner and his deputies. Ted Keitel, his own exec, was there looking discomfited in such exalted company, but the fourth man, a trim-looking Ivy Leaguer was a stranger to the detective.

Walker accepted the vacant place at the

table and braced himself for an encounter which bore all the hallmarks of an unofficial Departmental trial. As he sat down he unbuttoned his jacket to reveal the worn wooden grip of a .38 Special in its scuffed leather holster riding on his hip, silently emphasizing the uncompromising symbol of the street cop to this bunch of desk jockeys.

Chief Hanson was eager to draw first blood, scowling as he launched into the attack. 'Well, Mr Smartass, you want to explain why you disobeyed explicit orders and nearly got two of my people wasted?'

'With all due respect, Chief,' Walker replied evenly, 'they're my people too and they got the collar. The decision to keep the SNU undercovers going was mine alone.' He glanced at Keitel and saw the captain wince. 'It was in my judgement an operational imperative.'

The word 'operational' stung. 'Operational imperative my ass,' Hanson snorted indignantly. 'Since when did precinct detectives dictate Department policy? When I say I want the patrol force on the streets in uniform, that's exactly what I want, do I make myself clear? In uniform, not skulking around acting the fantasies of some jerk-off detective.'

'Begging your pardon, Chief,' Walker responded without rising to the bait, 'if we don't have some leeway on the precincts on how we deploy our people, then pretty soon this city's going to be drowning in its own sewers.'

Rooney smirked. 'Sounds like you're going to run for mayor making speeches like that.'

Walker looked at him. 'How'd you manage to speak with your head shoved up your ass, Quent?'

The colour rose on Rooney's cheeks and across the table Keitel moved in to head off trouble.

'I think what Walker is trying to say here, Chief,' he addressed Hanson, 'is that he apologizes for misinterpreting your orders, that it won't happen again and that he offers the capture of an armed robber in mitigation.'

'Thank you, Captain,' Walker said, 'but I feel I ought to add for the Chief's benefit that all of us around this table had better understand that the vast majority of crime in this city is drugs-orientated and my SNU operation was hitting 'em where it hurts before the Chief in his wisdom pulled the plug.'

Hanson's eyes narrowed. 'That's a big chip you're carrying on your shoulder, Walker, maybe too big for this Department to accommodate. That's the bottom line.'

'Chief,' Walker responded, throwing caution to the winds, 'crack is the propellant that's going to blast this town into orbit if we don't get a grip on it. *That's* the bottom line. Now we can sit here forever debating the finer points of Department policy. You blow some smoke, I'll blow some smoke, and pretty soon

50

all we'll end up with here is a smoke-blowing contest.'

'You're out of line, Walker,' Hanson blustered, his face flushed, but Walker cut him off, suddenly sick of the Star Chamber treatment. 'No, Chief it's you who's out of line. I was getting results. This thing with the Bandit was just a sideshow you're going to use to can me. But before you do, I'm going to tell you the story. One day some coyote out there in the jungle, Colombia, Bolivia, wherever, hears about the latest drug the yuppies are snorting on Wall Street and he looks out of the window and he sees the coca crop coming up good and he thinks to himself: "I'm going to have a piece of that action." So he gets his trusty Teflon pan, and he mixes in the powder, the baking soda, fries up on a slow heat till it all starts popping and he's got himself the product. Next thing you know, this guy's running around East Harlem in a stretch Caddy running a distribution network which would make the US Mail green with envy. And overnight we've got a crack epidemic that's going to put this town into outer space. That's the real world, Chief.'

Hanson glowered across the table. 'I'm going to have your shield, mister —' he started to say when the fourth man, an amused expression on his face, gave Walker's little speech a slow handclap and spoke for the first time. 'Get off your high horse, Eric,' he said to

Hanson. 'Can't you see your man here's got the balls for the job. Let's cut the crap and talk some business here.'

At The Tombs, Detective-Sergeant Tony Rowley followed a corrections officer up to level six for his reunion with the *capo di tutti capi.*

The echo of his footsteps from the bare floor of the galleries mingling with the clatter of the prison, Rowley recalled his first encounter with Frank Spinelli on the rooftop of a derelict warehouse in London's dockland. It had been there that he had succumbed to Dad Garratt's posthumous legacy of old world CID pragmatism and had finally sought out the undertaker's patronage to stay the death sentence hanging over him.

In the days when detectives cultivated active criminals, Spinelli, the linch-pin of London's underworld, had been Dad's ally in the world of organized crime, and had readily agreed to take his protégé under his wing, but not until they had performed the age-old ritual of kinship, the mingling of blood. The detective had become the gangster's blood brother. Rowley had crossed the line to save his own hide.

When they reached the detention area, Rowley was escorted to the visitors' cage where Spinelli was already waiting for him. The old man looked more fragile than Rowley remembered him, a slight figure, hook-nosed and Latin-featured, with bright bird-like eyes in a seamed and pock-marked face. In this area of The Tombs inmates were permitted to wear their own clothes and Spinelli's sombre suit seemed to hang loose as though the man inside was withering away. Or was it just the surroundings which had shrunk the capo's stature?

Once they were alone, Spinelli seemed genuinely pleased to see his visitor.

'Hey, Tony!' He embraced the sergeant with a cry of delight. 'How'd I know it was going to be you?'

'Oh, I'm just the advance guard, Frank,' Rowley said disengaging himself. 'The heavy mob from Extradition will be around later. You're going to have all sorts of exalted company.'

Still looking pleased with himself, Spinelli shook his head and said, 'It don't matter, you're still Dad's boy, Tony. I would've put money on you coming.' He laughed. 'Hey . . . hey . . . that Snow Man, wasn't that something? You got the credit for that, Tony, lots of exposure, good for your career.'

Rowley was taken aback. Here was the baron of the drugs conspiracy, the man he himself had arrested with the biggest shipment of cocaine ever to hit the streets of London, congratulating him on the bust as if he'd just read about it in the papers.

'I did what I had to do,' Rowley replied, but the capo cut him short. 'No hard feelings on this side, Tony. We took the vow of *omertà*, remember? The vow of silence. Only I don't need it any more. Can we talk like men, like brothers?'

Rowley sat down on the bench, remembering those other times when he had worn a wire whenever he met the capo. 'Frank,' he said, opening his jacket so that Spinelli could see he had nothing to hide, 'no tapes, no tricks, not this time. You and me, we're just a couple of pilgrims a long way from home.'

'There were times —' Spinelli watched him shrewdly — 'when it was all happening, when I wondered, you know what I mean? When I really wondered.'

'Well, you didn't have to worry in the end,' Rowley said.

Spinelli shook his head. 'I couldn't be sure, though. With Dad I wouldn't have had any qualms, but with you, Tony, I'd hardly got to know you, so I had my doubts.'

'Forget it,' Rowley said. 'It was easy.'

'You think so? Let me tell you my brief was saying I hadn't a prayer, no chance I'd get bail. You mind telling me how you swung it?'

Rowley shrugged. 'The file got lost, the CPS twerp went on cold and your brief ran him off the road.'

Spinelli's eyes sparkled. 'How does a file get mislaid?'

'Who knows? Happens all the time.'

'So here I am.' Spinelli waved his hands around the mean detention room as if he was in the best suite at the Pierre. 'Home of the brave and land of the free.'

'My people're going to move heaven and earth to get you back,' Rowley said. 'They'll go for extradition, and it could be a long fight.'

'It doesn't matter,' Spinelli said, still amused, 'I've got an ace left up my sleeve. All those years I never gave up my Sicilian nationality, always hung on to the threads of the past.' He leaned forward. 'The only way the law says this is going to work is deport me to country of origin, and that means they're going to have to send me to Sicily. What they're going to do when the lawyers finish with the beanfeast is drive me out to JFK and put me on an Alitalia out of here. I'm going home, Tony, home to sit in the olive groves for the rest of my life and watch girls in peasant skirts give me a glimpse of thigh and I'll be back dreaming of when I was a young stud.'

Frank Spinelli stared deep into the detective's eyes. 'You want to know the truth Tony? I've had the hassle, it's crushing the life juice out of me, all this dancing around trying to get people you don't trust to do things you don't even want to do any more. In the old days when Dad and me had our understanding, you had the savvy, you had respect. Now everybody's into drugs and it's like walking around in a chemical factory. They get themselves a chemist, they're making designer product, crack, rock all the stuff, and they're strutting around like they invented the world. They've got accountants running the rackets and they're dressed like they just stepped out of the boardroom, hooking up dinky computers and talk . . . talk . . . on the car phones. I don't need any of that. The trick in this life is knowing when to quit while you're ahead. When to step off. When to retire.' He spread his hands. 'I'm going home.'

'Well, that could be a problem for me, Frank,' Rowley said, broaching the subject which had brought him to The Tombs.

'You mean The Twins?'

Rowley nodded. 'They're mad dogs. They want my head on the stake, and with you out of the picture, they're off the leash.'

'I've been giving that some thought. I've been thinking about the mad dogs.' The capo gnawed his lip, watching Rowley, then he said, 'You came through for me when I needed you, Tony. Today I could've been rotting in Brixton gaol. We're of the blood, you and me, so now I'm going to stand up for you. Only this time I'm going to have to pull strings by remote control and ever since that Snow Man thing my best people have gone to the mattress, so what I have to tell you is that my options are limited.'

Rowley leaned forward. 'That doesn't sound optimistic, Frank.'

'Oh, it's no big problem,' Spinelli reassured him. 'Only it's not just a matter of pushing buttons any more. What we're going to have to do, you and me, is get our heads together and come up with a way we can dispose of your problem . . . permanently.'

'How would we do that?' Rowley asked.

'There are two ways,' Spinelli replied, his geniality undiminished. 'Either you kiss all this goodbye and come with me to Sicily.'

'And the other?'

The capo smiled. 'Or one last funeral,' he said.

At Police Plaza the fourth man had the floor. Into the tense silence around the conference table he introduced himself as Earl Mulholland, East Coast Regional Director of the United States Department of Justice Drug Enforcement Administration, his smiling eyes never leaving Walker's face.

Beyond the window, as if on cue, the lights of the Brooklyn Bridge came on, strung across the East River like a necklace in the November night.

'When the Bandit called Uncle,' Mulholland said, 'he called one of my guys on his confidential phone, straight to his desk, a direct number which maybe only half a dozen people have access to. My guy called me and I grabbed the first shuttle out of Washington.' Mulholland kept his gaze on Walker's face. 'Which I hope will give you some indication that this is no ordinary stick-the-piece-in-your-face-and-snatch-the-dough robber. This individual is one of ours —' he paused for effect — 'and his welfare is important to us.'

Walker couldn't believe what he was hearing. The Brown Bag Bandit working for the DEA? Government bonded!

'We've been running him for a long time, mainly undercover out in Colombia and Bolivia, and he's been making major cases for Uncle Sam. So now we've reeled him in and we're waiting for the moment to insert him into another cocaine-running operation. The Enterprise is currently shipping eighty per cent of the product and we can't get within a mile with conventional methods — cut off a head, another grows.' Mulholland's eyes glittered. 'But a maverick like the Bandit, he can go right into the heart, carry the stake for us. Now I know what you're thinking, this is dirty pool, only look at it this way: your crack epidemic out there, I can absolutely guarantee that somewhere up the line the whole thing is wired to The Enterprise. I'm telling you all this so that you'll understand our overriding priority. We have to protect our investment. There's no way we can let you have the Bandit.'

Walker shook his head. 'I don't believe this. Here's a guy robs a bank, comes out shooting, does his damnedest to waste a couple of cops, and if I read you right, you're telling me this mother has some kind of government immunity? You want to watch the networks in this town, every night screaming about rising street crime and what the hell are the cops doing, and here we collar the number one most wanted and you're telling me, hey not so fast, this is really an Ollie North look-alike doing good deeds for his country. In my book, that sucks. And I tell you something else Mr DEA Director: you've got to be kidding. This is the stone killer, and the only place he's going is to jail.'

The easy smile still on his lips, Mulholland said, 'We thought we had him house-trained, all that Sundance stuff has gone to his head. I have to admit he does have an unfortunate proclivity to freelance, but that's nothing we can't take care of.'

'Like hell you can,' Walker snorted. 'He's my prisoner.'

'Not any more,' Chief Hanson interjected. 'NYPD's off the case. You're turning him over to DEA!'

'I don't believe any of this,' Walker exclaimed, throwing Keitel a despairing glance. The precinct captain, looking uncomfortable, slowly shook his head in a silent signal to lay off. This was not the ground on which to do battle.

'Think yourself lucky you've still got your shield,' Rooney said from across the table, smiling smugly.

'Shut your face, Quent,' Walker snapped, ignoring Keitel's semaphore. He turned back to Mulholland. 'I'm taking him to the DA,' he announced stubbornly.

'He won't prosecute,' Mulholland replied easily. 'Let me draw you a picture. The DA's listening to Uncle. It's election year, remember? Besides, he sees it our way, a small sacrifice to the higher priorities of criminal justice.'

'Very patriotic,' Walker sneered. 'Then I'll go to the media, tell 'em what kind of lousy deals are going down.'

'You want to be an ex cop,' Chief Hanson growled, 'fine, be my guest. It'd give me the greatest pleasure to make your wish come true.'

'Apart from the embarrassment that would cause your Department,' Mulholland said thoughtfully, 'you can take it from me our man would be long gone and so would your credibility.' He leaned his elbows on the table. 'Look, Walker, before you blow your stack, let me put it to you like this. The Enterprise in running product and we can't get near 'em. You think a few cops are going to make so much as a dent in an operation of that magnitude? We've got to sneak inside, drive the stake through the heart. The Bandit can do that, he's our main chance. OK, so the guy's hyperactive, with basic criminal tendencies, but he's still the only one can do it. Our target is The Enterprise. We've got manpower tied up half way across the world on this Centac.'

'You interfere with my case and I'll talk to Channel Five.' Walker returned to the offensive, but the threat was just a bluff for he knew full well that his loyalty to the job would prevent him from turning the affair into a media circus.

'Thinks he's Kojak,' Rooney sniggered.

Helplessly, Walker turned to Keitel, 'What am I supposed to do, Captain?'

Keitel gnawed his lip. 'Look, why don't we take a break, see if we can work something out.'

'Terrific! What about the Bandit?' Walker asked bleakly, rounding on the others.

'Whatever your Captain comes up with to absolve your conscience,' Chief Hanson told him, jabbing the air with his finger, 'the Bandit walks.'

CHAPTER 4

At The Tombs, the birdlike capo was intent upon improving Rowley's education. Spinelli laughed unexpectedly, the dry cackle cannoning off the bare walls of the interview room, mingling with the background clatter of the prison.

'So here we are,' he told the DS mirthfully, 'the bail jumper and the cop, sitting in jail working out how best to eliminate a couple of crazy East End blaggers who don't have the brains of a baboon between them. Doesn't that strike you as ironic?'

'Frank, I wish I had your sense of humour.'

Spinelli took a handkerchief out of his pocket and dabbed at his face. 'Look, Tony, all I've got to do is sit here and let my lawyers do their stuff. It does me good to have a problem to chew on.'

'There's something else,' Rowley said. 'Before we get started, there has to be a spin-off for my firm, a quid pro quo.'

'Of course,' Spinelli agreed, as though it was a foregone conclusion. 'Naturally there has to be something in it for New Scotland Yard, most famous police in the world. Something to crow about.'

Disguising his unease, Rowley said, 'So what d'you think?'

'I've got an idea might be worth considering,' Spinelli said with a cunning smile. 'What you have to work on is a set-up so dazzling, everybody involved is blinded to the true purpose.'

Rowley shrugged. 'How d'you suppose we could do that?'

Spinelli hunched forward, rubbing his hands together. 'Let's play a game,' he said. 'You're the new hustler on the drugs scene, hungry to make your first million. What do you do?'

'Get a few people around me that I can trust and start shipping product.'

'OK, so you're running in grass in the cigarette boats, getting what you can off the freighter off the coast. What comes next?'

'Bring the freighter right in to the dock and offload the bales on to trucks.'

'So you're ready to expand. Which way do you jump?'

'Look for new product, more percentage.'

'And more risk.'

'Life's a risk.'

Spinelli cracked dry knuckles. 'Now you're talking,' he said. 'You move up a notch into the cocaine business. Open up new markets and impress everybody. Where next?'

'On up the ladder.'

'Because you can't afford to stand still. So, you tap into some established distribution networks, the old mobs, cautious people. You start dealing with people in South America who have private armies to protect their business interests. You're a mover and they like your style, only the market's reaching saturation point, you're shipping product so fast.'

'So I need to expand.'

'Right! Otherwise you're going to lose your new friends. You're already into Europe, going like an express train, and you can see the real market is the UK. But suddenly you've got a cashflow problem.'

'So I get some new collateral.' Rowley smiled. 'Like Nigerian bullion. That would do nicely.'

'Neat move, only you've expanded so fast you make the UK jump before you're ready. Get the picture?'

'Sure,' Rowley said. 'I get busted by Scotland Yard.'

'The Snow Man bust,' Spinelli said. 'After which suddenly the phone doesn't ring any more. So where are your associates? Getting their heads together, wondering if you didn't bite off more than you could chew and choke on it, and maybe they shouldn't do business any more with such a reckless individual. You've got to think of some way you can re-establish your credibility — and fast.'

Rowley shrugged. It was Spinelli's game plan now.

'There's one way,' the capo said. 'First you've got to prove you're still an action man. But more important than that, you've got to save

64

face. That's what it's all about, credibility.'

'How am I going to do that, Frank?'

'Snatch back your shipment. What is it worth to you? Twenty million in Colombian superfine, a hundred mill on the street, currently stashed away in some police strong room where it is Exhibit A in the case of the Crown versus one Francis Spinelli and others named on the indictment, alleging conspiracy to smuggle a prohibited substance.'

Rowley said, 'Aren't you forgetting the guardians of law and order?'

'They're your ace in the hole. Those very guardians are going to help you to repossess your merchandise.'

'Why would they do that?'

'Because you agree to trade in a couple of your low-echelon sub-contractors.'

'The Twins?'

'The Twins.'

'Wait a minute,' Rowley said. 'Assuming all this was possible, you'd need a man inside the force to make it work, someone who could pull the strings. You have any thoughts who that might be?'

'I'm looking at him,' Spinelli said.

It was Rowley's turn to laugh. 'Come on,' he retorted sceptically, 'I'm just a DS. I don't have the pull.'

'You don't need it,' Spinelli said. 'All you need is to be in a position to sow the seeds. Look, what are your people greedy for? Big cases. Show the politicians what a good job they're doing. You feed in the possibilities, they'll jump at it, you know they will. What did you learn from Dad, eh? You can do anything you want provided you wrap it up and sell it the right way. Am I right?'

Rowley nodded. 'And that's how we get The Twins?'

'In the bag. They'll be my parting gift to you, Tony.' The capo was silent for a moment, holding the sergeant in a speculative gaze. Then he said, 'So that's it. The bullshit session's over. It's up to you now. Do you want to do it or what?'

'Let me think about it,' Rowley said.

'Certainly,' Spinelli agreed. 'Only don't take too long. You lose the edge now and it could be gone forever. I'd hate to read about this detective they fished out of a reservoir with his feet cast in a hundredweight of concrete.'

He rested a hand on Rowley's shoulder. 'It's all a game. Survival of the fittest. What would Dad have done in his heyday? What was the last thing he told you to do?'

'Keep the faith,' Rowley recalled.

The capo spread his hands in a wordless gesture, his point already made.

'You dumb Mick,' Keitel told Walker as they waited in an ante-room on the Chief of Department's floor at Police Plaza, the rebuke alluding to the fact that whatever his nationality, every cop in New York from the newest rookie right up to the PC himself became by tradition an honorary Irishman the moment he donned the blue suit. 'You pull that media stunt, tell him you're going to the TV; you've been on the street so long it's addled your brain.'

The meeting stood adjourned. Chief Hanson had taken Mulholland through to his own office with Rooney tagging along, and Walker had been left with his executive officer to watch over him. It felt as if the court had adjourned prior to delivering its verdict.

'Don't ever apply for the diplomatic corps, Vince,' Keitel said, a pained expression on his face. 'You pushed the Chief into a corner so he's got no room to manœuvre and the last thing he can afford to do with the DEA breathing down his neck is leave a loaded cannon like you running loose on the gun deck. If we don't come up with a compromise, Hanson's going to fry your sorry ass.'

The Captain fished a cigar out of his pocket, jammed it into his mouth and rolled it around without making any attempt to light up. A deep frown creased his forehead. 'Sweet Jesus,' he finally exclaimed in exasperation, 'I come down here out of the kindness of my heart to mediate, keep the Chief who has the power of life and death over detectives from making you eat your gold shield, and what do I get for my trouble? All you do is give the man attitude. Goddamn it, Vince, you're pre-historic.'

Walker said, 'What am I supposed to do, Ted, sit there while a guy who wouldn't last five minutes on the street trades off my prisoner to the Feds?'

'Look,' Keitel said, 'don't go getting the notion this is the real world. Police Plaza runs on different rails. Now Hanson's got you under his heel he's going to grind you out of existence, probably tell the Chief of Department what a bunch of dummies he's got running around Midtown. The way this is panning out, instead of saving your hide, I'm going down with you.'

'Captain, I'm truly sorry for fouling up your career in the interests of justice.'

Keitel sighed at the sarcasm and found a match for his cigar. 'What the hell,' he exclaimed, puffing smoke, 'justice is a four-letter word. But I tell you something, Vince.' He held up thumb and forefinger about half an inch apart. 'This SNU thing's put you about this far from getting washed out of the force. You're deep in Department politics and that's like swimming with the sharks. Either we find a way to make you a deal or you come out with zip.'

After a while Mulholland called Walker back into the conference room. The DEA Director had removed his jacket and now looked every inch a Capitol Hill sharpie in his striped shirt and red suspenders. Mulholland was alone in the room, and with the distinct feeling that he was being manipulated by unseen forces, Walker gained the impression that some tough talking had taken place in his absence.

'I wanted to see you alone for a moment,' Mulholland began with a paternal smile. 'I understand you don't have much time for the DEA so I feel I owe you an explanation. To be frank, you've got Chief Hanson so pissed off I had to tell him that I didn't think we'd get anywhere with this little problem, not even if we batted it around the table until hell freezes over. So I craved the Chief's indulgence so that I could set the record straight with you, because I happen to like your style, Walker, because I hate to see a good detective with old-time principles going to waste.'

Mulholland sank into a chair as though a heavy burden had fallen on to his shoulders and motioned Walker to sit own. Then he said, 'Believe me, Vincent — you don't mind if I call you Vincent? I know how you feel about the Bandit. In your shoes I'd probably feel the same, so on that basis I reckon I owe it to you to tell you something about this prisoner of yours so that you have the complete picture.

'You want to know why we're making such a fuss about this guy? Well, I'll tell you. If this was some regular stoolie, even with mileage still left on the clock, I'd give him up in a minute, you can take my word on that. But this Bandit is like —' he cast around for the best descriptive phrase — 'like a magician. Everything happens just the way he says it will. He delivers on the button. Now that kind of performance is unique in my line of work. It means I can't let go, not even if I have to roll over a good cop on the way. I have to protect my man come hell or high water and you're just going to have to accept that as the base line.'

Walker said drily, 'Let's not pussyfoot around this, Mr Mulholland. What you're talking about is perverting the course of justice.'

Mulholland shook his head. 'The issues are not cut and dried like that. Hear me out a moment longer, OK? I think maybe there's a way we can sneak out of the woods without the old bear getting the scent. Only first we have to trust each other. You want to give it a try?'

'It's your territory,' Walker said. 'All I ever saw was a screwball with a gun who gets his kicks sticking up banks and shooting at cops, and I've got him cold.'

Mulholland waved a hand in a conciliatory gesture. 'First let me tell you the story. You've heard of Carlos Lehder, the Colombian drugs king? We've hunted Lehder for the best part of a decade, but we couldn't get near him, he was always that well insulated. He ran his cartel backed up by a lot of firepower and the political clout to match. In the end we put together a task force to hit Lehder, called it Operation Storm. A hundred and sixty agents went in and they got slaughtered, only ten came out alive. The rest Lehder's men picked off in the boonies.

'Now that got our dander up. There was even talk of an air strike, CIA coordinated, unmarked Phantoms, wipe his outfit off the face of the earth once and for all, only sanity prevailed. Instead we sent in the Bandit, into the badlands, and he gave us Lehder on a platter. Flew him into Tampa airport cool as you please, gift wrapped.' Mulholland shook his head at the recollection. 'We had the runway surrounded with machine-guns and bullet-proof jeeps, everyone was so nervous. The Bandit got him when no one else could.

'You heard of David Medin, chief bagman for the mob in Detroit? Another big product mover, out of Bolivia, used to have his capos meet the Bolivian intermediaries at fancy hotels the world over. We sent the Bandit into Bolivia and he walked out with Medin, turned him into the best stoolie we ever had and saved a lot of lives into the bargain.' Mulholland spread his hands. 'Put it this way: if I had to, I could get our friend an absolute pardon no matter what he did. Say he walks in here and wastes everyone in sight, I could still walk into the Oval Office and the President would sign the paper. That's the debt of gratitude Uncle Sam owes this guy. This thing of yours is strictly small potatoes.'

'What d'you want me to do, whistle the Star-Spangled Banner?'

'What I am saying is we've both got ourselves caught in a bind on this, so why don't we look for a way to help each other?'

'I've got an idea what's coming next,' Walker said. 'If I get the feeling I'm about to get set up, d'you mind if my Captain comes in on this? I think I may need a friend.'

When Keitel joined them Mulholland said, 'I'm going to give it to you straight from the shoulder, no bullshit. What I see opening up here is a window of opportunity. On the one hand, we're marking time waiting to insert the Bandit into an operation worthy of his talent, and on the other . . .' The Director looked from one to the other, then he said, 'OK, I'll level with you. On the other hand I've got to admit we've got a little snafu of our own to overcome. You've heard of this European thing, Narcotics Enforcement Liaison? Well, they're grabbing a lot of prime cuts, and we're under heavy political pressure to contribute, looks good for Uncle to be on a winning team. The trouble is, the first agent we sent over fouled up and got one of their undercovers killed, so naturally they're leery of any more direct DEA involvement. So we're at stalemate right now. But what if we offer them a street cop with our interests at heart? Then I'd guess we could swing it with the Brits and cover all the bases at the same time.'

Keitel said, 'Uh-huh. And if that street cop just happened to be a certain first grade detective NYPD, he'd probably escape the wrath of his superiors, might even cover himself with glory.'

'I was thinking out loud,' Mulholland said. 'I was thinking I could probably convince your esteemed Chief of Patrol that it'd be in his interests too. How about a personal note from the White House via the PC thanking him for his patriotic cooperation?'

Keitel chewed on his cigar. 'Kiss-ass, that'd clinch it,' he confirmed.

'Let's get this straight,' Walker said. 'You want me to go to London and play footsie with the Brits just so the DEA can score points with the White House?'

'Any clown could do that,' Mulholland said. 'No, what I'm saying is I believe you're smart enough to maximize our potential over there.'

'What did you call that before?' Walker asked, not bothering to conceal his sarcasm.

'A window of opportunity.' Mulholland repeated the expression, unfazed by Walker's jaundiced response.

Walker turned to Keitel. 'You see the catch, Captain?'

Mulholland smiled. 'There's no catch,' he said cheerfully. 'All you're going to have to do is swallow a chunk of pride, Walker. You're going to have to work with the Bandit.'

CHAPTER 5

A black Rover Sterling was running the lights down Park Lane in the scramble of the London rush hour, the driver judging the sequence to a hairsbreadth, catching each signal on the change to green without slackening speed. Jumping the lights was just one of the little tricks he had picked up at the Metropolitan Police driving school out at Hendon, and scoring points in the rush hour was one of the few pleasures left to a hotshot traffic man whose tour of duty with VIP protection was largely spent hunched over interminable hands of nine-card brag in the drivers' restroom at the Yard.

In the back seat Commander Larry Drake sank deeper into the hide upholstery, and closed his eyes, allowing the Rover to carry him the last half-mile past the Palace and down to Broadway, where one glass and concrete tower lorded it over its highrise neighbours by virtue of the rotating triangular silver sign which carried the legend New Scotland Yard, headquarters of the Metropolitan Police. As he passed a moment or two in self-indulgent reflection, Larry Drake imagined himself a Cæsar returning triumphant to Rome. The indignity of his banishment to a grubby District in the northern wasteland of the MPD slowly dissolved into sweet triumph. For far from accepting his fall from grace when the Snow Man bust had blown up in his face, Drake had outwitted his adversaries in the patronage-riddled reaches of the Met hierarchy and was returning to the power game with even more clout than he had wielded as the Yard's charismatic drugs supremo. Sweet was the victor's return.

The black Rover which swept into the service road denied to all but the privileged few and glided to a halt outside the canopied entrance to the Yard carried none other than the new Commander of SO 12; Special Branch.

Larry Drake waited until the driver came around and opened the rear door, then eased himself out of the car, reached for the briefcase which never left his side and with an affable nod to his chauffeur crossed the pavement to the glass revolving door, beside which a constable on security watch stiffened as a mark of respect.

To all outward appearances, Drake fitted the image of a stockbroker, banker, corporate lawyer; something successful in the City in his impeccable blue-grey nailhead double-breasted suit worn with a crisp white shirt tailored in the old-fashioned style with a high stiff collar into which was knotted his striped

Police College tie. Drake had always been a high flier, soaring easily to the rank of Commander without losing his boyish features which now sported a clipped Guards-style moustache. Behind this Boy Scout exterior there lurked formidable cunning, for Mr Smooth was the consummate operator, manipulator of a system so convoluted that it defied all but the most assiduous players.

Drake allowed the inertia of the rotating door to waft him into the spacious lobby, the 'back hall' of the Yard, a cavern littered with chrome fittings and black couches where visitors waited inside roped-off pens while the girls behind the reception desk chattered endlessly into the internal phones and filled out passes which allowed non-members of the Yard's closed community to cross the threshold to the banks of lifts which provided the only access to the interior of the building.

Crossing the lobby, Larry Drake was obliged to pass the white marble plinth on top of which the eternal flame burned beside a book of remembrance containing a roll-call of officers who had fallen in the line of duty. Idly he wondered whether the name of the girl detective-sergeant whose death had sparked off the Snow Man case had yet been immortalized on the page. Curiosity almost made him pause, but as the girl's name escaped him, his stride did not falter and he pushed the tiresome recollection aside, showed his ID to

the security guard and joined the crush waiting for the lifts. Dwelling on events of the past
was not one of Mr Smooth's preoccupations.

Back in the lobby two men observed the
arrival of the new SO 12 Commander with
particular interest.

'What'd I tell you? You just lost your bet,'
remarked the shorter of the two, a stocky man
peering through heavy-rimmed spectacles and
wearing a light camel overcoat.

'I wouldn't have believed it,' replied the
other, who was dressed in the green of the
Royal Ulster Constabulary. 'I heard Drake
had been banished to the wilderness.'

'You've been reading the wrong hand-outs,
Bill. And that's a tenner you owe me.'

'I heard he got banished, epaulettes torn off.'

'You heard wrong. Does he look like he's in
disgrace? Didn't I tell you, Drake's a survivor.'

'What's he do for an encore?' the soft Irish
brogue remarked. 'Walk on water?'

The man in the camel coat chuckled. 'You
bog-trotters, you're like babes in arms. Why
d'you think I asked you to drop by on the way
back to the Emerald Isle so that you could see
it for yourself? Now I'm going to complete your
education on the mysterious ways of the Metropolitan Police.' He folded his arms and the
artificial light glinted off his spectacles.
'Drake overstretched himself on Snow Man,
that's all, went a bridge too far, as they say,
and came a cropper. But you don't join the

circus until you've checked the acts first, and Drake had to have some space to lick his wounds, just a little breather to remuster his forces. You know Peter Ashworth?'

'At the Home Office?'

'The Sloane wanker. Look, Bill, as far as the Met's concerned the world is flat and it ends at the edge of the MPD. You go out beyond the super-eight, you drop off into oblivion. Drake went to the rim, looked over, and then gave Ashworth a bell, all in the interests of promoting the illustrious career of Commander Lawrence Drake. Are you getting the picture?'

'Ashworth ... Ashworth ... Minister of State at the Home Office?'

'You're not listening to me, Bill. Here I am giving you the crash course on the power structure, and you're not listening.'

'Where's Ashworth fit in?' the Ulsterman asked.

'Drake's got him in his pocket, probably something to do with choirboys or the midday specials you don't get with luncheon vouchers. Piccadilly urinals, something like that. So Drake gets a bloody nose on Snow Man, but right away he's angling for a come-back, and if he's got a politician, better still a Minister of the Crown in his corner, then where's the place he's going to have the most influence? The poor old SB.'

'I thought ... What about Mason? Isn't he

still running the Branch.'

'Ah, Bill.' The man in the camel coat shook his head sadly. 'Where the hell have you been? Jesus, somebody ought to hang you out to dry. Mason was a straight up and down copper, didn't spend his nights at the Lodge, didn't suck up to the politicians. That's why he's gone across the water with no extra rank to knock some sense into your lot. They shipped him into the RUC by the back door just to create an opening at SB. Who slips into the slot? None other than Larry Drake. And who pulled all the strings?'

'Peter Ashworth?'

'You're catching on, my friend,' the bespectacled man congratulated him. 'Now, much as I'm enjoying our little tête-à-tête, I'm going to have to get up there because the manual for new SB Commanders says that the first task you have to perform when you walk into the office for the first time is to call in your trusty lieutenants and start kicking butts just to show 'em who's the boss. As I anticipate our freshly baked leader will be doing just that any minute now, I'm going to have to dance attendance or I'm going to find myself hiking down the Falls Road with my belly-button jammed up against Ron Mason's back and both of us rolling our eyes and wondering how the hell we got sandbagged. But I'm going to do one thing before I go up there. One thing that's going to give me the greatest of pleasure.'

'And what would that be, I wonder?' the RUC man replied pleasantly.

'Relieve you of one crisp ten-pound note,' said the man in the camel coat with considerable satisfaction.

Drake rode upwards with the anonymous crowd in the lift clutching his briefcase tightly in front of him as though he feared that at any moment it might be snatched from his grasp by one of the secretaries or pasty-faced messengers who seemed to spend their lives in transit between floors delivering bulging folders. The familiar dusty bureaucratic scent of the Yard was already sweet in Drake's nostrils. The electric tingle reached him even here, sandwiched in the crush of humanity between the aluminium walls of the lift, and when he stepped out on to the Specialist Operations floor the full jolt surged through his body. He was back where he belonged, in the corridors of power, for it was here that the cream of the nation's crime fighters had their lairs, the synthesis of the Met's finest talent, the tungsten-hard cutting edge. And he was back among them, reclaiming his rightful place, ready to lead them to greater glory.

Drake began to walk down the featureless passageways, grey composition floor underfoot, light grey walls studded with dark grey doors with little metal holders into which were slotted stencilled cards identifying the occupants of the hive. A uniform world of drab Civil Service grey illuminated by ceiling light panels which stretched before him in one continuous overhead ribbon of white light panels which stretched before him in one continuous overhead ribbon of white light.

As he walked with the measured step of a victorious gladiator, Drake allowed his thoughts to consider the species which inhabited Specialist Operations. First there were the squads of SO 1, the serious crime squad and task force detectives, who spent their time racing around town smashing in doors at three in the morning and hauling pathetic examples of crime's dinosaur age, the wham-bam blaggers, out of their beds for a grilling on the latest series of armed robberies. But in Drake's book even the most apelike member of SO 1 outpointed the Neanderthal types of SO 8, the flying squad, with their tasty tickles, their ramps and fit-ups, their vulgar spivvy suits and sheepskin coats, loud voices and whisky breath. These heavy mobs lived cheek by jowl with the effete denizens of SO 6, the company fraud branch, who looked like accountants and carried copies of the *Financial Times*, or the weirdos of SO 11, the crime intelligence branch, who seemed to spend most of their time impersonating telephone repairmen, plumbers or sections of privet hedge. Down the bright tube of the corridor their doors were open, offering glimpses of cluttered, ill-organized offices, left open deliberately so that the occupants could visit and banter at will. Frequently knots of detectives from various squads would mingle in the corridor itself, leaning against the walls to compare notes and score off each other, so puffed up with their own importance that they missed the true game plan of Specialist Operations, which was all about power. The ultimate power, not simply the ability to deprive an individual, however lofty, of his treasured liberty, but more significantly, the power to work the levers which operated the complex machinery of the Metropolitan Police.

As he walked down the corridor, nodding here and there to a familiar face, enjoying the incredulity in their eyes, Commander Larry Drake almost laughed out loud at the absurdity of their tiny world.

At the far end of the passageway he turned the angle into the domain of the security sections, SO 13, the anti-terrorist branch and the various protection groups. Here the doors were not only closed, they were secured and triple locked for this was an area into which no one ventured without a cast-iron reason, where messengers scurried in and out as though passing through an alien zone, where every movement was recorded on closed circuit television and security was obsessive. Nowhere was the code more solemnly observed than within Special Branch, where the true warriors waged their relentless war against the enemies of the state, where secrecy was standard operating procedure and fragments of information were disclosed on a need to know basis only.

When he reached his own suite of offices Drake drew himself up to his full height and allowed his features to settle into a firmly composed expression of authority before making his entrance into the ante-room, where a clutch of typists, all positively vetted, toiled under the direction of his personal secretary, the formidable Joyce Swallow, very business-like this morning in a charcoal two-piece and white blouse. She wished him good morning from behind her word processor with that haughty, proprietorial I've-been-through-all-this-before-so-don't-give-me-any-hassle look favoured by the Yard's senior office staff.

'Good morning, Joyce,' Drake replied, easing on a smile as he fished his keys out of his pocket and crossed the general room to the door of his own office.

Joyce Swallow waited until he had the key in the lock before speaking to his back. 'I got your message, Commander Drake,' she said primly, obliging him to turn to answer her.

'Message?'

She smiled, confirming to her underlings that she had scored the first hit in the battle for control of the office.

'Why, the Earl Grey of course,' she replied archly.

'Ah yes.' Drake turned the numbered security key in the lock, recalling his instruction that the fragrant tea was to become a feature of his routine, 'Yes, of course. Perhaps I could have a cup, if it's not too much trouble?'

'But of course,' Joyce replied. 'I'll have one of the girls put the kettle on right away.'

Drake warmed up his smile. He understood just how important it was to win the respect and loyalty of a personal secretary, for they ranked high in the canteen mafia and could be treacherous adversaries if crossed. Idly he recalled that there had been a rumour that his predecessor, Ronald Mason, had had something going with Joyce Swallow and for an instant he imagined her body, stripped of its demure grey, spreadeagled beneath the bantam figure of Ron Mason and he almost guffawed as he thanked her and went through into the inner sanctum. Inside, Drake surveyed the spacious office with profound satisfaction. It occupied a lofty corner position with windows on two aspects providing outstanding views over the dense London skyline.

In accordance with his instructions, the pale green Axminster had been freshly shampooed. The leather upholstery of the visitors' armchairs actually gleamed and the dark wood of the massive reproduction antique desk glowed from a fresh waxing. In the space behind and to the side of the desk, a computer terminal stood beside a communications console and a black cabinet which contained a shredder. To the right, bookshelves displayed several yards of leather-bound legal tomes and Force manuals and a bow-fronted cabinet with brass handles held a television set and video-recorder.

Drake crossed to the desk, lifted his brief-case on to the pristine blotter and released the locks. He took out a fat leather Filofax, a portable cellphone and a chromium-plated wrist-exerciser with red plastic hand grips, all of which he placed on top of a thick folder which contained his briefing papers.

Joyce Swallow came in with his tea and a brown manilla envelope with red wax seals stamped several times with the word SECRET. She placed both on the desk in front of him and with just a hint of a superior smile announced, 'Morning prayers are at ten.' Pointedly she consulted her wristwatch and added, 'So if you want a staff meeting you'll have to look sharp about it.'

Drake eased himself into his big high-backed swivel chair. 'Thank you, Joyce, I'll buzz you,' he responded dismissively and she swept the desktop with a disapproving glance, then strutted back to her own domain.

Larry Drake sipped his tea and allowed himself a smirk of pleasure. Morning prayers . . . what an exquisite reminder that he had regained the citadel. Morning prayers was Met-speak for the start of the day conference when the chosen were summoned to the Commissioner's imposing oak-panelled office which resembled a galleon's wardroom to chew over immediate problems and offer advice. Even in his heyday with NEL, Drake had not been a member of this inner cabinet, but now as head of Special Branch, he automatically accompanied the AC Specialist Operations to the Commissioner's morning briefing. The smirk grew into a warm glow but just as quickly began to cool as he was reminded of the po-faced expression with which the Old Man had greeted Peter Ashworth's finagling of his appointment. True, no Metropolitan Police Commissioner in his right mind would cross swords with the limp wristers from the Home Office, particularly not a Minister such as Ashworth who was a favoured son at No. 10, and even more particularly when the Commissioner in question was still awaiting the customary knighthood which went with the job. So although he was prepared to accept the request which sent Ron Mason unceremoniously on his way to Belfast and in the same sleight of hand brought Drake in from the cold, he couldn't completely conceal his distaste for the wheelers and dealers at Queen Anne's Gate. Drake, his antennæ tuned, had detected the chill and now that he was in the chair at last, he knew he couldn't afford to leave anything to chance. He needed to consolidate his position quickly and decisively, and that meant producing something so outstanding from the hat that the assembled company at morning prayers would be dazzled by his brilliance.

Drake flipped open his dossier and began to leaf through the documents it contained. On top was a telex describing the current state of security alert. The Bikini Alert. There were three stages of readiness: Bikini Black, the normal state, if anything could be described as normal with Irish terrorists and lunatics from the Middle East always likely to pull some stunt when least expected; Bikini Orange, when cars carelessly parked near sensitive buildings were apt to have their boots blown open by a remote-controlled contraption called a wheelbarrow; and Bikini Red, the highest state of alert, which presaged Armageddon and sent everyone scurrying for the bunkers. Drake scanned the message. Bikini Black. He set it aside and began to burrow into the colour-coded paperwork. There were the usual rosters showing the deployment of the Branch, two- and three-men teams assigned to cover emerging political situations and visiting delegations from questionable countries, the embassy schedules and the bread-and-butter activities at the ports and airports, sit-reps on the covert surveillance currently in place, and a sheaf of progress reports on specific target operations. Nothing out of the ordinary, nothing to stimulate the imagination, nothing to sink the teeth into. With a sigh, the SB Commander pushed the folder aside.

Looking up, Drake allowed his eyes to explore the office until his attention focused on the computer console waiting obediently for his command, and felt a twinge of resentment. More at home with the electrode green data displays than with musty files of paperwork; he had been the genius behind 'Little Nel', the ferociously powerful intelligence computers which ran Narcotics Enforcement Liaison, the most brilliant drug-busting operation ever conceived, culling the cream of Europe's top detectives into one unit; but even this array of talent was a mere appendage to the electronic wizardry at the heart of the grand design. Little Nel, the data cruncher, his own creation.

The resentment became an ache as Drake sipped his Earl Grey and stared at the VDU. He picked up the wrist-exerciser and began to clench the springs in his hand to relieve the tension the memory had created. They had contrived to make a fool of him with that Snow Man débâcle, plotted to overthrow him, those rapacious Germans of the Polizei so besotted with their notions of clinical efficiency. Chopped him down and raped Little Nel! The dance of the chrome springs in his hand increased with righteous indignation and he fixed the computer screen with a baleful stare as if trying to project his own brain cells into the microchip before he reached out, turned on the power and watched the terminal run through its diagnostics, checking itself out in a series of challenges and responses which built up on the screen. The ache continued to grow as his fingers went to the keyboard and tapped in his personal security code, opening up access to all the formidable computer power of the Yard's data banks with executive override into PNC, MET COMCON and the highly classified systems. SB was the only department with a mandate to snoop through the entire complexity of the system under the prerogative of national security and in theory nothing could be hidden from the SB Commander's eyes. But NEL, cloaked in its own layers of security, was protected by access codes denied even to The Branch.

But now that he was roaming the system the idea crystallized into stark clarity. Would the Germans who now lorded it over NEL have taken the precaution of erasing the personal signature of the creator from Little Nel's memory? Without further hesitation Drake tapped in the code and his finger hovered over the execute key. Intent on the VDU, he stroked the key and immediately the NEL duty state began to march across the screen.

Stealthy as a thief, Drake scrolled through the data, his eyes narrowing in disbelief. Jesus, they were into everything! Raw crime data from every corner of the world rolled down the screen, page after page, each batch accompanied by a progress summary and target projection. On and on he scrolled, ripping through acres of field intelligence. Those double-dyed squareheads were having a ball with his creation!

Outrage seized him, but he retained the presence of mind to log-off before his intrusion could be detected. Staring at the cursor blipping on the screen, the SB Commander felt he had been personally violated, as if an unseen molester had reached out from a crowd and goosed him.

Mortified, he turned back to his desk and alighted on the manilla envelope with its red seals and gaudy SECRET stamps which Joyce Swallow had deposited on his blotter. Still nursing his impotent fury, he broke the seals with a thumbnail and withdrew a single sheet of powder blue paper from the stout envelope. When he read the heading it dawned upon him that this was the first time in his police career that he had actually set eyes on a document so highly classified that no more than a mere handful of mortals were privy to its contents.

The heading said Box 500, the innocuous Security Service euphemism for the Curzon

Street headquarters of MI5. Typed underneath was the title *Threat Assessment*, and as he read what followed a tingle ran through his fingers. He was being entrusted with the innermost secrets of the realm, and the jolt of excitement which ran through his body was as though he had been jabbed with a cattle prod. A subheading half way down the page of single-spaced typing leaped out at him. It said *Snuffbox* and he read the paragraphs below, consuming the wisdom of some anonymous INTCELL analyst with a rising fever of anticipation.

'. . . reliable sources in the Middle East indicate a growing propensity for criminal activity, notably racketeering, to seed new extremes of quasi-political activity. Symbiosis of criminal and terrorist activity has already been identified particularly within the infrastructure of groups such as Abu Nidhal. This leads to the hypothesis that a new wave of hostage taking/assassination of prime targets funded by criminal enterprise may now be imminent. There are positive indicators that the drug-related criminal subculture of the United States may be particularly susceptible to manipulation by terrorist organizations.

Drake stared at the paper as at a vision. Racketeering . . . drugs . . . terrorism . . . prime targets . . . *Snuffbox!* The vision blinded him, and immediately he saw how he could reflect that brilliance and dazzle his peers at Morning Prayers.

Quickly Drake scooped the *Threat Assessment* into the document safe bolted to the floor under his desk, twirled the combination, and cast a conspiratorial glance around the office. That was it!

His debut would be outstanding. He could hardly contain himself. But first he had to delegate some of the dross, otherwise the great SB machine might slip a cog. He pressed the intercom buzzer and Joyce Swallow came on the line.

'Get Superintendent Bailey in here the moment he arrives,' he commanded curtly.

In the outer office the man in the heavy-rimmed spectacles threw his coat over a chair, winked at Joyce Swallow, nodded towards the door leading into Drake's office and asked, 'Well, what's your verdict on his nibs then, Joyce?'

Joyce Swallow lifted her eyebrows in an expression of distaste, 'Mr Smarm himself. Stuck-up poser if you ask me, Don. Thinks he's God's gift.'

'Any particular bee in his bonnet?'

'Search me. Probably wants you to help him hang some pictures of himself shaking hands with God.'

Joyce sniffed and Donald Bailey, the detective-superintendent who acted as the SB Commander's right-hand man, rolled his eyes sympathetically.

'You'd better get in there,' Joyce advised him, 'It's ten minutes to show time.'

CHAPTER 6

'God's teeth, Andy.' Don Bailey voiced his exasperation.

'Will you wipe that smirk off your face and talk to me? I get you down here so that you can mark my card on this maniac we just got lumbered with and all you do is sit there with that told-you-so grin.' The Special Branch Superintendent took off his spectacles and wearily massaged the pressure marks on the bridge of his nose. 'I mean, Ronnie Mason was no great shakes, spent most of his time in the office lusting after Joyce, only he was so preoccupied with the call of the loins that at least he left the rest of us to get on with the job.' He shook his head. 'Never knew what hit him when the knives got him clean between the ribs. But I tell you, he seemed like Einstein compared to this lunatic who comes waltzing in today, first day aboard, mind you, starts giving everybody the evil eye. Now don't get me wrong, Andy, I don't mind that, I can take all the flak they dish out, I mean, in my time I've been jerked around by experts, only this twerp, he tells me to muster the troops for his pep talk and then he comes bowling out of there with this look on his face like he's just come down off the mountain with the tablets of Stone and roars off to The Box like he's got a flame up his arse. Leaves me sitting there with the lads all spruced up without so much as an apology. I felt a right prat, I can tell you.'

The words came gushing out in a torrent of myopic indignation, then Bailey replaced his spectacles and gave his companion a beseeching look. 'So what I want, old mate, is some good SP on this joker, and what I don't want is to be sitting there being treated to a smug cat-that-got-the-cream smirk, because you and me go back a long way and I'm entitled to some respect and consideration.'

Barnes laughed. 'Don, you're priceless. I was just thinking when you were rabbiting on there, how everybody was busting a gut to stuff this particular genie back into the lamp and we got him in there and we slammed it shut and by Christ if he didn't pop straight out again and land in your lap. Somewhere down the line you must've upset the gods, my friend, because what you have got there is the original Walter Mitty. He was bad enough with us, but with your lot, all that cloak and dagger stuff . . .' Barnes shook his head and pursed his lips to hide the grin. 'I've got to tell you, he's going to be in his oil tot.'

It was noon and the bar of the Feathers, a Victorian tavern down the street from the

Yard, was practically deserted. The pub with its dark furniture and extensive bar had long been a favourite haunt of detectives who could only take the claustrophobia of the Dream Factory in small doses. After the morning fiasco, feeling indignant and humiliated, Don Bailey had fallen back on his CID instinct and had immediately determined to get something on the source of his discomfort. Casting around for a confidant who might be able to furnish the goods, he had picked up the phone and called his old friend Andy Barnes. They'd been sergeants together in the Clubs Squad, so he felt justified in cashing in a favour by requesting a meet at the Feathers.

Now they sat on stools at one of the round beer-stained tables, a non-alcoholic lager and a tonic water with ice and lemon between them for appearance's sake as Barnes, now a detective-superintendent with Narcotics Enforcement Liaison, took his time enjoying the chagrin of his host before he began the serious business of briefing him on possible chinks in the armour of the new SB knight errant. Observing the rules of the game, Bailey was obliged to lay on the agony. This ritual he continued to perform with outraged gusto.

'You're not going to believe this, Andy. I mean, I wouldn't have believed it myself if I hadn't seen it with my own eyes.' Bailey hunched forward over the table and lowered his voice. 'He won't use the phone.'

Barnes cocked an eyebrow at this latest snippet of eccentricity. 'How'd you mean, he won't use the phone?'

'Honest to God —' Bailey's head wagged in mournful disbelief — 'he won't use the phone. He's got this pocket gizmo, portable cellphone, and he's walking around with this thing making calls right there in the office and Joyce is so amazed she says to him why doesn't he use the ordinary phone, we've got scramblers and everything, and he looks at her straight-faced and he says there's no way he's going to end up on some KGB phonetap. He actually said that! Joyce couldn't believe it. This is his first day, first couple of hours in SB, and already he's way out of his tree.' Bailey's head shook more rapidly. 'A pocket phone, in the office, can you believe it?'

'That sounds just like our man,' Barnes replied. 'When he was with NEL he was very keen on conspiracies, always looking over both shoulders at the same time. He's got this runaway imagination, the slightest thing can set him off, and he's in cloud cuckoo land. And the media, oh boy, has he got a yen for the media. You watch, something happens and he'll start playing it to the gallery, sees himself as some kind of megastar.'

Barnes took a sip of tonic water. 'I mean, we're still living with his cock-ups, they're like mines, keep popping up to the surface, you never know when another one's going to go off. Our main prisoner on that job, Spinelli the mafioso undertaker, jumped bail and skedaddled to the States and I had to send one of my people over there to try to get him back — all because the file took a walk at the critical moment. It's a pound to a penny somewhere down the line I could lay that balls-up at your man's door. He's from another planet.'

Bailey stared into his alcohol-free lager. 'You remember back when life seemed so simple, what the hell did we do to deserve a clown like this?'

'Search me,' Barnes said, 'and count me out, you've got him now.'

'So help me,' Bailey appealed, rolling his eyes behind the thick lenses. 'I've got to clip his wings before he makes us a laughing-stock. Give me something good and heavy, Andy, so when the time's right I can hit him over the head with it and do us all a favour.'

Barnes frowned, drank some more tonic and then leaned forward so that they were both hunched over the table. 'Well . . . he's a computer freak, that's his real claim to fame. Now a strength could be turned into a weakness if, you play your cards right. Then there's this DS of mine I've got over in the States on the salvage job, he was on your man's personal team when he was pulling some swift strokes. Good D. Soon as he's back I'll sound him out, if you like.'

'What's his name, this DS of yours?'

'Rowley,' Barnes said. 'Tony Rowley.'

Bailey frowned. 'Don't think I know the name.'

'Was skipper to Dad Garratt.'

'Jesus!' Bailey blinked and they began to plot in earnest. The kidding around was over. It was time to get down to serious business.

At that same moment Commander Larry Drake was sitting in a windowless shoebox office squinting under ferocious neon glare and trying hard not to show the dismay which accompanied the shattering of his most cherished illusions.

The day had started so well. Morning Prayers at the Yard had exceeded even his expectations. They had trooped into the Commissioner's conference room and had taken their places in the easy chairs which the old Man believed gave the proceedings a chummy air of informality but in fact served the purpose of checking on fashions in natty socks as trousers rode up calves of men seated so low that it was difficult to maintain a dignified posture. Legs crossed and uncrossed, jackets bunched up around the neck as deliberations on topics of the day ranged around the group which collectively represented the highest policy-making organ of the Metropolitan Police.

When his turn came Drake launched into his grand strategy with all the verve of a maiden speech, linking organized crime with the ravages of terrorism. To his immense satisfaction, his audience was attentive to the point of hanging on his every word and by the time coffee had been served and they were balancing cups and saucers on their knees with as much social grace as possible, Drake treated them to the spectre of the next armed robbery financing a terrorist outrage of unprecedented proportions. He reminded them gravely of past horrors, the Iranian Embassy, the Libyan People's Bureau, expounded solemnly on the ratchet effect of crime-sponsored terrorism, became expansive on the subject of illegal narcotics, and rounded off a brilliant performance with a pledge that henceforth SB would address this newly identified threat to the very fabric of society with unrivalled zeal now that he was at the helm.

Austere and aloof by nature, the Commissioner was never one to interject directly, preferring to allow some consensus to emerge from the discussion, but when Drake caught the Old Man's eye whilst at his most fervent he believed he had been rewarded with a nod of agreement. Only McKenzie, the vinegary Deputy whose penchant for stamping on the unorthodox was legendary, cleared his throat in the long silence which followed Drake's oration, and then asked with some apparent difficulty, as though his voice was somehow constricted with emotion, 'Commander Drake, what evidence do you have to support this — this —' he was having difficulty selecting an appropriate noun — 'this notion of yours?'

Drake looked over at the Old Man with the smugness of a shared secret and replied evenly, 'Oh I'm afraid that's classified information, need to know eyes only, including the Commissioner of course.'

The Deputy seemed primed to explode. 'Poppycock!' was all he could manage to splutter as he choked on a mouthful of coffee, and in his best paternal manner the Old Man brought Morning Prayers to a close.

Brimming with enthusiasm, Drake had hastened back to his own office and had instructed Joyce to make him an immediate appointment at The Box, so anxious was he to expand upon the prediction succinctly outlined in the *Snuffbox Threat Assessment*. He had to talk to the INTCELL analyst who had identified the link, pump the well dry before the toadies on the staff of the Deputy, who was obviously motivated against him through envy, could undermine his credibility. He had to be fireproof.

But one thing was missing from the meteoric career of Larry Drake. He had had no previous dealings with the Security Services and as his appointment to head of SB had been a political conjuring trick on the part of his Home Office patron, there had been no time for the careful grooming process which would normally have presaged the crowning of a Special Branch overlord.

Consequently, when he arrived at the non-descript building in Curzon Street which housed the INTCELL cadre of Box 500, Drake was totally unprepared for what was to follow. His illusions began to crumble when he was greeted not by some steely-eyed Cold War warrior of British Intelligence, but by an insignificant individual in a Wind-in-the-Willows waistcoat and spotted bow tie who made a cursory examination of his credentials and gave him a paper pass. There were no codes, passwords, cunning security challenges, just a glance down a list on the desk officer's clipboard.

'What if I were an impostor?' Drake put the question with growing irritation at this cavalier attitude to the defence of the realm.

'You wouldn't be on my check list then, would you?' the DO replied, treating the inquiry with the contempt it deserved and flourishing his clipboard as though explaining elementary logic to a recalcitrant child. 'Besides, nobody's going to be stupid enough to impersonate The Branch, now are they?' Before Drake could catch the double meaning the waistcoat set off at a fast trot leading him down a labyrinth of dreary corridors before depositing him at the door of the intelligence analyst with whom he had requested an audience. The whole experience was so mundane, so prosaic, that Drake was already feeling deflated.

Now that he was on the other side of the door squinting in the excessively bright artificial light which blazed off the bare white walls of the tiny room, his bewilderment was complete. For across the cheap desk which filled most of the floorspace sat the INTCELL analyst who had so successfully fired his imagination. He had expected a cool military type with a firm jaw and a crisp Sandhurst manner. Instead he found himself confronted by a woman of indeterminate age, although he put her in her early forties, with frizzy ginger hair and a face so freckled that her complexion reminded him of a piece of mouldy linoleum.

She looked up at him. 'What can I do for you, Mr ah-hum?'

'Drake,' he reminded her. 'Commander Drake.'

'Ah yes, of course, The Branch.' She made it sound like something in the Forestry Commission. 'I'm Anthea Gibson. So what brings you to our little outfit?'

'I wanted to talk to you about the threat assessment you wrote, *Snuffbox*.'

'Oh really?'

'It touched an area I'm particularly interested in, you see, the correlation between organized crime and terrorism.'

'Oh really?'

'Hmm, yes indeed. My last job was in charge of narcotics investigation. You've heard of NEL?'

'Nel?' She was becoming monosyllabic.

'Narcotics Enforcement Liaison,' Drake explained. 'PanEuropean, big computer operation, concentrating on what I call the multinationals of organized crime. Although I say it myself, it was my concept, you know, crime in the big league is no respecter of national borders, yet the police response has traditionally been parochial and . . .' He shrugged, suddenly aware that he was sidetracking himself. 'Anyway I've handed that on now, but it occurred to me when I read your, I must say most persuasive, assessment, that we, the police, and in particular my own people in SB, should be giving this possibility really serious attention.'

'How interesting.'

He tried to look behind the freckles to see if she was teasing him, but there was no obvious sign. 'That's why I wanted to talk to you.'

'For what purpose precisely?'

'To see what more you can tell me.'

Anthea gave him a tolerant smile. 'Mr Drake, I'm afraid you may have slightly misunderstood my function here at The Box. I'm an analyst, you see. I take the raw intelligence which comes in through our network and try to make some sense out of it, look for trends, try to predict patterns of behaviour. Oh, I've got stacks of stuff on Abu Nidhal, Hezbollah, all the factions currently in vogue in the Middle East, the mavericks, the mercenaries, the political manipulators. I've got extremists, agitators, anarchists, stacks and stacks of it. I've got speculation and possibilities from our people in the field and all sorts of statistics. I can even tell you the size and brand of Gadaffi's underpants. All of this I sift through searching for some direction, and when I think I've identified something I report it in the Threat Assessment.'

'And you saw a trend linking organized crime to terrorism?' Drake asked eagerly.

'Most certainly, but if you'll pardon my saying so, Mr Drake, I'm not looking at this material as a policeman might. Facts are your job; mine tends to be very much in the abstract.'

Drake felt a sinking feeling in his stomach. 'But surely with this wealth of information you can give me some pointers, get me started?'

'Well, I can certainly try. But where to start, that's the question.' Her eyes roved around the little room and settled on the ubiquitous putty grey screen of an IBM compatible on a metal stand to one side of her desk. 'I tell you what, why don't I have another run through the stuff on my computer, dump anything that looks worthwhile on to a floppy and you can run it through your system and see what comes up?'

'Sounds good,' Drake said, and the swarm of freckles glowed into a smile. 'You know, this is most heartening. We beaver away here in our own little world, and well — to be frank — nobody in The Branch has ever taken any interest in the Snuffbox before. I put them in largely for my own satisfaction. I didn't think anybody bothered to read them, let alone take them seriously.'

Drake blinked, taken aback at what he assumed to be a poor attempt at iconoclastic humour, but before he could respond a low rumbling from the corridor outside captured their attention and Anthea Gibson, face suddenly ablaze, glanced at her watch and in a flurry of activity wrenched open the bottom drawer of her desk, grabbed a half-pint enamel mug from some deep recess and flew out of the room as though Drake no longer existed.

Dumbstruck, Larry Drake stared after her and was treated to the sight of an ancient tea-trolley complete with urn trundling down the passageway under the command of a matronly figure in a white overall. Figures swarmed around the trolley as men in Fair Isle pullovers and women in knitted cardigans fell upon it from all directions. Before his eyes, Anthea elbowed her way through the scruin and became embroiled in a heated argument with the stout tea-lady. Before the SB Commander could react, his new-found ally, the INTCELL analyst, custodian of the innermost secrets of the most famous intelligence service in the world, came stomping back into the minuscule office, slammed a mug half full of thick brown liquid down on the desk and began to beat a furious tattoo on the partition wall, freckles blazing.

'Fergus, you dickhead!' she screamed at the occupant of the next cubicle. 'I'll get you for this!' She turned to Drake as though seeing him for the first time. 'Little creep had the last bacon roll off the trolley. He knows I can't exist without my bacon roll!'

CHAPTER 7

Barricades surrounded Herald Square, holding back the holiday hordes outside Macy's. Long planks slotted into the saw-horse supports were freshly painted blue with the legend in white: *Police Line — do not cross.* Of all the cops on crowd control duty only the motorcycle patrolmen could still perform the black leather swagger. New York city fathers had long since decreed that such macho garb was too aggressive for the corporate image of The Finest and so the officers on foot patrol or crewing the blue and white RMP cars found it beneath their dignity to swagger in blue nylon jackets, even for the Macy's Parade.

There was a good-natured carnival atmosphere in the square as the moment approached to light up the mammoth Christmas tree shaped out of millions of tiny bulbs which rose up the frontage of the store. From the backs of TV trucks, camera perches were lofted above the crowd on extending red calipers, the platforms shrouded in polythene sheeting looking like aliens from another world.

The moment came, and in a ripple of yellow

fire the great electric Christmas tree flared into life, sweeping upwards through a trillion tiny filaments. For an instant Con Ed had deposed Santa Claus as the patron of Christmas.

Overhead huge inflatable fictional figures ducked and lurched as the parade bunched up for the finale, whooping and barnstorming around the block like Indians circling a wagon train.

When they'd had their fill of the razzmatazz, Walker and Rowley slipped away and headed for the nearby Midtown South precinct house. They turned down West 35th Street. Away from the glitz of the parade, the pavements running down the flank of Macy's had been roped off with miles of orange tape to protect pedestrians from the crumbling superstructure of the store, and although he was becoming familiar with the honeycomb of Manhattan neighbourhoods, each little community defending its space with the ferocity of a village, Rowley still found it difficult to comprehend the squalor which so quickly manifested itself within a few minutes' walk of the main thoroughfares.

Sensing the Brit's fascination with the idiosyncrasies of the city, Walker gestured towards a space no greater than ten feet wide between two buildings.

'You see that alley there? They're going to build in that. It's the latest thing, sliver development, going all the way up. You know the real racket around here, Tony? Not buildings; air space. They're breaking their necks bidding for the air space over anything one, two storeys, so they can build up. That's where the smart real estate money's going these days. Air space. Unbelievable, huh?'

At the precinct there was the usual circus in the foyer with a predominance of blue suits on double shift to cover the parade. Under the 'Busiest in the World' banner a dishevelled young patrolman, his belt festooned with equipment, his face flushed and sweaty, slammed his cap down on the desk and protested to a sergeant: 'How'm I supposed to do the hundred yards sprint with all this junk? No way, man. The little punk grabbed the handbag and he was gone. I mean, Jesus, it was embarrassing!'

Walker took Rowley through to the CO's office and put his head around the door. As he had expected, Ted Keitel was behind the desk, standing in for the Old Man. The Deputy Inspector who commanded the precinct was a believer in the privilege of rank and therefore seldom worked on a public holiday. The captain looked up from the reports he was initialling and waved Walker in.

'I've got Tony with me, Captain,' Walker said. 'Tony Rowley, the sergeant from Scotland Yard I was telling you about.'

'Bring him on in, Vince.' Keitel pushed the

paperwork aside and as Rowley came into the office stretched across the desk and offered his hand. 'MY XO, Captain Ted Keitel.' Walker made the introduction and Rowley glanced around the office, his eyes coming to rest on the precinct street map almost obscured by its rash of red marker pins.

Keitel said, 'I've got the Chief believing the crime status off the computer, only he don't trust it. Sticks pins in a map. He's about as prehistoric as your buddy here.' He came around the desk and gave Walker a playful poke in the chest. 'How'd you like this character, Tony? The original knucklehead New York flatfoot, nuts like footballs, but a brain like this —' he held a thumb and forefinger a quarter of an inch apart. 'Only wants to indict a character who's wired to the Government, top echelon snitch on the DEA payroll, and for what? Shooting up a jar of ketchup.'

'Ah, come on, captain,' Walker protested. 'That Bandit was doing his damnedest to waste a couple of our people.'

'Who shouldn't've been there.' Keitel turned to Rowley. 'You know this town, Tony? One mean mother, so mean the feds don't want to work here any more. Those guys, FBI, they'd rather resign than get posted to New York, claim they can't afford to live here on a special agent's *per diem,* but what it is, they don't have the gonads for this mother. Now this guy —' he gave Walker another playful poke in the chest — 'he's got 'em, only he thinks he can dictate to the brass how to run the Department and then wonders why they want to kick his ass. And where does that leave me?'

'Looking after my interests, Captain,' Walker said, grinning.

'Damned right,' Keitel said. 'Damned triple-A goddamn right!' He turned to Rowley. 'So I go into the lion's den downtown, Police Plaza where they eat precinct captains for lunch, and stand by this guy, which does not exactly endear me to my superiors, and I cut a deal for the schmuck, line him up for a nice vacation over in London with your outfit just until the dust settles, and is he grateful? Hell, no! Dummy's playing hard to get.'

Keitel rounded on Walker. 'I hear it's nice out at Breezy Point this time of year, Vince. How'd you like to put on the blue bag, walk around there a little, watch the grass grow?'

Walker said, 'Captain, it's Thanksgiving, headquarters'll be like a morgue. You'll have my answer by the time Chief Hanson's back in his office Monday morning.'

'Well, I'd better, Vince,' Keitel said, a frown clouding his face. 'Otherwise I wash my hands of you and you sink without trace all by yourself.'

The captain turned back to Rowley, 'Nice meeting you, Tony. See if you can't talk some British horse sense into this clown.'

'Ted isn't a bad boss,' Walker said as he took

Rowley up to the squad room. 'Just rank conscious. You get over lieutenant and even the best guys start getting nervous of downtown.'

The detectives' squad room was crammed with a collection of battered desks which looked as if they had been bought as a job lot from a surplus store, with eight-drawer filing cabinets wedged in between to form a kind of grey metal maze. Light filtered dimly through dusty meshed windows and yellow foam oozed out of splits in the worn-out chairs. Paperwork spilled from stacks of wire baskets, and in marked contrast to the depressing shambles of the place a young man in a cream safari suit who was talking rapidly into the telephone gave them a clenched fist power salute as they edged past and squeezed into an alcove between the metal cliffs. A collection of mugshots taped to the side of the cabinet stared down dull-eyed on the two detectives.

'So what are you going to do?' Rowley wanted to know.

'First off,' Walker replied, stretching back and resting an ankle on the corner of the desk, 'I'm going to let my good friend the Captain down there stew in his own juice a while. Ted Keitel knows I'm the best detective he's got on this lousy squad, and unless he wants the CO to have a hernia when his wall disappears under those goddamn marker pins, he'd better start giving me some insulation from those comedians downtown. Nah, that's unfair.

Ted's an OK guy underneath that stuffed shirt. Me and him go way back, only now he's got the career disease, sees himself commanding a precinct all his own one day, so he's not about to get himself into a bind with the brass over some dumb gold shield who won't toe the line.' He smiled ruefully. 'And to tell you the truth, Tony, in his shoes, I don't blame him. He got captain out of playing the system, so there's nothing to stop him going all the way.'

'Same thing at the Yard,' Rowley said. 'Good coppers, good at their jobs, start getting a little rank on their shoulders and it's like they've had a personality transplant the way they start fawning over the guv'nors. Becomes a full-time job.'

'You said it,' Walker agreed. 'They're running around all over the place trying to latch on to some gimmick that'll shoot 'em into high orbit and in the meantime it's the street cops who're getting on with the job.'

'Poor bloody infantry,' Rowley reflected.

'Sure.' Walker clasped his hands behind his head. 'And here's another one. Why is it that a cop gets stomped for bucking the system while a Bandit gets star treatment? Check that one out.'

Rowley reflected on his own experience at the hands of the Yard hierarchy. 'Well, they certainly don't write that into the words of wisdom when you take the oath to uphold the law.'

'No, but it sure as hell comes with the territory. You know what a cop's life's worth in this town? I tell you, kill a police officer, you're going to bargain a plea, probably take a little involuntary manslaughter off the DA, and you're going to be out again in five years maximum, every punk on the street knows that. So here you have the Brown Bag Bandit, robbing a bank just for kicks because he thinks he's the Sundance Kid.

'Now bear in mind this is not just your everyday psycho, this is a hundred per cent sociopath, no conception of right or wrong, the most dangerous animal you're ever going to come up against out there. So this Bandit does his damnedest to deep six two of my people and where is he now? In the slammer? No way. Turns out this Bandit is cosy with the government, and now the DEA have got their playmate stashed away while they do the job on me. That's irony, New York style.'

'I've had some of that irony myself,' Rowley said. 'We've got the same brand back home.' He returned to his original question, 'The point is, what're you going to do about it, Vince?'

Walker said, 'Well you know what they say, Tony, don't get mad, get even. What I'm looking for now is what our friends the feds call a window of opportunity.'

Rowley thought about that for a moment, then he hunched forward, resting his elbows on his knees as he turned a possibility over in his mind and at the same time wondered just how far he could trust this renegade stretched out in front of him. In the end it was Dad's voice which spurred him on.

'As it happens, I may be able to help you settle that score.' He paused and waited for the gleam of interest to show in Walker's eyes. 'See, Vince, I didn't tell you the whole story on my bail jumper. Spinelli is amenable.'

Walker raised an eyebrow. 'Amenable to extradition?'

Rowley shook his head. 'Forget extradition. Think of a wily old villain with lots of connections. Wouldn't it be a waste to turn him off now, when there's still something to bargain with? This is a guy who could wake up one morning and if the signs were auspicious, he could deliver a good slice of The Enterprise.'

Walker swung his legs down, suddenly attentive. 'The Enterprise. Are we talking about the product shipper the DEA's drooling over?'

'The very same,' Rowley said. 'That's why I've got to move carefully, these are very dangerous people.' He frowned. 'Put it this way, Vince. The understanding I have with my capo is personal and fragile. Whatever I do with him, I have to do myself, and he has to be fully protected, only what I'm thinking, the way things are turning out, you could have half the ingredients for the recipe already.'

'You mean the Bandit?'

'The DEA's star turn, you said it yourself,' Rowley said. 'With my capo and your Bandit, I was just thinking, we could put something together, something that'd work to our mutual advantage.'

'You got something in mind?'

Rowley nodded. 'But I've got to see Spinelli again before I know for sure. All I'm suggesting is, that if you were to bite the bullet, take the offer and come over to my firm, I think we might just be able to do some business.'

'You know, Tony,' Walker began slowly, 'I always had you Brits pegged for the stiff upper lip types, play the game according to the rules no matter what.' He looked into Rowley's face with renewed interest and said, 'Don't tell me I'm beginning to detect a man after my own heart?'

Rowley said, 'You ever hear the expression agent provocateur?'

'We'd call it entrapment,' Walker said.

'You've got it,' Rowley said, hearing Dad speak to him again. 'It's for those times when the law and enforcing the law have got nothing to do with each other.'

'Walker regarded the errand boy from Scotland Yard in a new light. 'You're full of surprises today, Tony. So tell me about it and maybe you'll get yourself a new partner.'

Much later in the solitude of his room on the seventh floor of the Madison Towers Hotel in the quiet business section of Manhattan, Detective-Sergeant Tony Rowley felt the shakes begin, the familiar involuntary trembling spreading through his limbs. Depression sapped his resolve, and when he caught sight of himself in the dressing-table mirror he was instantly reminded of the source of the inner turmoil which threatened to tear him apart. The badger streak which crowned his head, the tuft of white hair which transported him back to the Bow Street courtroom where The Twins, screaming from the dock, had sentenced him to death. The picture changed and he was once again in the hospital intensive care unit looking down into Dad Garrat's blue-tinged face. Click of the camera in his mind and he was back in the street, flung against a brick wall by the searing gust of the fireball as a bomb blasted his patrol car and all but took his life. The Twins were determined to kill him, and after the car bombing he had surrendered himself to post-incident stress counselling to massage away the trauma. At least that was the theory, but all those calm reassurances couldn't dislodge the fear which had etched itself into his subconscious. Threats were an occupatinal hazard, but only cops with no imagination could shrug them off.

Rowley paced the hotel room, striving to conquer his agitation. He turned on the TV, losing himself in the blare of sound and the bright images on the screen, but still he couldn't settle. He wandered to the window and looked out over the nightscape of Manhattan. Velvet darkness shrouded the junkyard of nearby rooftops, but beyond, the city had on her sparkling cape of electric light and for a long moment he stared at the blue neon of the Pan Am building and listened to the rumbling of the traffic way below his window.

Rowley observed the scene but was not soothed by it, knowing that at any moment the passive trembling would be replaced by involuntary spasms of anger as his emotions yawed from one extreme to another. Come on, he demanded of himself, come on, get a grip!

But they were there inside his head and he couldn't dislodge them. The Twins, not just twins but identical twins, feeding off each other's ego and paranoia, the mercenaries of organized crime who would hire out to the highest bidder whenever robberies worthy of their talents were plotted.

The Twins had modelled themselves on the old robber barons who ruled their territories with a rod of iron, so far down the road to criminal insanity that they had no fear of the law and scorned 'the filth' with such open contempt that the pragmatic detectives who valued their lives gave them a wide berth, for they would not think twice about throwing acid into the face of the wife or child of any D foolhardy enough to cross them. Of all the swashbuckling detectives on the glamour squads, only Dad Garratt had had the nerve to pursue The Twins with the same relentless vanity. And when he had them bang to rights on the Heathrow bullion robbery, stitched up on the word of a supergrass, fate had intervened, and with Garratt dead The Twins had turned their rage upon his protégé.

Even now their evil influence reached to a hotel room on the other side of the Atlantic and, standing at the window, blind to the spangled glory of New York, Tony Rowley shuddered as he felt their feet dancing on his grave.

CHAPTER 8

Larry Drake was back in The Box, perched on a chair in the cubbyhole inside the honeycomb of the INTCELL section engaged in earnest conversation with the freckle-faced analyst. In the normal course of events the SB chief would have dealt with MI5 at director level as demanded by the etiquette of rank and Civil Service protocol, but his weakness for intrigue had led Drake to cast aside such niceties. He wanted to be tapped in at source, so desperate was he to ensure that his theory of the symbiosis of organized crime and terrorism should not leak out before he could engineer an opportunity to put it to the practical test and thereby reap the glory.

Larry Drake, intent upon making a sensational comeback, was besotted with the Plain Jane of a woman who had composed the Snuffbox Threat Assessment.

'How'd you get on with the floppy, Commander Drake?' Anthea wanted to know.

'Call me Larry,' Drake responded, trying hard not to leer as he endeavoured to win her confidence. 'I mean, we're friends, aren't we — colleagues at least — no need to be stiff and formal.'

'Well . . .' She blushed, a little flustered, 'I mean, you know . . . I'm not accustomed to being treated like . . . well . . . like a person.'

'Anthea,' Drake's voice boomed off the walls as he seized the opening, 'I happen to believe that there's just too much pomposity and, well, I'll say it, chauvinism in this security service of ours.'

'Amen to that,' she replied, and Drake knew he had touched the right chord.

'I mean, you've got a fine mind, Anthea,' he ploughed the furrow. 'An outstanding mind. I don't stand by and see someone with your qualities held back just because of the old boy network. Now I'm going to make sure you get recognition for this, you're doing your country a great service.'

By now it had become a leer, but Anthea was too flattered to notice. She was quiet for a moment and then said, 'You know, that's the first time anyone said anything like that to me in all the years I've been cooped up in here.'

He reached out and placed a hand over hers. 'Anthea, we're going to change all that.' His voice still rang with sincerity. 'The head of Special Branch has got a certain amount of clout and — I know I can tell you this in confidence — as it happens I have some particularly good connections in government circles. Strings can be pulled.'

He patted her hand. 'So, are we friends?'

The frizzy head nodded hesitantly and Drake moved in to consolidate his position. 'I have to tell you, Anthea, I found the data on the disk you sent me quite exhilarating. It fitted in with so many of my own ideas. We're absolutely *ad idem,* as the lawyers would say.'

'Oh, it was just routine stuff.'

'Routine!' Drake echoed the self-effacing word. 'Routine perhaps in terms of raw field intelligence, but I'm talking about the interpretation, Anthea, the analysis, the path ahead. That's what I mean by brilliant. I was most impressed.'

'It was nothing.'

'Let me be the judge of that.'

Anthea Gibson, basking in this acknowledgement of her talent, couldn't resist telling her newfound disciple, 'Umm, Larry —' she tried his Christian name for the first time — 'honestly, that was nothing compared to the material just in, the deep cover predictions nobody's really tried to make any sense of, the long-range assessment.' Her voice trembled at the excitement of at last discovering a true confidant, someone she could actually talk to on the same wavelength. 'I wouldn't say this to another living soul, Larry —' the familiarity came easier the second time — 'but it's mind-blowing, absolute dynamite, or should I say Semtex. So hot it can't even be classified.'

'Your secrets are safe with me, Anthea,' Drake said, eyes ablaze with sincerity.

She giggled. 'If I can't trust the head of the Branch, who can I trust? I mean, it's not like spilling the beans to the *Guardian*, now is it?' The giggle became a self-conscious little laugh.

Drake nodded sagely before replying, 'Ah, if only a few others I could name had your sense of loyalty, my dear.' He shook his head, allowing body language to reinforce the point. 'Now what were you saying about predictions?'

The colour rose in her cheeks and her voice slipped back into a confidential tone. 'You were asking me about a link between organized crime and the terrorist community. Well, have you ever heard of an international drugs syndicate called The Enterprise?'

The Enterprise! Drake felt as if he had been stung.

'The Enterprise,' he mused, concealing his excitement. 'Would that be a multinational with principals in Colombia, Bolivia and Florida, shipping cocaine into the USA?'

'That's it,' Anthea replied, delighted that Drake had caught on so quickly.

'Now looking to ship in crack from the Continent,' Drake expanded in his best urbane manner. 'Oh, back in my drugs days we crossed swords with The Enterprise all right.'

'Splendid,' Anthea enthused. 'Now watch

this!' She swung around to the computer at her elbow and fed a disk into the drive, tapping keys to run the program. Immediately lines of green data began to slide across the dull grey screen. Drake watched the eruption of encrypted information swarm and scatter as she scrolled through the pages, his fascination growing. Despite his familiarity with computer programs, this one appeared so elegant that it eluded his grasp and a frown began to furrow his forehead.

'Don't worry,' Anthea explained as her fingers danced over the keyboard. 'You won't be able to follow this unless you have the cypher, but once you're in it's childishly simple.'

'What is it?' Drake asked, eyes glued to the screen.

'Coded traffic intercept. Langley through GCHQ, SIGINT stuff mostly, George Two, that's a CONCOM satellite the spooks popped out of the shuttle, geostationary over the Middle East. George is pretty long in the tooth now, but you give him a sector and he'll listen to telephones until the day he falls out of the sky. We always monitor Langley traffic just to keep tabs on our American cousins. They copy most of the rubbish to us anyway, but that's the first rule of this game: never trust your friends.'

'What about the Special Relationship?'

She gave a delicate little snort. 'Don't you believe it, Larry, that's just icing on the cake.

In the intelligence world you hunt alone.'

He looked back at the screen. 'You were going to explain?'

'Oh yes.' Anthea bit her lower lip and added, 'You know something, Larry? You're the first person to take me seriously. Let me explain. You remember Irangate?'

'Arms to the Ayatollah, cash to the Contras?'

'Right. The Ollie North show. We were watching it for ages before it blew up. They were so careless, the Yanks, they ruined a perfect covert operation, fleece the baddies to fund the goodies, textbook stuff, depending which side you're on, naturally. Well, when it all collapsed around their ears, certain people did certain things in the interests of self-preservation. And that's when the wild cards started to fall and the ace was Islam.' Her eyes glittered. 'You see, the spooks had a little ploy up their sleeve all along to cover their tracks if Ollie blew it, and while the Colonel was on TV making his patriotic speeches, someone deep in the field pulled the rip-cord and they all bailed out. Someone, God knows who, put Hezbollah in contact with The Enterprise, that was the wild card. So here you had the spooks, the American Central Intelligence Agency no less, actually making a deal with bandits in return for access to the political machinery of Colombia, which in turn could open the back door and send in supplies to the Contras and keep the White House happy.'

Anthea leaned her elbows on the desk. 'Nobody here would believe a word of it of course, Langley had them brainwashed, but I'm convinced they kept up the supplies to the Contras by arranging for The Enterprise and the Sword of Islam to do business. They just switched the rails from Teheran to Beirut. Of course I could never prove it, but my instinct tells me that's what happened. While the Marine and the Admiral faced the music, nothing stopped, it just burrowed a little deeper underground. What d'you think of that, Larry?'

Drake smiled and made a pretence of appreciating the complex plot, when in truth he had more or less lost interest. The machinations of the Middle East had always struck him as incredibly boring.

'Anthea, I'm sure you're right, but isn't this just a trifle . . . well, academic?' He made a dismissive gesture. 'I mean, when you wrote that Snuffbox assessment I naturally assumed —'

'Larry, you've missed the point,' Anthea broke in. 'I'm like a chess player, I'm looking for the end game while I'm still playing the opening gambit. I did some work on another batch of intercepts, this time stuff we got from 6, and the same pattern turned up again. The way I read it, those connections are still as strong as ever and now that the Syrians are in Beirut hell bent on discrediting the Jihad, what do Hezbollah need most?'

This time she didn't wait for him to answer. 'A boost for their battered image. And what better than to assassinate a soft target right here in London, on centre stage. Now they aren't stupid enough to use their own people, they wouldn't get past the airport, so who do they turn to to do them a favour? Their new friends The Enterprise! A gesture of goodwill, loan of a mercenary assassin, an American who can walk in unchallenged and do the job for them.'

Larry Drake blinked as his imagination clicked back into gear. This was more like it. 'Well, now you're talking,' he enthused. 'A coup for the mad mullahs, eh? Yes, I can see that.' He leaned across the desk drinking in her rapturous expression. 'So tell me, Anthea, this assassination attempt, where and when?'

The gauche question caused her eyebrows to lift in astonishment. 'Larry . . . look, I'm an intelligence analyst, that's what I do. I try to make some sense out of the stuff we steal from everyone else. But my work is in — how can I put it? — intangibles, predictions, scenarios, options. We don't have any powers of investigation or arrest here at The Box. Surely the wheres and the whens are the province of The Branch?'

'Oh yes, yes, of course.' Drake hastened to recover from his faux pas. 'It's just that I value your opinions, Anthea. What I meant to say was . . . well, how seriously should we take

Hezbollah? Aren't they just a bunch of Beirut bandits?'

'Bandits! Hezbollah is The Sword of Islam, the most potent terrorist force in the world today.' Her voice grew breathless and a pulse began to beat in her throat. 'Martyrs of the Jihad, parading to glory with their own blood streaming down their faces, marching to world domination in the name of Allah . . .'

To his amazement Drake found himself mesmerized.

'Hezbollah are the prime movers,' Anthea rushed on. 'Of all the active terrorist groups, only Hezbollah have the capacity to manufacture an IND . . .'

IND? The acronym skittered around in Drake's head. Where had he heard that before? One of those military briefings, some plum in the mouth major talking in a riddle of jargon. IND . . . got it! The explanation blazed inside his head like a neon sign. Improvised Nuclear Device!

He opened his mouth, but she was still in full flow. '. . . so exciting. I mean, I've cracked this all by myself, a real breakthrough to actually predict the first IND, the ticking bomb!'

Watching her, the question burning a hole in his mind, Drake felt a twitch in his loins as he blurted out, 'Anthea, this is incredible! You have to tell me more!'

Instantly her expression blanked and her

eyes narrowed. 'Oh no. Not even for you, Larry. This is mine, all mine. The terror nuke! I'm going to get my regrading on the strength of this. Oh boy, are those bastards going to sit up and take notice for once. I'm going to get an SEO out of this, get a flat in Kensington.' She wagged a finger. 'And no more flogging in on the lousy tube!'

Don Bailey walked into the Feathers. Behind the spectacles his eyes took a moment to adjust to the cosy gloom inside the already crowded bar and he was obliged to squint in order to make out the figure he was trying to locate.

Andy Barnes, his NEL counterpart, was standing at the end of the bar near a blackboard on which was chalked the day's pub lunch specials. Recognizing the serious drinking posture, Bailey eased himself through the crush and when he was close enough remarked, 'Looks suspiciously like the ritual drowning of the sorrows.'

Barnes turned around as Bailey emphasized the comment by pointing to the depleted gin and tonic in the other's hand.

'You ought to be a detective, Don,' the drugs chief observed drily.

'Be an improvement on what I'm doing now,' Bailey replied with feeling, turning his back on the neighbouring drinkers in order to give their conversation a degree of privacy. 'I've been looking for you all over, and what do I find? A Perrier man nursing a double slug of gin with a good portion of the working day still to go. So I wonder.'

'Are you asking me?'

Bailey shook his head. 'Nope. I already know the answer. I was looking for you in Disneyland —' he referred to the Special Operations Centre in the bowels of the Yard which was currently occupied by Narcotics Enforcement Liaison — 'and a little bird told me they're shipping you out, lock, stock and barrel.'

Barnes finished his drink in one long swallow, pulled a face and then signalled the barmaid for two more.

'Ice and lemon,' Bailey said. 'How'm I doing?'

'You'll make CID yet.'

'Meet interesting people, have meaningful conversations on the mysteries of life, then lock 'em up and throw away the key. So what's the SP?'

Barnes sighed. 'Polizei paranoia. Ever since the Germans took over NEL we've been having running battles. All they're ever looking for is intrigue. Got a bee in their bonnet we're out to pull some kind of flanker, complaining it's all too cosy bottled up in the Dream Factory, lobbying all the time for neutral ground.'

'The Old Man doesn't buy that, does he?' Bailey seemed genuinely astonished.

'You know the score as well as I do with the Commissioner, Don. New man. He's not going to rock the boat now, is he? Might sink his K. So he's doing his celebrated sitting on the fence routine while the jackboot hordes are stomping all over us.' Barnes grimaced at the recollection. 'Of course they want to take the whole shebang over to Bavaria where they'd have total control, but as you can imagine, the Carabinieri won't wear that one, so they're screaming Rome, and the French are hollering Paris, and everybody's throwing a tantrum. In the end we've got to placate 'em with a compromise.'

'And where've you come up with, Bermuda?'

'Basingstoke,' Barnes said flatly.

'Basingstoke?'

'Slap bang in the middle of the golden corridor. Silicon valley. We're going to Basingstoke.'

'Jesus!' There was awe in Bailey's voice. 'That isn't even in the MPD.'

'The Krauts scouted it out and found a place which looks just like a blockhouse, all yellow concrete with a perimeter fence. Used to be an Audi warehouse, so they felt at home right away.'

The fresh drinks arrived.

'They're busy lacing in the computers right now and then we'll be on the road,' Barnes went on. 'Polizei paranoia. Any wonder I need a drink?'

Bailey shrugged. 'Well, you know what it's like in the job these days, Andy: ninety per cent jockeying for position, ten per cent bragging about it. If that much time and energy was put into feeling collars we'd have the crime rate licked.'

'You never said a truer word,' Barnes said bleakly. 'So. You were looking for me and now you've found me. What we can do now is sink a few gins and put the world to rights, or you can tell me why you're so keen to seek out the convivial company of an old drug squad hack, as if I didn't know it. The Boy Scout's flipped his lid again, right?'

Bailey's face crumpled into an expression of anguish. 'Andy, Andy, this lunatic's driving me nuts. Two days is all it took, and I've got a mutiny on my hands. Let me give you a for instance. He tells me to get the troops together and then he comes bouncing in, starts telling 'em how he wants 'em to turn in all their PIRA informants so they can be programmed into the computer. My lads are sitting there and they're rolling their eyes, for God's sake. Everybody knows you put Paddy on disk and you're going to find him on the doorstep with his kneecaps blown away.' Bailey sighed. 'Now Ronnie Mason, he had his faults, but he was a good copper. This clown is a meddler, poking his nose into everything. A lazy incompetent I can deal with, but an incompetent enthusiast, that's the kiss of death. Drake's got everybody so riled up there's dark rumblings on the lower decks, so I've got to clip his wings before he can do too much damage.'

'You're dealing with a very tricky individual there,' Barnes warned, momentarily deflected from his own troubles. 'Drake's got a lot of clout in all sorts of surprising places. If you cross him, you're liable to get hurt.'

Bailey flapped a hand. 'OK, OK, you don't have to draw me a map, I've been around guvnors with delusions of grandeur before, you can usually leave them be and they'll burn out all on their own. Only this one's getting right up my nose.'

Bailey turned further around and leaned towards Barnes to give his next remark an even greater degree of privacy. 'There's worse. Andy, look, don't breathe a word of this. Drake's got himself involved with a bird at The Box.'

Barnes raised an eyebrow. 'Shagging?'

The SB superintendent shook his head. 'No, that I could cope with. Far as I'm concerned, he could be having it off with the entire traffic warden corps, male and female. Matter of fact, that would be ideal. Slip that to the *Sun*, bugger his PV and he'd be on his bike. No, this is worse. This is some biddy those fruit-cakes in The Box have got beavering away on threat assessments.' He lowered his voice. 'Straight out of *Alice in Wonderland*. So way out we shred most of 'em. Anyway I hear from a mate of mine over at 5 that Drake's gallop-ing round there all the time and he's closeted

135

with this nutcase for hours on end. Now I've got it on good authority that the big turn-on is the Snuffbox assessments.'

'Snuffbox?' Barnes queried the unfamiliar term.

'They're sort of assassination predictions, who Abu Nidhal's going to knock off next. You ask me, they get 'em out of cornflake packets.'

'Snuffbox.' Barnes toyed with the word. 'You learn something new every day.'

'Well, that's what's giving Drake the gigantic hard-on,' Bailey said testily. 'And any minute now, when he's got up a good head of steam, he's going to start screaming for action. That's why I've got to nip him in the bud.'

Barnes pursed his lips. 'You ought to think about that very carefully. I've seen our friend in action, remember, very smooth, very plausible. He's probably got the Old Man in his pocket by now and he's definitely well connected with the Home Office. You get out on a limb with Larry Drake, he'll saw the bough off and you'll be gone.'

Anguish further distorted Bailey's features. 'Why'd you think I came looking for you? Look . . . what you said before . . . I need this DS of yours to help me set up a game plan, before the wheel comes off.'

'Rowley?'

'Yeah. What's the chances?'

Barnes sank his second gin and tonic and exhaled the perfumed fumes. 'Right now Sergeant Rowley's in the Big Apple,' he replied. 'Cooking somebody else's goose.'

CHAPTER 9

Saturday was traditionally a quiet time in the civic area around City Hall in downtown Manhattan. The throng of bureaucrats moving between the bleached white municipal buildings had departed for the weekend, and on a public holiday the wide streets and little parks were even more noticeably deserted, with only a handful of workaholics heading doggedly for their offices.

Tony Rowley left the grim entrance of The Tombs and came down the shallow flight of steps. Even the constant low of traffic on Canal Street had slowed to a trickle. Such tranquillity under the leaden November skies came as something of a culture shock, for in his brief encounter with New York Rowley had experienced nothing short of manic activity.

He looked across the street and was relieved to see Vince Walker lounging against a fire plug, a midnight blue Buick V8 with a buckled front wing parked beside him at the kerb. Rowley hurried across and the two detectives got into the unmarked police car.

Rowley said, 'Atlantic City.'

Walker leaned on the wheel and looked across at him.

'That's what the man said,' Rowley continued, 'Atlantic City.' He shrugged. 'Where the hell's Atlantic City?'

Walker started the engine. 'Over in Jersey. Down the cast a-way, on the ocean.'

He eased the car into gear and pulled away. 'Gambling town,' he said, 'Cæsar's Palace, Bally's, lots of bored housewives go down there, and the orientals, Chinatown Friday evening, you can't move for the buses loading up for the weekend jaunt to slot-machine heaven.'

Rowley began to laugh. 'That's Spinelli all over, everything a drama. In London I had to meet him on the roof of a warehouse at dead of night. Now he wants to gamble.'

The car began circling a forest of slabsided highrise apartment blocks and emerged into a desolate tract under the elevated highway beside the East River. Driving one-handed, Walker began to thread the Buick down the rutted, rubbish-strewn wasteland between the concrete piers of the South Street Viaduct.

'This capo of yours, is he on the level?'

Rowley rocked a hand. 'The trouble with Spinelli is, everything's a riddle.'

Walker parked under the El near a collection of discarded oil drums and, turning up their coat collars against the damp breeze wafting in from the river, the two detectives began to walk down the deserted and shuttered fish quay towards the Fulton Street fish market.

Suddenly, cheek by jowl with the wasteland, the area took on the smirk of New York chic with old ware-houses transformed into collections of boutiques around cobbled plazas scattered with wrought-iron pavement furniture. Mullioned windows glistened under fresh coats of varnish and cosy interiors beckoned through bullseye panes.

On the edge of this transformation stood Sloppy Louie's, onetime hangout of the sailors and fishermen who toiled on the quays, which had also been given a face lift and now positively beamed with affluence. Inside, Walker steered Rowley through the crush to a booth at the rear and told him, 'This used to be an ordinary place, good and ordinary. Original New York low life. Now what d'you get? Bunch of yuppies think they're slumming and a bus load of Japanese tourists.'

But the bowls of chowder cheered Walker's mood and he returned to the business of the day. 'So he says Atlantic City. Well, that makes sense for an old-time capo. It used to be a mob town way back before the families split with tradition. Guinea gangsters parading up and down the boardwalk . . . Only those days are long gone. The mobsters are in corporate offices now looking like millionaires.' He cast an eye around the gleaming, mellow bar and lamented 'Everything's gone cockeyed respectable, you know? All the rackets these days, I tell you, they all have teams of legal eagles polishing their corporate images. Some Don wants a guy whacked these days, he don't have a hit man put a twenty-two round behind his ear any more and toss the body in the river. Just cancel his AMEX and he's dead. That's progress for you.'

Rowley said, 'Spinelli'll be OK. It's just . . . well, we're going to have to humour him. All this theatrical stuff is one of his quirks, but underneath he's rock.' He spooned some of the thick soup and wiped his lips on a napkin. 'Right now he's sitting in The Tombs thinking he's Jimmy Cagney and casting you and me in the supporting roles.'

Walker drank beer from a frosted glass. 'You don't have to tell me, buddy, this is tinsel town, remember? So what's real any more? Half the traffic's snarled up because some movie outfit's shooting a remake of *Naked City*. You don't see it on TV, it didn't happen.'

Rowley said, 'There's more Spinelli showbiz to come, Vince. We're going to have to meet a man in Atlantic City, a go-between. Some lawyer called Deegan, Maurice Deegan.'

Walker slapped a palm against his forehead. 'Are you kidding me?'

'Mean something to you?'

'Oh, that's beautiful! He actually told you Maurice Deegan?'

Trying to keep irritation out of his voice, Rowley replied, 'Something I ought to know?'

'Well, you could say that,' Walker said, 'because unless I miss my guess, and some other Maurice Deegan crept into the sewer, the rat we're talking about here is no other than Mighty Mo Deegan, star of the Grand Jury, who's got the Fifth Amendment tattooed on his black heart. Jeez, I didn't know that buzzard was still practising law.'

'I gather you know him, then?' Rowley disguised his inner alarm.

'Mighty Mo? Everybody knows him. He was an old-time rackets lawyer, mob mouthpiece, was with the DA's office but defected to the other side. That's got to be . . . what? Fifteen years ago. You sure you got the name right?'

'Unless there's some other Maurice Deegan,' Rowley said. 'I just got the name. My bail jumper didn't hand me a pedigree.'

Walker began to shake his head in disbelief.

'He did tell me something else, though,' Rowley began with a rueful smile. 'Don't choke on this, Vince. First there's the Greyhound bus.'

Like a sleek silver creature rising from the depths, the Greyhound bus emerged from the subterranean level of the West Side Port Authority Terminal, slithered into the crosstown traffic and then dived again, departing the island of Manhattan by the Lincoln Tunnel to surface once more on the far side of the Hudson River. As the muscular skyline of New York diminished in the distance, the bus with its complement of card players, crap shooters and slot jockeys snorted its air brakes at a toll plaza guarding the entrance to the highway beyond and then began to cruise through the flatlands of New Jersey. Half way down the bus, the two detectives were engaged in murmured conversation.

Walker's early scepticism had turned into outright disbelief. 'If this is what I think it is,' he said, 'this has got all the hallmarks of a set-up. Mo Deegan is about as cunning as a barrel full of rodents. You know why we're taking this ride? Not to see the Jersey countryside. He wants us outside NYPD jurisdiction when he pulls whatever stunt he's going to pull. You know what happens when we meet up with this character?'

Rowley said, 'Two or more persons put their heads together and start discussing the possible commission of a crime. That's a conspiracy.'

Walker said, 'You'd better believe it, because once we do that, Deegan's going to have us right there.' He clenched a fist. 'Conspiracy to commit a felony. You ever stop to think that's why your fugitive has set this up, so we don't know what's going to happen next? So he can cold cock us. Conspiracy to pervert the course of justice.'

Rowley looked out of the window, and watched the traffic on the turnpike. After a while he said, 'You don't have to do this, Vince.'

'Oh, I wouldn't miss it for the world,' Walker replied. 'Only I'd feel happier if I knew where the meeting was going to be so I could put in an unofficial stake-out, even up the odds.'

'Well, however it works out, it's down to me,' Rowley said defensively.

'Thanks,' was Walker's sardonic response. 'Even though we're running blind, I feel happier already.'

The rest of the journey was uneventful until a road sign announced their arrival on the outskirts of Atlantic City and the first rendezvous which Spinelli had ordered with his penchant for melodrama began to shape up. The mystery tour was beginning.

On the edge of town the bus pulled into a compound crisscrossed with high chainlink fence into a series of pens. From Rowley's window, a trick of the light caused the interweaving diamonds of heavy gauge wire to ripple as though water was cascading across the expanse of the pens. But no sooner had the wheels stopped turning than the purpose of the stop became apparent as the casino scouts came tripping on to the bus, men in tuxedos with slicked back hair, girls decked out in white boots, pleated red miniskirts and spangled waistcoats. They carried satchels and weaved down the aisle distributing complimentary tickets to the various gambling emporiums.

A girl with flufly blonde hair and a dazzling smile leaned over and gave Rowley a ticket. When he looked at it he saw that a business card had been slipped into the fold. The complimentary announced: *Bally's, Number One for Slots.* The card read: *Maurice Deegan, Attorney at Law.* Rowley looked up, expecting something more, but the swinging pleats of the miniskirt had already moved on.

Walker took a look and merely grunted, then bent down in the confined space between the seats and slipped his off-duty weapon into the elastic gusset of his boot. The pistol was a Glock 17, 9 mm. automatic, so slim and lightweight that it ideally suited the undercover purpose. But the real beauty of the Glock was that it was made of plastic and could pass through sensors without a murmur. Many a time Walker had stood in line at an airport security check and watched a flustered passenger divest himself of body jewellery, then walk through the arch with the Glock in his boot without a peep from the metal detectors. He settled the plastic pistol inside his boot and muttered, 'Lock and load, here comes the bullshit tour.'

When the scouts had finished their rounds the bus moved off again, and Walker squirmed around, peering out of the window. 'Why do I get the feeling we're going to be dealing with old-fashioned button men? All we're going to know is what they want us to know when they want us to know it. If these people are truly wired to The Enterprise they're going to be checking us out every step of the way. They see something they don't like, any little thing, they're going to cat and mouse us, and we're going to see our pictures in the papers, law enforcement officers consorting with criminals, and that's always assuming we get out of this with our hides intact.'

'These are just cautious people,' Rowley said, feeling the same apprehension. 'They're bound to protect their backs.' He was still pinning his hopes on Frank Spinelli.

Walker gave him an old-fashioned look and a few moments later the Greyhound pulled into the bus terminal and jolted to a halt at its stand. As they prepared to get off Walker said, 'Well, I hope you're prepared for the runaround. Right now it's showtime and if you want my considered opinion, Sarge, what we've got there is the old conjuring trick: now you see 'em, now you don't.'

'If you don't like it, Vince, sit this one out,' Rowley said stubbornly. 'It's my neck on the block if this deal falls apart so I'm going to have to take the risk, but you don't have to.' He looked around the cavernous terminal. 'Have a cup of coffee. If I don't come back, get back on the bus and forget any of this happened.'

Hands thrust in his coat pockets, Walker stared at the Yard DS, wondering at the Brit's obstinate naïvety. Here he was walking into what could easily be an ambush set up by a bunch of gangsters who would dispose of a cop with the same casual disregard as swatting a fly, and an unnerving thought crossed his mind. Perhaps the crazy British who worked without a gun actually didn't understand how cheap life could be in America.

'Hey, Tony . . .' He wanted to explain the age-old lore which had been passed down generations of street cops, but the instinct for self-preservation was just too subtle to be expressed. So he gave up with a vigorous shake of his head and instead gave Rowley a comradely slap on the shoulder as he said, 'Come on, partner, you're determined to do this, somebody's got to be there to make sure you don't end up in the city morgue with a John Doe tag on your toe.'

They walked down Atlantic Avenue to the boardwalk where the fairground of Atlantic City ran bang up against the ocean. The casinos dominated the boardwalk, and the winter-grey Atlantic thundered in, its steely rollers toning down the glitz of a resort caught in an out of season yawn.

The two detectives made their way down the ancient promenade, heading for the pink-

147

blushed greenhouse of Bally's. Under the mauve awning a giant black man wearing a candy-striped blazer the size of a tent stepped out, eyed them with a keen glance of inspection and then said, ' 'Scuse me, gen'lemen, you looking for Mr Deegan?'

Walker rolled his eyes. 'Here comes the first con artist. Didn't I see you before, in a circus?'

The giant looked down on them impassively. He said to Rowley, 'This dude with you?'

Rowley said, 'Yes, he's with me, and yes, we're looking for Mr Deegan.'

White teeth gleamed in the black gorilla face, 'Hey, man, you talk pretty, where's you from, Georgia?'

'England,' Rowley said. 'So where can we find Mr Deegan?'

The giant jerked a thumb. 'He's in the coffee shop, table at the back.'

As they moved away Walker gave the doorman a flinty stare. 'No . . . I got it now,' he said, snapping his fingers. 'It wasn't a circus, it was a freak show down The Garden.'

'Yeah,' the giant responded, 'I went the distance with Sonny Liston, now you just take care, bro'.'

Even at this early hour Bally's was a humming hive in which the coffee shop proved to be a centre of tranquillity. It was here that battle-fatigued housewives on an afternoon binge retired between bouts at the slots to gorge themselves on pastries, each mouthful accompanied by the prayer bell jingle of bangles and charm bracelets.

Mighty Mo Deegan was sitting alone, sipping juice and nibbling a chocolate croissant. The lawyer was wearing a lilac-coloured suit over a navy blue shirt, Gucci'd with body jewellery.

'Well, well,' Walker said as they reached the table. 'Who'd have thought it, the scourge of the South Bronx done up like a Christmas tree.'

A faint smile touched the lawyer's lips. He looked first at the Englishman.

'You're Rowley, right?'

'Right,' Rowley said.

'I've been expecting you,' Deegan said. He looked at Walker. 'And I was expecting you to come alone. Who's this?'

'Vince Walker,' Rowley said. 'He's OK.'

Deegan looked puzzled. 'Do I know you from somewhere?'

'You wouldn't remember, Counsellor,' Walker said. 'You were a legend when I was a rookie in the job, about a million years ago.'

'You a cop?'

Rowley said, 'Does it matter?'

Deegan shrugged. 'Not to me.' He waved a hand. 'Sit and we'll lay down some ground rules. If everything goes all right, we'll get down to business.'

They sat down and Walker said, 'You in the messenger boy business now, Mo? That how you're making the bucks?'

'Everybody to their own trade,' Deegan said easily. 'I'm just a lawyer representing a client's interest. Now we can either horse around and I'll finish my snack and that'll be that. Or we can cut the crap and talk about the thing we're all here to talk about and maybe get some business done. Either way makes no difference to me.'

Rowley said, 'Don't mind my cousin here, Mr Deegan, he's a little short on the social graces after a long bus ride.'

'Yeah, no offence, Counsellor,' Walker smiled.

'None taken,' Deegan retorted. 'Can I assume that we're going to have a serious discussion?'

Rowley said, 'We have a mutual friend who would appreciate that. Unfortunately he can't be with us today, his bus pass got cancelled.'

Deegan nodded. 'Too bad, but let me say to you right off, this acquaintance of ours is here in spirit and his wish is that we should get along together.'

He gestured with his fork. 'I must also tell you that my principals habitually shun any kind of exposure. You could say they're like rare exotic blooms, the slightest change in temperature and they disappear.'

Deegan hunched forward. 'Now your *bona fides* are not a problem, but what we do have to address our minds to is the question of how we're going to protect the interests of my clients. You have to understand that these are suspicious people, they don't like strangers, they don't take risks, you get my drift?'

'Absolutely,' Rowley said. 'We didn't come here to rock the boat.'

'Provided we understand each other from the outset,' Deegan said. 'My people are apt to get overwrought if things don't turn out the way they expect. They tend to get jumpy and that can be very dangerous.'

Rowley nodded. 'That's understood. We're anxious to do business, not cause trouble.'

The flamboyant lawyer cocked his head. 'What sort of business?'

'Lost property,' Rowley said. 'We have access to some merchandise to which your people have some claim. We might be in a position to reunite them with the mislaid item. I believe they would be quite anxious to secure its return.'

Deegan smiled at the skirmishing. 'It's all a matter of face.' He shrugged eloquently. 'We Americans, and I imagine you British, are rather more sanguine over reversals of commerce. Others —' he spread his hands — 'tend to take it personally, a blow to their reputations. Very personally.'

Rowley said, 'Let's just say we have it in mind to restore their self-esteem.'

'My people are curious,' Deegan said. 'They

want to know why you would want to do a thing like that.'

'Because I badly need some bodies.'

'Bodies?' Deegan raised an eyebrow.

'Just a figure of speech,' Rowley reassured him. 'We say bodies on the sheet. You, I think, would say collars.'

'Arrests, you mean?'

Rowley nodded. 'There's a couple of your people's associates, mechanics, labourers, heavy muscle. We would like to see them out of circulation.'

Deegan's eyes narrowed 'We? As in the royal we?'

The Yard DS shook his head. 'No, just me.'

'Let me get this straight. Am I to understand that this is a freelance operation, no official sanction?'

'That's it in a nutshell.'

Deegan looked at Walker. 'And where do you fit into this, my friend?'

'Oh, I just came along for the ride.'

'You'll have to improve on that.'

The New York detective shrugged. 'OK, Counsellor, you want it straight, I've got a score of my own to settle.'

Deegan thought about it for a moment. Then he said, 'Well, well. A couple of maverick cops. I'm sure my people will find the prospect — what shall I say? Intriguing.'

'So do we talk?' Rowley wanted to know.

Deegan leaned back and beckoned to a passing waitress. 'I'm forgetting my manners. What can I get for you fellows? The croissants are delicious.'

They continued the discussion in the same vein as they ate and drank coffee and when the lawyer seemed satisfied that the foundations had been laid he wiped his mouth on a paper napkin and said, 'I'm just the advance man. Why don't we take a little ride, meet the guy who's going to have to take the decision on this? What d'you say?'

Walker rolled his eyes. 'Not the goddamn mystery tour again?'

The faint smile returned to Deegan's lips. 'These are people who prize anonymity. They may be intrigued by your proposition, but stupid they are not. They want me to set this up like Harry Houdini, that's up to them, they're the client; you've got to make the sales pitch. Any time you want, Detective, we can shake hands and call it quits. It's no big deal.'

Rowley stepped in. 'What my friend means is, we don't want to take too many risks ourselves. We need a guarantee of safe passage.'

Deegan laughed. 'These are businessmen, Mr Rowley. As I said, they don't want any trouble or to attract attention to themselves. They just want to get on with the running of their business. They bear you no ill-will, take my word on that.'

'The word of a fink,' Walker said. 'You're just the gofer.'

Deegan got to his feet wiping crumbs from his lips with a napkin, the smile still playing on his mouth. 'You're right,' he agreed amiably. 'That's what lawyers do. So you want to go ahead or what? Meet the guy who makes things happen?'

'You're going to take us to the man, counsellor?' Walker asked.

'Right.' Deegan nodded. 'Provided I'm happy with your proposition, I'm empowered to take you to him. Otherwise this is a cut-off, right here and now.'

'And you're happy?' Rowley wanted to know.

'Ordinarily I wouldn't touch either of you characters. You wouldn't even be here if you hadn't come highly recommended.'

Walker said, 'How'd you know we don't have half the Jersey troopers out there all fired up to grab your smart ass?'

Mighty Mo's smile widened into a grin. 'Because psychology tells me you want this deal more than we do, and besides we've taken precautions. I was in law enforcement myself, remember? I can tell when guys are lean and hungry.'

They left Bally's by a side exit and Deegan took them around to an alley where a black stretched Cadillac was parked. A uniformed chaufleur leaning against the coachwork straightened as they approached. Walker took

154

one look at the limo which had the rear compartment blacked out and groaned, 'Oh, pure bullshit!'

Unperturbed, Deegan ushered the detectives into the back and spoke rapidly to the driver. Inside, blinds were down so they could not see out of the car, which moved off smoothly and after what Rowley guessed to be about half a mile the wheels began to shudder over an uneven surface.

Presently they came to a halt and Deegan got out first, holding the door open. They found themselves inside a disused casino, partly gutted, its former glory evident from the dusty one-armed bandits still lining the slot alleys like platoons of saluting soldiers. Deegan appeared nervous. 'For your own sake, gentlemen,' he murmured, his tongue flicking over his lips, 'be very careful. My free legal advice is, don't make any moves which could be misinterpreted.'

Squinting into the gloomy interior of the casino, Walker tensed as he caught sight of figures leaning against exposed girders on the upper levels, the unmistakable silhouette of the M16 assault rifle suddenly etched on to his retina.

'What the hell . . .'

Rowley had spotted the guns too and quickly laid a restraining hand on the New York detective's arm. 'Easy, Vince,' he cautioned, feeling the same helpless tension ripple across his abdomen, but knowing they still had to play the game.

Walker rounded on the lawyer. 'Some reception committee!'

Deegan, looking pale, said, 'Don't worry . . . you're among friends.'

'Terrific!' Walker snorted. 'Friends with firepower — that I can do without.'

'It's OK, truly it's OK,' Deegan strove to reassure them. 'Don't get excited . . . just security, that's all. They're going to sweep you with the detectors, that's all, make sure you're not wearing wires or carrying hardware. Hey, look, it's just security.'

Walker was scowling into the shadows.

Fearful that his charges might over-react, Deegan gripped Walker's shoulder. 'Trust me a minute, then we can all relax, OK?'

The detective shook him off and for a while they stood there under the guns and then a Latino in a shiny black suit and patent leather shoes emerged from the shadows and began to run the wand of a metal detector over each of them.

When his turn came, Walker gave the black beetle-like figure a hard stare and hissed, 'Get out of my face, roach!' knowing that the low-power hand-held detector wouldn't pick up the plastic Glock auto tucked inside his boot.

The Latino leered, displaying a gold tooth, and then waved an all clear to the gunners. That was the signal.

Down the aisle between the rows of slots came the honcho, unmistakably Colombian, his lean face topped with a thatch of hair the colour of steel wool. Black eyes sank into the dark sockets of his skeletal features and in sharp contrast to the flamboyantly attired lawyer this executive of the drugs empire presented a spartan figure in a loose grey track suit and jogging shoes, a towelling sweat rag around his neck. The honcho looked lean as a wolf in winter, but it was the dog straining ahead of him on a choke-chain which demanded their immediate attention.

The dog was a pit bull, one of the notorious fighting breed reared purely to tear an opponent apart. The dog snarled as it lunged towards them, teeth bared, blood lust blazing in its eyes, tugging and twisting as the chain snapped taut.

The honcho let a few links slip through his fingers as he came towards them, watching expectantly. Deegan, wheezing audibly, backed off towards the safety of the limo, but the detectives exchanged knowing glances and stood their ground. This killer dog, lunging at them, eager to rip into their flesh, was the test, they could see that in the honcho's eyes. The guns were just window-dressing, the real test of nerve, the test to see who would lose face, was the only question which mattered now. That's what the eyes said.

The flat bone of the dog's forehead quivered,

ears flattened, teeth bared, every muscle in its powerful body straining against the leash. The honcho let the chain run and the pit bull leaped at them with a bloodcurdling snarl. The great muscles rippled down its back and bunched into its massive neck. The chain jerked taut again and the pit bull, brought up short, shuddered, shook its bucket head, prepared to make the final leap.

The honcho was standing in front of them, the question glittering in his eyes, and Rowley felt the cold sweat of fear jump from his pores as he tried to calculate the odds of surviving an encounter with such a murderous beast. The chances were remote. He was about to raise his hands in a gesture of surrender when Walker moved, dropping into a crouch so suddenly that for an instant Rowley imagined he was going to wrestle the animal in some lunatic display of bravado. But the detective's hand had gone for the Glock hidden in his boot and in a reflex blur he came up with the pistol levelled at the pit bull's head.

'Try me now, m'man,' he urged, his voice heavy with menace, 'and your pooch dies first.'

At the sight of the automatic in Walker's hand the tableau froze, tension crackled like high voltage, and then the shutters clicked down on the Colombian's eyes as he lazily turned away from the challenge and his hooded gaze fell upon the one who had been a smirking spectator at the show. The Latino was gaping at the gun in Walker's fist in abject dismay, his face the colour of parchment. The standoff collapsed as the honcho met Walker's unremitting stare and gave him a small nod of acknowledgement, thin lips pulling back to reveal tombstone teeth.

Walker lowered the Glock and the man in the tracksuit bent to the dog which had quietened but was still straining at the chain. The Latino who had sealed his own fate when he failed to find the concealed weapon began to scream, a high keening wail, as the honcho murmured a new command to the pit bull and slipped the leash.

Coiled like a spring, the terrier took off in one ferocious leap, a powerhouse of muscle and fangs, going for the throat, and hit the petrified Latino full in the chest.

They went down, thrashing in the dirt, the man's frantic screams and the dog's guttural snarl mingling into one howl of terror.

The honcho turned to the detectives as though nothing had happened and extended his hand in a quaintly formal greeting. 'Well now, gentlemen,' he said in a voice which was only lightly accented, 'I believe we have some business to discuss.'

The honcho's name was Fabio Rey Blanco and although he had been born and raised in Medellin, the Colombian cocaine capital, he had earned an early reputation as a fearsome adversary in the jungles of Bolivia where he was known to the peasants tending the coca crop as a trader who dealt in sudden and violent death. Ruthless and ambitious, his career had taken him from freelance crop scout to the highest echelons of the Medellin cartel. An elusive field commander in the cocaine wars, agents of the US Drug Enforcement Administration had simply labelled him Snow White.

On this November day in Atlantic City, New Jersey, with his retinue of armed guards watching over them, Snow White led the detectives deeper into the disused casino. In a room stripped to the brick where roulette wheels had once spun there stood a conference table.

They followed Blanco to the table and when they were seated Blanco looked at Deegan.

'These are the two who come on the personal recommendation of Frank Spinelli, Mr Blanco.' Deegan indicated Rowley. 'Mr Rowley here is from England . . . New Scotland Yard. He's the guy was instrumental in facilitating Frank's recent travel arrangements.'

Blanco said softly, 'I've known Frank Spinelli a lot of years. You and Frank are of the blood?'

Rowley said, 'We have that understanding.'

Blanco nodded, satisfied. He looked at Walker. 'And this one, what's he, champion of the Canine Defence League?'

Rowley said quickly, 'I'll vouch for him.'

'You handled yourself pretty good out there, you got some style for a New York bull.'

'Sure,' Walker replied, 'I open on Broadway any day now.'

Blanco showed his teeth. He returned to Rowley. 'You were responsible for the Snow Man bust?'

'I'm the officer in the case,' Rowley replied.

Blanco seemed satisfied. 'You know what they taught me when I was at college? Your business is only as good as your last deal. Your reputation hangs on it. Now that piece of work of yours, myself and my associates we lost a lot of prestige over that, our reputation took a hard knock at a time when we could least afford it. It would be no exaggeration to say that we were not delighted. Now that's not good for business, so the only reason you're here is we understand you could be instrumental in assisting us to regain our status in the market.'

Blanco leaned back and gripped the ends of the towel draped around his neck. 'So I have a few things to tell you, gentlemen, sketch in the background. The first is that I am taking time out of my schedule to meet with you here today only through the good offices of my friend Frank Spinelli. That trust becomes my trust, and if you betray that trust you will be my personal responsibility, a responsibility that I shall be obliged to discharge.

'The second thing I have to say is that if I like what I hear, I shall make a speedy decision. Needless to say, this conversation has not taken place.'

Snow White looked at Rowley and his wire wool thatch bobbed in a pedantic nod of satisfaction. He turned to Walker. 'For your personal safety as an NYPD cop I have to warn you that I am — how shall I put it? — well connected with certain agencies. We look after each other's interests in difficult areas. We swim like fish in the sea.'

Walker's face remained impassive. He made no reply.

Blanco spread his hands on the table. 'Well now,' he said, 'I am at your disposal.'

Trying hard not to let the tension across his chest reflect in his voice, Rowley said, 'I think it's important at the outset, before we get any deeper into this, to make it absolutely plain that we each of us here have to do the thing we have to do for particular reasons. I don't propose to go into those reasons and I imagine you wouldn't want to either, but it's important for each of us to recognize those reasons exist and they are the basis of our discussions.'

Blanco nodded.

'Basically,' Rowley said, 'I'm not going to insult anybody's intelligence by concocting some story to give credibility to a suggestion which under normal circumstances you would not expect to hear from a police officer.'

'Let's take it as read,' Blanco said. 'We're all honourable men.'

'Good,' Rowley said. 'I wouldn't want anybody at some future time to hear things which may or may not be true but which may lead them to believe they hadn't been given the total picture.'

'No problem,' Blanco said.

'Because essentially, what I'm going to propose is that we get our heads together to commit armed robbery.' When Rowley finally said it he could hear his own voice, but it was Dad Garratt talking. It was Dad he could hear inside his head working him like a ventriloquist.

'You say you were embarrassed by the Snow Man bust,' he heard the voice say. 'Well, the case isn't over yet, not by a long way. Right now the cocaine we seized is sitting in our Forensic Lab where it has been analysed and certified. It is contained in two aluminium cases, like the kind you'd carry camera equipment in, and each case is locked and sealed. The contents of each case is documented and certified as evidence in the prosecution case of Regina versus Francis Spinelli and others who stand jointly charged with illegally trafficking in a prohibited substance.'

In his mind he could feel Dad Garratt weaving the web, 'Now as I said,' Rowley said, 'this is the real McCoy, and one of the little quirks of the British legal system requires that the

163

evidence linking the accused to the crimes of which they are charged must be preserved, the sequence of events and continuity of evidence documented, in order that it may be presented uncontaminated to the jury at the criminal trial. But before that happens, the judicial process requires that the evidence must be presented before a magistrate who will test the strength of the prosecution case and determine whether to commit the accused for trial. That's called the committal proceedings.'

He looked over at Deegan. 'You're familiar with the British process of justice?'

The lawyer pursed his lips. 'Our jurisprudence is based on yours, Sergeant: the adversarial system, innocent until proven guilty.'

Walker smiled as though enjoying a private joke.

Rowley said, 'When the committal takes place those three cases will have to be transported to the court. That's the time of maximum vulnerability, and the best opportunity for repossession?'

'One moment,' Blanco interrupted in a soft voice. 'Who will know the exact timing of this transportation?'

'The officer in the case,' Rowley said.

Blanco smiled.

Rowley said, 'The route and timing are the key, because at a point on the journey I'm going to suggest that certain people might find it opportune to ambush the vehicle.'

Blanco rubbed his chin with thumb and forefinger. There was a glint of interest in his eyes.

'There are conditions,' Rowley said. 'The raid will be led by an American, put up by my friend here.'

Walker said, 'A DEA stoolie, works both sides of the street.'

Blanco began to frown.

'Don't worry,' Rowley reassured him. 'We need this man as our inside contact, to make sure everything goes according to plan. The other condition is that you'll arrange for a couple of robbers I'm going to nominate to complete the gang. They all have to be expendable.'

Blanco nodded. 'We heard that from Frank, that'll be OK. It's the American I don't go for. Frank didn't say anything about that.'

'You'll love him,' Walker said. 'He's your kind of guy, done you a whole lot of damage in the past. This could be your chance to put his lights out.'

'You see,' Rowley said, 'what we want out of this is to grab all three for armed robbery. Only when they ambush the vehicle, in the confusion you'll snatch the drugs.'

Blanco said, 'Explain that a little more?'

'It's easy.' Rowley spoke the words Dad was feeding into his mouth. 'We're playing the system. Everybody comes out in credit. We get bodies on the sheet, you get your product back and your reputation.'

Blanco was nibbling at the hook, striving to keep any shade of excitement out of his voice, but his eyes were the give-away. 'You're wasted on a sergeant's pay,' he told Rowley admiringly. 'When can we do this?'

Rowley said, 'Now Spinelli's out of the bag, my people are anxious to get this show on the road. The next move will be in London. So I need your answer very soon.'

'You shall have it,' Blanco agreed readily. 'Naturally I shall need to check out what you have told me with our independent consultants and if it all shapes up I'll get word to you through Mr Deegan here. But as things stand, I'd say we go ahead.'

Blanco rubbed his hands on the towel and, reading the almost imperceptible changes in his expression, Rowley guessed that the Colombian was making the mental transition from academic interest to practical considerations, committing himself to the outline of the plan. The hook had sunk deep.

Blanco smiled showing his teeth. 'You know what a cut-out is?'

Rowley nodded.

'This'll be a cut-out,' Blanco said. 'We don't like any detail of this, you won't hear from us again.'

Later on the journey back to Manhattan

Walker said to Rowley, 'I've got to hand it to you, Tony, you hit him where it hurts, he couldn't get enough of it.'

'You think he bought it?' Rowley asked.

'Oh sure,' Walker said. 'He looks at you, what he sees is a Boy Scout gone bitter. With your tame capo in your corner how could you lose? He's grabbing for it.'

Rowley looked out of the bus window. 'Well it's more or less on the level,' he observed, turning back to the NY detective, 'We've got a multi-defendant conspiracy without the prime mover, so the committal's got to be a fight, bunch of briefs screaming *Habeas corpus,* only with Spinelli gone we don't have a body to produce. So we're on to a loser anyway. But the consignment still has to go to court, there's no other way.'

Walker said, 'And you're going to give the wise guys a chance to hi-jack it.'

'I've got to nail The Twins,' Rowley said. 'Otherwise it's my neck.'

'You'll actually go through with it?' Walker pressed the point.

Rowley stared off out of the window. Up ahead a string of tail lights stretched like a red ribbon towards the looming outline of Manhattan.

'As long as Blanco believes it, that's all that matters,' he said finally. 'As far as he's concerned, I'm ready and willing to compound a felony.'

'And put 100K of product back on the street,' Walker said. 'You know what that'd be?'

'Yeah,' Rowley sighed, his eyes still on the ribbon of lights. 'That'd be a crime.'

CHAPTER 10

In a penthouse apartment in the castellated Manhattan enclave of Tudor City, the Brown Bag Bandit slouched on a sofa legs outstretched and ankles crossed. He was wearing blue jeans and a Western-style shirt with a bootlace tie clasped at the throat by a small gold replica of a skull.

'San Vicente was just a blind, a cover to throw the Pinkertons,' he said. 'You ever been to Bolivia?'

'Flew over it a couple of times in a Huey looking for coca cook-ups,' his DEA shadow, a husky young man in a sports coat, replied affably.

The Bandit clasped his hands behind his head and stretched. 'You got to get down on the ground, old buddy, get down there and see how them peons live, you want to understand. Man, I know, I've been there.'

The DEA man said, 'I've seen enough of the territory coming in over the jungle with the M60s ready on the door mounts and the rotors chewing the top of the canopy. I've seen all I want to see of Bolivia.'

'Well, that's my point,' the Bandit said. 'You

want to know how the hog lives, you got to get down on your hands and knees and root around in the shit same as he does. Bolivia, man, you tell me Sundance went down at San Vicente, I'll tell you you don't know squat. You got ten dollars in your pocket, you could buy half the Bolivian army back in those days.'

'What about the bodies?' the DEA man said. 'They identified the bodies.'

'Same thing,' the Bandit said confidently. 'Gringo bodies are cheap and all you've got is the Bolivians' say-so. All that whole thing was, was a ruse to throw the Pinkertons. Sundance didn't die at San Vicente, no way, no day.'

The DEA man glanced at the door to the adjacent room which was ajar. He could hear the murmur of voices. 'OK, smart guy,' he said, leaning forward, 'so if Longabough didn't go down in the Andes that time, just where the hell did he go?'

'Why, right back where he came from,' the Bandit replied easily.

The DEA man shot another glance at the partly open door. 'Right to hell, you mean?'

'Back to the hole in the wall,' the Bandit said.

The DEA man's eyes narrowed in his young face. 'How come you're so all fired keen on the Sundance Kid anyway?'

The Bandit stretched and yawned. 'You're looking at him,' he said.

Beyond the partly open door Earl Mulholland, the East Coast ranking official of the DEA, looked from one to the other of the two detectives sitting across the room, hooked a thumb into blue suspenders spangled with little silver stars and said, 'My oh my, you've been busy as beavers.'

They had outlined the sting, Vince Walker doing most of the talking with Tony Rowley adding a detail here and there, following the strategy they had rehearsed. The New York detective knew how to exploit their position and was rewarded by the light of interest flaring in Mulholland's eyes every time he mentioned the drugs cartel called The Enterprise. When he threw in an oblique reference to Snow White the DEA chief almost fell out his chair.

'So you see,' Walker continued, 'right now we've got the hook, the slide and the button is what we need to talk about, assuming you're interested.'

Mulholland had at first been dubious, but his scepticism evaporated as Walker fired his imagination, though he reined in his enthusiasm. 'The thing that worries me,' he said, turning to Rowley, 'no disrespect, Sergeant, but we're going to be operating on foreign soil. London isn't like Washington or New York, you know. After that Snow Man problem we don't exactly have a cosy relationship with you Brits.'

Rowley sought to reassure him. 'Mr Mulholland, there's nothing can go wrong. I've done the spadework, and we'll be looking after your interests.'

'I don't know.' Mulholland shook his head slowly. 'We've had stings go wrong before, the stinger gets stung.'

'Then you can disown us,' Walker suggested. 'If it goes sour all you have to say is you knew nothing about it, just a couple of street cops got in over their heads. We're going to be taking all the risks for you. You've got nothing to worry about. If it all goes right you get your picture on the cover of *Time* Magazine.'

Mulholland said, 'What I've got to do is weigh up the probabilities, and if it comes up with a more than fifty per cent chance of success, then we're in business.'

'What did you say before?' Walker reminded him. 'Something about looking for a window of opportunity to use that cowboy you've got tucked away in there. Well, the window's wide open.'

Mulholland thought about it. Then he said, 'I knew I wouldn't be disappointed in you, Walker. The moment you spit in Chief Hanson's eye when he was about to bust you, I knew you had what it takes. So I tell you what I'm going to do. I'm going to give this proposition of yours priority consideration, clear the decks for action, and in the mean time I'll have you transferred to my office on special assignment so that Hanson can't get his claws into you and we'll just see how it all shapes up.'

Walker said, 'What we have at the moment is a flame and a few stands of straw. What we have to do is make ourselves a fire.' He inclined his head towards the door. 'For instance, how would you handle the Bandit?'

'That's the least of our problems,' Mulholland replied. 'Uncle's got a bunch of paper corporations, we just take our pick and put the Bandit into the London end as an executive vice president so that he can operate with lots of status and no hassle. Anybody checks him out, friend or foe, the cover runs deep. One of the things you've got to remember with the Federal agencies, Uncle takes good care of his people.'

Walker said, 'That's OK as far as it goes, but if I'm going to have to work with this pistol, I need to know something about him. All the records we pulled drew a blank, like the guy never existed.'

'That's understandable,' Mulholland said. 'That name you booked him under is just one of his covers. He's got a string of names he uses, some we've provided, some of his own. Nobody knows what his real name is any more.'

'Terrific! So what makes him tick?'

'Let's just say he's a type which is very useful for the work we occasionally have to get done. He believes he's the born again Sundance

173

Kid.' Mulholland smiled. 'Got the ideal profile for his line of work, delusions of grandeur, heavy machismo, the lone ranger against the world.'

With disgust in his voice Walker said, 'So give me a for instance. How'd you handle a whacko like that?'

'Simple,' Mulholland said candidly. 'We exploit those traits, slot him into a drug-trafficking operation, give him his cover, bankroll him, and if we feel it's important for him to believe he's invincible then we let him pull off a few jobs.'

'Would that include homicide?'

'Could do.' Mulholland shrugged. 'If part of his profile is he feels somebody's got to be taken out in the scam, then we'd orchestrate it so that he'd be the one to hit the guy. I'm talking about someone who'd be hit anyway, I'm talking about the real world. If we had solid information that a certain person was going to get hit, we've talked to the people who are going to have it done, and here's someone we need who needs to feed his ego by whacking someone, then we're going to stage-manage it so that the two factors come together. Nothing wrong with that, just manipulating a situation which is going to happen anyway.' The drugs chief shrugged again. 'I have no problem with that, no ethical, legal, moral problem. I'm still going to sleep easy at night knowing the Bandit's out there doing his thing, even if it occasionally means taking somebody out of the ball game.'

'Did you know he was going to pull that stunt at the bank?' Walker wanted to know.

Mulholland shook his head. 'Absolutely not. That was a mistake for which he has been reprimanded.'

Walker gritted his teeth, aware that they needed this pragmatic DEA sharpie's cooperation if they were to get off the ground and further exploration of the Bandit's warped psyche might lead him to say something which would blow the deal. He contented himself with a cynical half-smile.

Feeling the chill, Rowley said, 'One thing, Mr Mulholland, the time factor. We're going to have to make decisions quickly now because the sequence of events back home is on a fixed timetable. We get one chance only, so we need to plan it so that when it happens, it goes like clockwork. We don't want any slip-ups.'

'I certainly appreciate your eagerness, Sergeant, very commendable.' Mulholland closed his eyes for a moment as though giving the Brit's words some serious thought when in fact he was mildly troubled. Here was a deal too good to be true, conceived overnight by a couple of street cops. Here he was being asked to believe they had come up with a strategy against a watertight operation like The Enterprise which had eluded the efforts of his best agents. Still puzzling it out, Mulholland opened his eyes and said, 'Scotland Yard? I knew a guy at Scotland Yard, a student of mine when I was out at Quantaco, the Academy. One of your shooting stars, on the way up. Real over-achiever, on a roll until he blew a circuit, had a nervous breakdown and we had to ship him home.'

Then, reminding himself of Rowley's relatively junior rank, he dismissed the possibility. 'Ah, you probably wouldn't have come across him.'

'It's a small world,' Rowley replied. 'Most everybody at the Dream Factory knows everyone else. What was his name?'

The DEA chief smiled. 'Oh, this guy was a regular fire-ball. You ever hear the name Larry Drake?'

In his office on the Specialist Operations floor at New Scotland Yard, Commander Larry Drake flexed his shoulders under the smooth cloth of his Savile Row suit, clasped his hands on the blotter which sat squarely in front of him. The knuckles of the clasped hands whitened, the pale blue eyes took on a stony glint as Drake regarded the subordinate standing in front of him as though he were some particularly odious insect.

Feeling the temperature in the office suddenly plummet, Detective-Superintendent Donald Bailey shuffled uneasily, and despite his long experience of the breed which made

Commander while still in nappies, found his resolve beginning to crumble.

'No disrespect, Guv'nor, but all I was trying to say . . . I mean, the point I was trying to make . . . well, the lads really, I suppose . . .' The sinking feeling expanded into dismay as he withered under the relentless gaze. 'Well, it's just that we've got a lot on at the moment what with PIRA, INLA, the Paddies, I mean the surveillance and the counter-measures, er . . . the er . . . routine . . .'

'The lads!' Drake seized on the expression of comradeship with a scornful snort. 'Good God, man, if the Metropolitan Police, or more importantly The Branch, operated according to the whim of The Lads, we might as well all pack up and go home.' His voice changed to a weary tone. 'Need I remind you again, Bailey, that it is our job to lead. To provide leadership; to stiffen the backbone, to crack the whip, to get the job done. Now I know it's not fashionable these days, but I happen to believe that people respond best to discipline, a firm chain of command, know where they are and what is expected of them. I don't know what went on under my predecessor, and to be frank I couldn't care less, but while I'm in charge of SB I will not tolerate the tail wagging the dog.'

Bailey swallowed, his face a frozen mask. 'Perfectly clear, sir,' he replied stiffly.

'Well, good,' Drake boomed. 'Because I don't want to have this conversation again. I don't want to have to remind a detective superintendent of your experience that I am entrusted with the task of writing up your annual report which will go into your docket forever to be read by the people who have the power of the Almighty over your future career next time you go up on a board. I am bound to say that as of now I am not impressed with your attitude, and unless you pull your socks up, I shall have no alternative but to put a black mark on your record. Not to put too fine a point on it, Mr Bailey, I have your balls in my hand and if I choose to squeeze, believe me you will feel pain.'

In front of the desk, Bailey rocked on his heels, felt the blood drain from his face and the black bile rise in his throat.

'What I particularly do not want,' Drake continued, 'is you swanning in here with some eyewash from the canteen mafia. What I expect is old-fashioned loyalty. Is that understood?'

Bailey nodded, not trusting himself to speak.

'Well, that's just fine,' Drake said. 'Now that we understand each other, we can get on with some work.'

The SB Commander rose from his chair and came around the desk, perched himself on one corner, a sly smile softening his expression. 'Donald, Donald, you look as though someone just piddled in your pocket. You think I enjoy having to come down on you like a ton of bricks? Damn it all, man, it's for your own good. The minute you passed DI, took the promotion, you stopped being a spit-in-the-guv'nor's eye detective and took on responsibility, responsibility of the rank. Now that still means something in the job. The glittering prizes, Donald, they're that much closer.'

Drake's dangling leg began to swing in mesmerizing fashion. 'Look, Don—' his voice continued to soften — 'I can help open a few doors. No reason why this time next year a man of your talents couldn't be ACPO rank, Assistant Chief of some cosy little force. You haven't done the senior command course yet, have you?'

Bailey cleared his throat. All he was thinking about was self-preservation, getting out of the office in one piece. 'I hadn't given it much thought, Guv'nor,' he mumbled.

'Well, it's high time you did, Don.' Drake's voice rose to a boom once more. 'Get the College under your belt, start making the right connections and you're on your way. You don't want to rot in a dead end for the rest of your life, now do you?'

Having accomplished this textbook piece of man management, first the stick and then the carrot, Larry Drake hopped from his perch and with a brisk businesslike air took a floppy disk from his briefcase and turned to the computer beside the desk. 'Now I'm going to show you something that will make your hair curl,' he told Bailey as though confiding in a bosom pal. 'Watch this.'

Mesmerized by the chameleon changes in Drake's demeanour, Bailey found himself watching the rainbow graphics which flared across the screen. The SB Commander was already engrossed in keying in the commands, and as he saw the target profile begin to take shape Bailey almost groaned out loud, for there was no mistaking the origin . . . it was another of those INTCELL jokes from The Box.

'Then you know what that condescending clown told me we were going to do,' Don Bailey spluttered between gulps of lager in the chintzy back bar of the George Hotel, Odiham, that evening. 'He said we were actually going to put on this pantomime he came up with in one of his wet dreams.'

'Well, Christmas is coming,' Andy Barnes replied. 'Why don't you tell him you'd rather do Puss-in-Boots instead?'

'This isn't funny,' Bailey scowled. 'Not funny at all. In fact, if I don't put the brakes on this nonsense, whatever credibility we've got left is going clean out of the window.'

'I thought you SB types were pretty cosy with The Box?'

'Shhh . . . not so loud.' Bailey cast an eye over the clientele. The place was full of eager young men in seersucker suits and trendy ties leering over bright young career women with complicated hairstyles, the exotic migrating species of the Golden Corridor dallying over drinks on their way home to the yuppie villages.

Then he said, 'How'd you feel in my shoes, Andy? You know what he had me doing? He had me standing there in front of his desk like a raw DC, and he started giving me this dressing-down, and then the next minute he's doing this old pals routine and telling me how he can fix it for me to make chief somewhere without so much as breaking into a sweat provided I play my cards right. I came out of there, I had to keep pinching myself to make sure it had really happened.'

'Sounds SOP for a thrusting new SB Commander. Give the troops a good thrashing so they keep in line and understand who's boss. If I had a miserable po-faced bugger like you working for me, Don, I'd probably give you a drubbing every morning just to see that beautiful hang-dog expression come on your face.'

Bailey shook his head. 'You don't understand, Andy. Look, what've we got between us, fifty years in the job give or take. We know what the hell's going on because we've seen it all before. Now Drake, he's the boy wonder with the golden touch. Hooked his wagon to some smooth-talking ponce of a politician. Only experience he ever had was hoisting the next rank on to his shoulders.'

Barnes fished the slice of lemon out of his gin and tonic, sucked on it and pulled a face. 'So what's got him stirred up this time?'

'Same thing,' Bailey said. 'This bird at The Box is feeding him one of her fantasies. She's even given him a new computer game to play with which produces comic book assassins and we're supposed to drop everything and go beating the bushes looking for this figment of an overheated imagination.'

Bailey lowered his voice. 'Andy, we all know this cloak-and-dagger stuff is pure eyewash. Our job is very simple, keep Paddy and the maniacs with tea-towels around their heads from blowing up the place, keep a weather eye on the loony left and the odd crank who's got himself a chemistry set, and everybody's going to be happy. I've been doing the job a long time and I never yet saw an assassin, never even heard of one, until we get a poofter for a guv'nor and he sees 'em lurking in every shadow. I tell you he's driving me nuts.'

'So why don't you get one of your cronies over at Five to give Drake's lady-friend a talking to?'

Bailey looked mortified. 'You think I haven't tried that? Apparently they shuffled this crazy biddy into INTCELL because she was sending everyone loopy over there. The only place they could move her now is somewhere she'd be even more of a menace. Nobody thought anybody'd be stupid enough to take these threat assessments seriously — you're supposed to feed 'em straight into the shredder. All I'm getting is a whole load of head-shaking and commiseration from The Box.'

'You've got a problem,' Barnes said.

'That isn't the half of it,' Bailey said. 'Drake's so taken with this fairy story he's started having tête-à-têtes with Mr Brown.'

'The SAS?'

'For Christ's sake keep your voice down,' Bailey pleaded, swivelling his head to see if anyone had latched on to the magic initials of the Special Air Service. 'All the shit-or-bust brigade ever want to do is kill people and golden boy is playing right into their hands. We've got this liaison officer — mad Major galloping across from MOD, closeted in Drake's office, and when he comes out of there, I've seen that gleam in the eye before. Mr Brown's getting psyched up to do the job MACP and you know what kind of scenario that's going to be. Take no prisoners.'

'You're kidding,' Barnes said. 'Military Aid to the Civil Power? That's not possible. It's London we're talking about, not bongo-bongo land.'

Bailey clutched his head. 'I know it sounds impossible, but it's happening. The checks and balances and all that malarky, forget it. Here you've got a big game hunter at the Home Office, a fantasy freak at MI5, a total numbnut in SB, and the gung-ho winged dagger's itchy finger on the trigger.'

'Light the blue touch paper, eh?' Barnes remarked, dropping the remains of the lemon slice back into his glass.

Bailey drank some lager and wiped his mouth with the back of his hand. 'So why do I do my health and temper a lot of no good risking my sanity in the rush hour on the M25 just so that I can enjoy a pint with my old mate out here in England's green and pleasant land? This is it, Andy, crunch time. Either I get some good ammo so that I can stop this bastard dead in his tracks or else I swear to Christ I'm going to end an illustrious police career dribbling in a rubber room.'

Barnes laughed at his friend's doleful expression. 'Squad commanders come and go, Don, but old war horses like you and me, we just go on forever.'

'What I'm asking,' Bailey said, 'is when are you going to stop mucking around and deliver your promise?'

'Promise? What promise was that?'

Bailey sighed his exasperation. 'This hotshot. Garratt's skipper. You know, this DS you said could clip Drake's wings.'

'Rowley?'

'Yeah, Detective-Sergeant Rowley.'

'Did I say that?'

'Oh, for God's sake!'

'As I recall, all I said was that Rowley had a run-in with Drake, that's all.'

'Look, OK, so I'm clutching at straws, it's all I've got. Now when can I talk to him?'

Barnes looked at his watch. 'As it happens, you're in luck,' he replied. 'Right about now he's forty thousand feet over the pond, winging home. Gets into Gatwick in about four hours.' He sat back and watched Bailey's face brighten. 'Why don't we go out there and meet him?'

'Well, what else can I do?'

Barnes shrugged. 'You could put your trust in prayer,' he replied with a straight face.

CHAPTER 11

No sooner was he back in London than Tony Rowley began to feel the old pangs of fear sapping his resolve. He tried sounding out his underworld contacts, the snouts and the grasses he and Dad Garratt had nurtured over the years, to discover if The Twins were still actively gunning for him, one part of him anxious to know the score, the other urging him to shut out the threat. But all he succeeded in doing was spreading his nervousness around like an epidemic until no one wanted to know him. None of his informants returned his calls. Now that he no longer enjoyed the protection of Frank Spinelli's blood-bonded patronage, he had become a jonah, a pariah, and the vision which haunted him was that one day he would pull up at a traffic light, a car would draw up alongside and as the light changed the window would roll down and he would catch sight of the snout of a sawn-off shotgun the instant before they killed him. It was a nightmare which jerked him awake at night, bathed in sweat. The horrors seeped and poisoned, but all he could do was wait for Walker and the Bandit.

Everything had been set up to follow a fixed time-scale and there was nothing he could do to speed it up.

Working on the file for the Snow Man committal helped to blunt the anxiety, for although the NEL task force had moved out to the Basingstoke bunker, a handful of detectives working on the case had remained at the Yard for ease of consultation with the CPS prosecutors who would present the evidence before the Metropolitan Magistrate at Bow Street on the appointed day. The pernickety lawyers, already peeved at the loss of the principal defendant, spent their time ripping holes in the case and flatly refused to traipse out into the wilds of Hampshire to do their demolition work. So, under protest, the Snow Man team was grudgingly permitted a corner of the National Drugs Intelligence Unit's ninth-floor quarters and it was here that Rocky Stone sought Rowley out.

'Got a minute, Skip?'

Rowley looked up from the sheaf of statements he was cross-checking. 'Rocky! How're you doing? Hey, did I hear right . . . you're putting your papers in?'

The big paunchy man on the other side of the desk shuffled uneasily. He had a few strands of hair scraped across an otherwise bald head and his florid face with its lump of a nose tinged blue from broken capillaries took on a sheepish expression. Detective-Constable Albert 'Rocky' Stone was a surveillance specialist with SO 11 who spent his time plotting the movements of the criminal fraternity targeted by any one of the cluster of crime squads based at the Yard.

' 'Sright, Tony,' Stone replied, fidgeting in the baggy telephone engineer's overalls he was wearing. Long ago as a fresh DC, he had shown a natural aptitude for undercover work, a talent which had stunted his career, for he had remained a rank and file detective throughout his service. 'Two more weeks and I'm out of this madhouse.'

'You fixed up?' Rowley asked.

'Couple of irons in the fire.' Stone fished a packet of Panatellas out of his pocket.

'Well, you're the best, Rocky, always have been.' Rowley pushed the ring binder crammed with statements to one side. 'Anything I can do . . . you know.'

'Thanks . . . appreciate it.' Stone stripped the Cellophane from his cigar. 'Thirty years I've been doing this, same thing, day in, day out. Bound to be a bit of a wrench.'

'The job's the loser,' Rowley said. 'Old stager like you, everybody expects you to go on for-ever.'

Stone shrugged his bulky shoulders. 'Yeah, well, in a way I won't be sorry. It's not the job I joined, Tony, not by a long chalk. Detectives these days . . . I tell you, son, I wouldn't give 'em the time of day. Like a bunch of bank clerks. Take my game. When I got started there was some skill involved, some craft in it, pit your wits against some blagger on the make. Policemanship.' He rolled the word around his tongue to give it emphasis. 'You had to be all about in those days, otherwise you'd show out and blow it. I mean, you had to be a bit of a thespian to do a decent tail or obbo. Times I've spent days on end up a tree watching some likely lad who was well at it. Now all you've got to do is fiddle around with a bunch of gadgets. Where's the skill in that?'

It was the protest of a craftsman and Rowley said, 'Rocky, you don't have to tell me, I was Dad Garratt's skipper, remember, I learned all the old dodges in the same school.'

Rocky Stone's gaze grew misty. 'Ah, Dad, where the hell are you now?' He glanced towards the ceiling, then stuck the cigar into his mouth and lit up with a cheap plastic lighter. 'I was on some capers with Dad back in the old days, before your time, Tony. Jesus, he had a sixth sense for villainy, Dad did. Times he'd had one nicked on nothing better'n suss and he's given me a bell and said, "Rocky, give me something I can stick on this geezer." And he'd do it with a straight face, and it'd stick too! There's a good few still doing long stretches on account of Dad's brand of nicking. "Only place for an active villain is rotting in the Scrubs," is what he used to say, and he meant it. The strokes he used to pull don't bear thinking about these days, but he got bodies on the sheet, he was the thief-taker all right.'

'You want to form a Dad Garratt appreciation society, count me in,' Rowley said. 'Only I don't suppose that's why you came looking for me, eh Rocky?'

'Not exactly.' The old-timer looked uncomfortable as he pulled on his cigar. 'Look, Skip, I don't know how to put this, but, Jesus, I've been loyal to this job a lot of years, taking orders, doing what I was told. Guv'nors know best, only . . .' His voice trailed off.

Rowley pushed his chair back. 'Only what, Rocky?'

'You haven't heard from my lot, have you, Tony?'

Rowley shook his head. 'Should I have done?'

'Gutless wonders!' Stone spat the words. 'I should've known they wouldn't lift a finger.'

'Lift a finger over what?'

'Guv'nors these days! I don't know how they can look at themselves in the mirror, all they think about is number one.'

'Rocky!' Rowley said. 'Something you want to get off your chest or what?'

'They told me they were going to give you the nod. I should've known they were slagging me off, what do they care?'

Rowley said, 'Who care?'

'The Owl and his cronies on the squad.'

Rowley flinched at the nickname of the Detective Chief Superintendent who commanded his old outfit, the No. 9 Regional Crime Squad. There was no love lost between them. 'What's the Owl up to?' he asked, keeping his voice steady.

'Putting your head in the noose, looks like,' Stone snorted. 'They said they'd give you the gypsies on this, swore to me they would. And then they didn't, probably never intended to. Must've thought I was born yesterday, they thought I was going to leave it out, just like that. Well, they've got another think coming!'

'Hey, take it easy, it's me you're talking to,' Rowley said, alarmed at the dark flush of anger on the DC's face. 'You going to stand there spitting blood, or you going to tell me what this is all about?'

Stone sighed. 'Look, I was on loan to the squad, wasn't I?' he began. 'Obbo, usual thing. They wanted a phone tapped, I won't bore you with the details, but it was a pukka job, warrant with a Home Office monniker and everything, good enough to go to court with. Only the thing is with phone taps, Tony, you get all sorts of crap as well as the stuff you're looking for. Well, I don't have to tell you . . . Anyway I stuck a voice-activated Nagra on the line, piece of cake, but when I was logging the tapes, well . . . your name kept cropping up.'

Something in Rowley's expression made Stone hurry on. 'Look, Tony, I shouldn't be the one to tell you . . .' The cigar had gone out and the dead stub was hanging from his lip. 'By rights, the Owl should've given you this, official, you know? I'm not supposed to pass on what I hear on phone taps . . .'

'It's OK, Rocky,' Rowley said.

'Nah, it's not OK . . . and anyway, that's not what I'm worried about. I mean, what're they going to do? Two weeks and I'm on the pension. What're they going to do, give me the boot?'

The DC's agitation was catching. 'Honest to God, Rocky,' Rowley protested, 'you want to put the frighteners on me, you're doing a good job. What the hell's this all about?'

'Like I said, this phone tap,' Stone sighed. 'We were wiring this villain —' he mentioned a name. 'You heard of him? Got a firm south of the river, a right nutter, only he's lived a charmed life up to now, no form, clean as a whistle, but he's active all right in the blagging stakes. So I'm tapping his phone and most of it was just bunny, him and his conies talking tough. Then all of a sudden he starts making lots of calls, something must've really got him going, and he's all excited about stomping the filth and I'm not taking much notice because I've heard all this a hundred times before, only that's when your name started cropping up.'

Stone's battered features creased into a scowl and Rowley felt the hairs on his neck begin to rise. 'It was The Twins,' Stone explained. 'Mick and Vic, suddenly they were all over the tapes bragging how they'd done for Dad Garratt.'

'Come off it,' Rowley said. 'Everybody knows Dad had a heart attack.'

Stone's head shook vigorously. 'These are mad dogs, Tony, they don't see it that way. Far as they're concerned, they saw off Dad and that's how they're putting it about. Ought to have been put down long ago, you ask me, if we'd got anybody with the bottle to do the job. It shouldn't be me telling you this, Tony, but I've got to mark your card, son, none of those other tosspots will, I mean I wouldn't forgive myself if . . .'

'If what?'

'If anything happened to you. See, they not only said they got Dad, they said they're going to do you next. Probably just a bunch of blaggers talking big. All I'm saying, Tony, is what I hear on the tapes and that's gospel. Those dogs were swearing they were going to do for you.'

Stone stood in front off the desk, fidgeting and looking embarrassed at the clumsy way he had expressed his concern for Rowley's safety. He shrugged. 'It's what I heard, that's all, so you watch points, you know what I mean? There's not many of us good 'uns left, eh? And besides I owe it to Dad.'

Stone rolled the dead stub of cigar around

his mouth, his expression a picture of disgust at the CID hierarchy's indifference to the welfare of their own. 'Guv'nors!' He spat the cigar butt into the waste-paper basket in a gesture of contempt.

If Rocky Stone's warning alarmed him, another equally unnerving event had caused Rowley to question both the ability and willingness of the Metropolitan Police high command to protect him. Everybody seemed so preoccupied with the scheming and intrigue which fuelled the central nervous system of the Yard from the canteen mafia to the serious rumour squad that if The Twins had walked into NDIU and hacked him to pieces right there at the desk, he doubted anyone would have raised an eyebrow. At least that was how it appeared when coloured by his overwrought imagination. It brought the other episode into sharp focus, an event which had occurred the moment he cleared Customs at Gatwick. His name was being called over the public address system and when he reached the information desk he had been surprised to find Detective-Superintent Andy Barnes waiting for him. Assuming his NEL chief had taken the trouble to meet his flight because of his anxiety over the abortive Spinelli extradition, Rowley had launched into a description of his New York experience only to find Barnes less than attentive, brushing aside the legal impasse with a pragmatic, 'Well, we got our result when we nicked 'em, Tony, so now we'll just let the lawyers slog it out. We put 'em on the sheet and CPS cocked up the remand, so they can take the flak for a change.'

Solicitously, Barnes picked up one of the sergeant's bags and began to steer him through the crush in the arrivals terminal towards a nearby Sky coffee shop, explaining, 'Come on, mate of mine's been busting a gut to get a quiet chat with you.' He patted Rowley on the shoulder. 'Been driving me round the bend, so you'll be doing me a personal favour if you can put him out of his misery.'

Barnes took him to a table tucked away in an alcove where Rowley found a pugnacious-looking fellow in hornrimmed spectacles giving him an unsmiling stare. Despite his dulled reactions, Rowley read SB into the man's demeanour even before Barnes completed the introductions. 'Superintendent Bailey here is with the Branch,' Barnes confirmed, adding in an amused way, 'But he's a decent bloke all the same.'

Rowley's eyes flitted between them, his expression puzzled. 'What's this about, Guv'nor?'

'Sit down, Tony, and take a deep breath,' Barnes replied. 'This'll tickle you pink. SB have got a new commander —' Barnes paused for effect. 'None other than your old chum Larry Drake.'

'Who's sending me potty.' Bailey spoke for the first time. 'And your boss here tells me you're just the lad to help me clip his wings.'

Rowley looked at Barnes, who now had a grin on his face. 'Is this straight up, Guv'nor?'

'It's on the level all right,' Barnes confirmed. He took his pipe out of his pocket and tapped it on the heel of his hand. 'Don here, in his usual unsubtle way, is asking for a favour, that's all. He's actually looking for a little advice.'

Barnes began filling his pipe from a worn leather pouch. Concentrating on the task, he said, 'Drake took you under his wing on the run-up to Snow Man, so you're bound to know a few things he'd like kept under wraps. A few skeletons in the old cupboard. Besides you're CID through and through, Tony, that's where your loyalty lies, so whatever you can do for Don here will be for the good of the cause, you can take my word on that.'

Barnes extracted a box of matches and lit the pipe. 'After all, we don't want comedians like Drake meddling with our side of the firm, now do we? So we'll just keep this in the family and I'll make it my business to see you don't lose by it.'

Feeling himself being backed into a corner, Rowley sank into a chair and drank some coffee to revive his brain. The last thing he wanted at this moment was to become embroiled in some senior officer's vendetta so he fell back on his first line of defence. 'Look, Guv'nor —' he looked from Barnes to the man in the glasses who was still sizing him up — 'Mr Bailey, I'm just a DS, what would I know about a Commander?'

'Nobody's suggesting you drop anybody in it, Tony,' Barnes replied, 'but you've had a taste of Drake's games so you're favourite for nobbling him. Put it this way, there are times in this job when you have to fight fire with fire.'

'If I'd wanted to fight fire I'd've joined the fire brigade,' Rowley retorted, but Barnes merely chuckled good humouredly, 'You're Dad Garratt's boy all right, Tony, so you know the strength better than most. You know who your friends are.'

Still trying hard to keep the incredulity out of his voice, Rowley said, 'Let me give it some thought. All I've got at the moment is jet-lag. Give me a day or two and I could probably come up with something.'

'That's more like it!' Bailey brightened at the prospect and began to heave himself out of his seat, saying, 'Come on, let's go somewhere we can get a steak and a decent drink. I'm feeling better already.'

Rowley cried off. 'Thanks all the same, Guv'nor, but I'm dead on my feet. All I could use at the moment is some shut-eye.'

CHAPTER 12

Then there was Cindy Miller. Buried under the Snow Man dossier in his corner at the NDIU, Tony Rowley picked at the scab of his own fear which refused to allow the wound of Dad Garratt's death to heal. The exhibit file he was working on began to blur and when he pinched the bridge of his nose, and massaged his eyes with thumb and forefinger he saw the image of Cindy Miller. Cindy, the West Indian nurse who had eased Dad's final days and had after his death kept her promise to seek out Rowley with his mentor's dying message. Cindy, warm and ingenuous, who had sheltered him without hesitation as The Twins and their hench men scoured the streets eager to fulfil the contract on his life. Cindy who took him to her bed after the car bomb shattered his nerves and rendered him impotent. Cindy who had given him back his manhood, whom in the end he had betrayed, skipping out of her life without so much as a farewell, rationalizing to himself that he did so to protect her, to distance her from the danger which dogged his footsteps.

Cindy was the talisman he had cast aside

and now at his low ebb Rowley felt a selfish desire to creep back into her arms so that she could soothe him once more.

On impulse he locked the case files away in the steel cabinet, invented an excuse for follow-up inquiries and borrowed a car from the CID pool. It was mid-afternoon when Rowley escaped from the Yard into the lull before the creeping paralysis of the London rush hour. He drove the unmarked Escort over the span of the Hammersmith fly-over, windscreen-wipers flicking at the heavy drizzle which obscured all but the tail lights of the car ahead, then took his chance in the rat runs of side streets to reach St Catherine's Hospital. He squeezed the Ford into the overcrowded car park and looked up at the concrete façade with its rows of dirt-streaked windows and felt the usual sinking depression which he always associated with hospitals. Rowley got out of the car and walked across the slicked tarmac to the casualty entrance and went through a pair of wire-glazed swing doors from which the varnish was peeling. Inside the hospital had that weary run-down feeling of a building required to function around the clock day in, day out, without respite. Even the fresh daub of emulsion and the colourful prints along the corridors could not disguise the jaded ambiance. Rowley made his way up to the Intensive Care Unit, eased open the door marked ICU Staff Only and slipped into a narrow lobby from which he could see into the unit through glass panels.

He wandered the floor, unchallenged by the white-coated automatons on duty and eventually found Cindy in the staff restroom, stretched out in a threadbare easy chair, with a magazine on her lap and a mug of tea going cold at her elbow. Her face looked so tired and drained that he was of half a mind to slip away when she opened an eye and caught him standing there.

'Tony?'

He spread his hands and grinned.

'Tony Rowley?'

He held the grin.

'No, this can't be the Tony Rowley who stepped out of my life two weeks ago and I haven't seen hide nor hair of since. He wouldn't have the gall.'

Rowley shrugged.

'So you finally turned up?'

'Yep,' he said, 'the bad penny.'

Cindy took a gulp of tea to hide her confusion and pulled a face. 'Ugh . . . that's the pits!'

Rowley said, 'Cindy . . . I just wanted to see you again . . .'

'You could've phoned.'

'You might've said no.'

'Damned right I would. What if I say no now?'

'Then be on my way.'

'Ah well, I ought to, you pig. I ought to, but

you'd probably remind me I knew the score from the start, how we always agreed, no strings, no complications.' Her eyes began to glisten.

'Just your regular everyday selfish bastard,' Rowley said, 'but I was your star patient.'

'Oh, I see,' she said, fighting back tears. 'Appeal to a nurse's better nature now eh? Just dropped in for a check-up?'

'Come on,' Rowley said, 'I'm doing my best to apologize.'

'Don't,' she said. 'Don't try, things'd get too complicated.'

'I had to go away,' Rowley said. 'The job.'

'And now you're back in town, you thought you'd look up Cindy, the good sport.'

'I wanted to explain.'

'Is that all you wanted?'

'I could use a sympathetic ear.'

'Like old times, huh?'

'Like friends,' Rowley said. 'So how've you been?'

'Oh, wonderful. Parties every night. Twelve-hour shifts work wonders for your social life. I've been having a ball.'

'Cindy, I'm sorry.'

'You don't have to apologize.' She flicked away a tear with an impatient swipe. 'I'm a big girl now.'

'Look, can we get out of here? Just to talk.'

'Oh, anything you say, Lord and Master.'

'Cindy, give me a break.'

She looked at him for a long moment and then her expression softened. 'Well . . . I get off at four . . .' She eased herself out of the chair, reached into a cupboard and threw a white nylon coat at him. 'In the meantime, by way of penance, you can do the bedpans.'

The nurses' home where Cindy lived was just around the corner from the hospital. The block had the same institutional atmosphere, flights of bare concrete stairs with metal handrails connecting drab anonymous landings. By contrast, Cindy had made her bedsit bright and cheerful; the cosy atmosphere soon lightened their spirits and despite their pact just to talk, soon the old chemistry began to work and she put her arms around him, burying her face in his neck and exclaiming, 'Why is it, whatever I promise myself, I can't keep my hands off you?'

Rowley felt the warmth of her body through the thin cotton shift. 'Whatever it is,' he responded huskily, 'I'm catching the same bug.'

'Come on,' she murmured, giving up any further pretence at displeasure. 'You've been missing out on your physio. We've got a lot of catching up to do.'

She drew him over to the sofa bed with its bright floral cover and sat on the edge, offering her back so that he could unzip her uniform.

'Like old times,' he breathed the words, but

as she unhitched her bra and slipped out of her briefs, Cindy suddenly collapsed in a fit of giggles.

Rowley leaned back on his elbow. 'What's the joke?'

Cindy bit a knuckle, still convulsed with mirth. 'You,' she said, 'you saying like old times, just reminded me, I just remembered Dad.'

'Dad? At a time like this.'

Cindy pushed him down, straddled his back and began to massage his shoulders. 'This is a secret, OK?'

'Scout's honour.'

'Well, Dad was very wicked, always trying to touch up the nurses. And you know what?' The giggles bubbled over. 'Swear you won't ever mention this to a living soul!'

The motion of her hands had relaxed him and Rowley said, 'Cross my heart.'

'Well . . . this is terrible really . . . Dad died with his hand up Sister's skirt.'

'What?'

'It was so funny. The ECG alarm went off and we all came running and Sister Roberts had the crash cart with the de-fib and when she leaned over and gave him the jolt, his hand shot straight up her dress . . . She screamed the place down.'

Rowley began to smile, picturing the scene. 'Sounds like Dad all right.'

'Sister Roberts was not amused, got very

sniffy about it, swore it was just a muscle reflex, only we all knew different. I never told anyone this before, but Tony, it really was funny. Dad cardiac-arrested giving Sister Roberts a grope.'

'That old buzzard,' Rowley laughed. 'Probably goosing angels right now.'

Cindy pulled on the mechanism which let down the bed and drew the cover over them. 'Men,' she said. 'You're all just little boys.'

'You wouldn't believe it —' the prosecutor wrinkled his high pale forehead to signify his disbelief, 'the DPP is the guilty one, burning the candle at both ends just so he can get the defence circus to lift reporting restrictions and he can put on a show for the media. Everything's political these days.'

'Which brings us back to your Director. What's got him so fired up all of a sudden?'

'Only some TV type who crept in under our defences and conned him into considering a six-parter on the rich tapestry of British justice, to whit a documentary series on Channel Four called *The Sword and the Scales* or some such mush. Turned his head, I'm afraid. Now he thinks he's Perry Mason and he's lying in the bath one night after a hard day toiling at the mill when he recalls our little Snow Man case and it occurs to him that this example of human frailty has all the ingredients of a meaty drama. He's so busy drooling over the prospect, he clean forgets we're a defendant light and the case is riddled with so many holes you could drive a bus through most of 'em.'

'That's the trouble with the telly generation,' Rowley said.

'Well, I'm afraid the old man's flipped his wig. Next thing you know, we'll be trying cases like game shows.'

'So what's the verdict?'

'Oh, very droll. The most we've got is circumstantial. If we don't get Spinelli back, the jury's going to throw the whole shebang out at Crown Court, and I wouldn't blame 'em. Tell you the truth, if it was up to me, I'd discontinue like a shot, cut our losses, only like I say, the Old Man's got the bit between his teeth, so we're going the distance.' The prosecutor's forehead furrowed. 'Play it to the gallery, and there's nothing like a mountain of cocaine piled on the exhibits table to stiffen the sinews of an old blowhard who suddenly sees himself on the box like the caped crusader.'

Rowley smiled. Going to be a white Christmas after all. Out there in the real world, drugs are flavour of the month. We'll get a result all right.'

'Very commendable, Sergeant. Ten out of ten for enthusiasm —' the phone on the desk between them began to ring — 'only you don't have to con me. Fact is we're on the calendar so we're going to court next week with all guns blazing . . .'

Rowley picked up the phone and said, 'DS Rowley.'

'. . . even if we do end up looking like a horse's rear end for our trouble.'

A voice spoke into Rowley's ear. 'We're going to do your black pussy, filth . . . and you're next!'

Clutching the phone, Rowley jerked upright, the blood draining from his face. 'What!'

Across the desk the prosecutor stared at him.

'Down payment, lover-boy,' the voice rasped and Rowley knew the message was delivered and the phone was going down.

'No! Wait . . .' But the line was already dead.

'Tony . . . Tony . . .' The prosecutor's voice was drowned by the scream which began to rise inside Rowley's head. The lawyer was staring at him, perplexed. 'You all right?'

But all Rowley could think about as his fingers stabbed the keypad on the phone was Cindy. You stupid bastard, he cursed himself, you drew her on to the sword!

The phone in the nurses' home rang steadily, without answer. Rowley put the phone down slowly, his hand shaking, and realized the prosecutor was sitting there, watching him.

'What's up?'

'I think a friend of mine's in trouble.'

The prosecutor stared at him. 'Something to do with the case?'

Rowley shook his head. He felt sick. Pushing the chair back, he jumped to his feet, grabbed his jacket, and explained as calmly as he could, 'I've got to shoot, Paul, can we pick this up in the morning?'

'Sure,' the lawyer agreed, an eyebrow arched. 'Dull it isn't, eh?' But he was speaking to Rowley's back as the DS dashed out of the office. He broke into a run in the corridor, burst through then nearest fire-door and clattered down the fire stairs.

In the underground car park below the tower block of the Yard, Rowley skipped around the lines of job motors, the black Jags and Rovers of the brass, knowing that it would be more than his life was worth to commandeer one of those. The Escort he had borrowed earlier had gone, but the squad 'spare', a battered Range-Rover which was routinely garaged at the Yard ready to bulldoze rush hour traffic if an urgent shout came in, was sitting in a corner slot with the keys in the ignition.

Without hesitation Rowley jumped in and gunned the engine, almost colliding with a concrete pillar as he swung the big four-wheeled-drive around and aimed for the exit ramp. Under full power the Range-Rover's wheels left the ground as it shot out of the garage and rocketed into the traffic with Rowley fighting the wheel as he accelerated furiously. The evening drizzle had consolidated into a heavy wet curtain blurring the yellow haloes of the street lamps, the flash of brake lights fragmenting into a million pinwheels as, briefly blinded by the dazzle, Rowley hit the wailer and the strobes. With the pedal flat down the big V8 took off, cutting a swathe through the traffic.

Jumping red lights and dodging the phalanx of taxis cruising the West End, Rowley drove in a haze of anger, the rasping telephone threat echoing in his ears. The Bayswater Road was jammed as usual, so without hesitation he swung out of the line and went racing against the oncoming traffic. A van flashed by just inches from his window and he stamped on the brakes as a coach suddenly loomed across an intersection, but the Range-Rover ablaze with police lights was sufficiently awe-inspiring to intimidate the crush of drivers who flinched over to let him pass the instant they saw the blue light in their mirrors.

The Park Lane cruiser rolled viciously as Rowley snatched at the wheel and plunged into the back doubles without letting up speed. The side-streets were cluttered with parked cars and he caught a blur of astonished faces as he hammered through the maze, the wailing siren echoing off the terraces.

When he made the turn into Nightingale Road, the Range-Rover finally balked at his heavy-handed driving, slewed broadside and almost clipped a car coming the other way, cannoned down the last hundred yards and slammed to a halt outside the nurses' home. Rowley jumped out, cold sweat trickling down his ribs, and ran towards the entrance, but stopped almost immediately, the power draining out of his legs. He knew instinctively that he was already too late.

In the wet street two area cars were angled across the roadway, blue lights flashing. An ambulance had pulled up, back doors flung open, its interior an oblong of white light blurred by the drizzle. Figures in fluorescent tabards were hunched over something in the road. The keening inside his head rising to a wail, Rowley pushed past the straggle of onlookers, brushed aside the arm of the PC who tried to bar his way, his gaze riveted on the rag doll flung into the gutter. Dull red splashes arced across the slick of tarmac. The rag was a nurse's uniform.

His head bursting, Rowley plunged into the orange scrum. Red-hot needles pierced his eyes. The face was turned towards him, a mask painted on a crushed eggshell oozing mealy brain matter. He gagged on the bile as the puddle of blood seeped around his shoes.

Rough hands hauled him back.

'What's your game, then?' The white face of a traffic patrolman was thrust into his as the grip on his jacket yanked him around.

'I'm in the job,' Rowley gasped, showing his ID.

'Oh, sorry, Skip,' the uniform apologized, acknowledging a kindred soul.

Checking his emotions as best he could, Rowley asked, 'What happened?'

'Hit and run,' the uniform replied in the flat tone of someone accustomed to the routine of scraping bodies from the street. 'From what we can gather, she came out of there —' he nodded towards the nurses' home — 'and the car hit her there.' He pointed to a scatter of headlight glass and paintwork fragments in the road. 'Callous bastard didn't even stop. Just put his foot down and kept going. One over the eight, probably. We put a general call out, but what chance have you got? Bastard's long gone.'

Stirred up now, the traffic man vented the rest of his spleen on the ambulance crew. 'Come on, you lot, get a move on, this isn't a sideshow!'

Rowley turned away, sickened, the threat hammering in his ears. The desire to scoop her up, absolve his guilt by cradling her shattered body, was overpowering. But he was rooted to the spot. The drizzle was turning to rain, wetting his face, mingling with the tears streaming down his cheeks. Cindy, so warm and vital, smashed to a pulp just to teach him a lesson.

CHAPTER 13

Detective Vince Walker kept his appointment with the lawyer on the observation deck of the Empire State Building. Now that he was officially seconded to the US Department of Justice Drug Enforcement Administration Walker felt himself curiously detached from the tide of street crime in which he had wallowed for the best part of twenty years. An artificial Christmas tree twinkled in the lobby as he followed the crocodile of tourists into the express elevator and rode the 1200 feet up to the viewing gallery.

Mighty Mo Deegan was waiting for him there, more conservatively dressed than when they had last met.

'Every time I come back I come up here,' Deegan greeted the detective with a touch of nostalgia, 'every time. Must be a sucker for the allure of the city. You get up here, you don't see the garbage in the streets, everything's pure, symmetrical, makes you feel good.'

Walker looked down on the scalloped art deco spire of the Chrysler Building batted in the soft glow of the misty sunshine. 'Yeah,' he agreed, 'I remember the days when you were an old romantic, Mo, shovelling that garbage for the DA.'

'Oh, and idealistic too,' Deegan said. 'Those were the days I'd put in eighteen, twenty hours straight, working my ass off for the city in the great crusade against crime. Got the old son of a bitch re-elected twice on my performance representing the people of this fine borough until one day I saw the light. Ideals don't pay the rent.'

'So you defected.'

'I was always good on my feet in front of the jury. I just went where the money was for a change.'

Recalling the memories of his days as an Assistant District Attorney brought a rueful smile to Deegan's face as he told Walker, 'I have to tell you, my friend, the man down the coast there —' he referred to the Atlantic City interlude — 'was so tickled pink by your pal from Scotland Yard he's buying the deal, even though I'm bound to say I was sceptical. A couple of street cops come strolling in with the sale of the century, I want to take a long hard look at the fine print before I go making an investment which even on conspiracy alone could send me to the slammer for five to life, only you know how it is with these macho types, all you've got to do is appeal to their vanity and they're blinded. Got a blemish on his reputation and you come in with a double

212

act and show him how he can polish it up again good as new. How could he resist it?'

Walker said, 'Like you said before, Counsellor, you lawyers play games, we cops play games. It's all the same game.'

Deegan's expression grew artful. 'I don't suppose you're going to tell me what's really happening, behind the smoke screen?'

Walker laughed. 'You're too suspicious for your own good. Put your fat fee in your pocket and walk away. You've earned your corn.'

'All the same,' Deegan said, 'I worked your side of the street, remember? I'm still curious.'

"There's nothing to be curious about,' Walker said. 'All the pieces fit together like the components of a watch. It'll tick like a Rolex.'

'Ah, but there's Rolex and then there's Rolex . . .'

'The deals which are irresistible don't come with a guarantee. You have to take a chance once in a while.'

Nodding at this pearl of wisdom, Deegan said, 'He's going to take care of the London end himself.'

'That'd be cosy.'

'Risky, too. Long, long way from home.'

'I thought this was a frontiersman?'

'Look,' Deegan said, 'I'm in a client relationship with the guy. Massaging some gangster's ego, is one thing, setting him up for the drop is another.'

'There's no set-up,' Walker reassured him.

'All the cards are on the table, we look after each other's interests, simple as that.'

'So why do I get the feeling there's something here you're not telling me?' Deegan cocked his head to one side.

'Because you're a suspicious buzzard.'

'I used to get the same itch when I was downtown, trying to make you guys look good in court.'

'Glory days,' Walker said. 'Long gone. Now it's dog eat dog.'

Deegan nodded. 'Maybe I've developed an allergy to smart cops.'

'With me it's shyster lawyers.' So what are you going to do about it?' Walker asked finally.

Deegan shrugged. 'The action-man's hungry. We're going to do it.'

'Give him what he wants.'

'Come again?' Don Bailey's face took on a disbelieving expression. Andy Barnes was leaning back, watching.

'If that's what he wants, give it to him,' Rowley repeated his advice, wondering why detective-superintendents could so easily be afflicted by deafness.

'That's it!' The eyebrows shot up, the colour rising on Bailey's cheeks. 'You pulling my plonker, son?' He wheeled angrily on Barnes. 'So much for your globe-trotting wonder boy. Is this the sharp operator you said could clip my man's wings without breaking into a sweat, or am I missing out on something?'

'Relax, Don, let him explain,' Barnes said easily and then turned to Rowley. 'You wouldn't want to pull anything of Mr Bailey's, would you, Tony?'

'Perish the thought, Guv'nor.'

'Oh, you're a right couple of jokers, you two are,' Bailey snorted unsmilingly. 'You ought to be on the telly . . . the twerp and his lifesize dummy.'

They were sitting in the long bar of the Farnham Conservative Club with its comfortable worn furniture and plain wooden tables. Bailey had signed them in and had handed the visitors' book back to the steward with the waxed moustache behind the bar. To Rowley's eyes the place was like a mausoleum, even down to the tobacco tins arranged on the tiled window-ledges in the Gents so that you could tap your cigar ash while taking a leak. The only sacrilege was that they were drinking LA out of steins designed for stronger stuff because everyone knew the Surrey Constabulary was red hot on drink and drive and it wasn't worth taking the risk.

Rowley leaned forward, his expression serious. 'Mr Bailey, with all due respect, you asked me if I would help you with your problem regarding the questionable sanity of Commander Drake. Now as it happens, my guv'nor here —' he nodded towards Barnes — 'is right when he says I can give you a lever. What you do with it when the time comes is your business, but in the meantime, if you seriously want me to help you, then you've got to give your imagination a little exercise and not fly off the handle even before I lay out my stall.'

'That's telling you, Don,' Barnes said, enjoying himself.

Bailey scowled. 'I tell you what I'm not used to,' he said, still sounding peeved, 'and that's jumped-up DSs talking to me in riddles. Only as you're so cocksure of yourself, Rowley, I'm going to make an exception to that rule and I'm going to sit here patiently and listen to you. All I can say is, it'd better be good.'

'What you have to understand about Larry Drake,' Rowley said, 'is that here you have the original techno-cop. He's seen the vision and he's blinded by the light. No more dirtying of the hands on humdrum police work, just crank up the computer and hey-presto.'

'Tell me something new,' Bailey sniffed. 'You want to be a DAC these days, you've got to have a gimmick. So Drake's a computer buff, so what?'

'I'll tell you,' Rowley said, expanding his theme. 'Computer buffs in the job have got one king-sized Achilles heel. They're seduced by the technology. Hit a few keys on a terminal, and bingo, you can look really smart. Absorb all the jargon and you're way out ahead. Only that's the crunch.' He looked from one to the other, Bailey still scowling, Barnes enjoying the show. 'If you'll excuse my saying so,' Rowley said, 'the higher the rank, the harder they fall, because at best you're talking about dyed in the wool coppers who just a moment ago wouldn't have known a floppy disk from a ballpoint. They don't understand the system, it's just so much gobbledegook, but they're scratching each other's eyes out to get in on the act, and once they're hooked and playing the game, the technology takes over, the computer can do no wrong, they're making magic.'

Bailey said, 'So we've got thickies and fantasy merchants running the Force. I don't remember when it was ever any different.'

'But the beauty of computers,' Rowley said, 'is that you can manipulate the system, and if you've also got somebody who already believes the computer is God and it's telling him to do this or do that, what's he going to do?'

Bailey dropped an elbow on to the table and braced his chin on his hand. 'OK, Rowley. You've drawn me the picture, now let's see you put Drake into the frame.'

Rowley said, 'If I understand you right, Drake is so mesmerized by this Secret Service fairytale that he's got your dedicated system trawling all the other data banks, trying to match a target profile. Now SB are the only people with that kind of clout, am I right?'

Bailey looked at Barnes. Barnes nodded. 'You could say that,' Bailey admitted grudgingly, for the Branch didn't surrender its secrets lightly.

'So it comes back to what I said,' Rowley continued. 'We give the man what he wants. We give him his target.'

'Oh, come on!' Bailey snorted, hardly able to contain himself. 'How'm I supposed to do that? All we've got is Mick bombers. I toss him a bog-trotter, I don't care how computer crazy he is, he's going to see right through that. The soothsayer at The Box says this mythical assassin's a Yank.'

'Then give him a Yank.'

'Like what? Like NORAID or something? Some rabble rouser who spends his time rattling the can in the Boston Irish bars?'

'Get me Drake's personal access code and I'll make you a present of the target.'

Bailey frowned. 'How're you going to pull that off?'

'Guv'nor, believe me, you don't want to know,' Rowley said. 'All you have to do is hang on to your hat and watch Drake drop like a ton of bricks on some poor unsuspecting tourist on a Christmas shopping trip. Nothing like an international cock-up to torpedo a fragile reputation. He'd have a job living that down.'

Bailey blinked. 'You can do that?'

'I can do that,' Rowley replied.

Bailey turned to Barnes for confirmation. 'Can he?'

The drugs chief grinned. 'How'd you want it — gift wrapped?'

At a little after eleven o'clock the next morning, Detective-Sergeant Tony Rowley sat in the NEL chief's office at the Basingstoke Bunker watching a green mosaic build up on the screen in front of him. It still amazed him how the whole world seemed infatuated with computers. You wanted money; you went to a keypad set into a wall, tapped in the digits and the computer gave you crisp new bank notes out of a slot. The same applied to law enforcement; you wanted a suspect, there was no longer any need to wear down shoe leather trekking around asking questions. No, you did what he was doing right now, sat at a console, pushed the buttons and waited for the data banks to give you the answers. Suddenly the entire world ran on computers and the lesson he had read to the SB Superintendent with the sour expression last night had been the new gospel. The smart set among the top brass at the Yard, of which Larry Drake was a prime example, was consumed with technology. The way they looked at it, an investigation, however major, wasn't worth the candle unless it could be run on a battery of computers. Rowley felt himself smiling grimly at the thought as he watched the luminous chains of data trickle across the screen. One of the early lessons he had learned from Dad Garratt was the psychological advantage of keeping one jump ahead of the guv'nors whenever humanly possible.

Rowley concentrated on the patterns, the chains and blocks of hieroglyphics which made up the operating system. As far as he was concerned, the sequence of symbols might just as well have been Sanskrit, but then he didn't need a hacker's skills to manipulate the system because he was already on the inside. All he needed was a modicum of computer know-how and the patience to wait for a gate to open as he scrolled through the data; a gate he could slip through unnoticed.

Without taking his eyes off the screen, Rowley drank some coffee from the mug at his elbow and waited for the electronic process to take its course.

The morning had already been busy. After his early meeting with the Snow Man prosecutor at the Yard, Andy Barnes had collected him and they had driven out to Basingstoke together. The NEL chief had swung his Cavalier Commander into an industrial park where a nondescript ochre-coloured blockhouse tucked away behind a high wire-mesh fence attracted little attention. However, on closer examination, concealed TV turrets could be seen scanning the approaches to the squat windowless building. The cameras tracked their progress as Barnes lamented the Polizei preoccupation with the gadgetry of security, sighing audibly as he escorted the sergeant through a series of counter-intrusion procedures, patiently entering combinations into keypads beside the doors as they passed through security layers into the new austere headquarters of Narcotics Enforcement Liaison. But once inside the blockhouse, the human scene was every bit the same as any other CID task force, with shirtsleeved detectives bent to the ritual, their painstaking efforts recorded on wall charts enlivened by mugshots of principal targets.

When they reached the sanctuary of his office Barnes gave Rowley a quick rundown on the new computer system. The NEL hardware was a McDonnell-Douglas capable of crunching data at a phenomenal speed. The core program was called Pathfinder denoting its ability to chart a course through the maze of names, physical descriptions, addresses, telephone numbers, bank accounts, business deals, registration numbers of cars, ships and aircraft which flooded in from around the globe. Every scrap of raw intelligence gleaned by the investigating teams, from a routine Carabinieri road check in a suburb of Rome to the suspicions of a border guard on the German frontier or an unexplained multi-million-pound deposit into a Swiss bank account, was fed into Pathfinder. Armed with such devastating computer power, NEL was beginning to live up to its concept of unravelling the conspiratorial webs which so cunningly obscured the activities of the traffickers — coming up with names and faces.

Such was the Pathfinder potential that a special shield had been devised to combat the risk of eavesdropping. Every terminal in the NEL complex was TEMPEST protected, clad in metal shields with wire-mesh screens linked by fibre optic cables to prevent any leak of telltale radiation. Only one other system rated TEMPEST protection, and that belonged to the Security Services at GCHQ which fed The Box and The Branch, the system with which Rowley was now preparing to duel. Glued to the terminal, watching for the gate to open, Rowley became so absorbed in his task that he almost forgot the superintendent at his elbow.

'You don't go much on Don Bailey, do you, Tony?' Barnes broke the silence.

Rowley was startled by the voice. 'I don't know him well enough to form an opinion, Guv'nor,' he replied.

'His bark's worse than his bite.'

Barnes watched as Rowley concentrated on the screen, flexing his fingers over the keyboard, and felt obliged to confide, 'Me and Don, we go back a long way. I wouldn't have involved you in this if he wasn't a hundred per cent.'

'That's OK, Guv'nor,' Rowley said, watching the diode green symbols, waiting to seize his chance. If, as Bailey had indicated, Drake had opened up the SB computer to comb all the other crime intelligence systems for his elusive target, then he could reverse the process and lock into Drake's system, but when the opportunity came he would have to work fast. There was a security pulse in the line and at any hint of unauthorized entry, the system would automatically close itself down.

'What I'm saying is,' Barnes was saying, 'Don's all right . . .'

But Rowley was no longer listening. There it was! On the screen in front of his eyes . . . the gate! His fingers moved rapidly over the keys. Quickly he opened a command file and entered Drake's personal code. The screen blanked and then reformed inside the SB program, issuing the routine challenge. Rowley's fingers spelled out the password Bailey had given him and the electronic sentry let him pass. And there he was, on the inside, like a burglar about to rifle the jewel box.

'You're a dark horse, Tony,' Barnes said admiring the sleight of hand. 'Where'd you pick up that clever stuff?'

'Playing space irivaders,' Rowley joked, busy with the keyboard as he scrolled through the priority targets, the most secret Special Branch hit list. And he found the man,

Drake's mythical assassin, right at the top of the list.'

Methodically Rowley plundered the file, erasing the physical description of the target line by line, then moving the cursor swiftly back to the prompts and tapping in a new physical, using the detail he had memorized from an NYPD rap sheet.

'Yeah?' Barnes said. 'Kids these days, it comes to them like second nature, all this computer mumbo jumbo.' The NEL chief shook his head and watched uncomprehendingly as Rowley picked his way stealthily back down the trail and as he passed through the SB operating system he slipped in a one-shot virus using the date numerals of the day for the Snow Man committal as the trigger. Then he retraced his steps to NEL and logged off. The computer screen subsided into a dull green sheen as Rowley sat back like a concert pianist concluding a bravura performance.

'That's it?' Barnes queried.

'That's it,' Rowley confirmed.

'You want to tell me what you just did?' Barnes asked, intrigued.

Rowley smiled. 'You can give Mr Bailey a bell and tell him Commander Drake's target is up and running. All he's got to do is be patient for a day or two, just bide his time.'

'You think it'll work?'

Rowley shrugged. 'We'll know soon enough.'

CHAPTER 14

At 4.30 in the afternoon Eastern Standard time the Pan Am shuttle cleared runway six left and began a steep climb out of La Guardia. No sooner had the blue and white Boeing 727 achieved its operating altitude of 14,000 feet and turned up the coast for the 40-minute hop to Boston than the flight attendants began the hectic process of plying passengers with drinks and snacks.

In the window seat the Brown Bag Bandit watched skeins of lights trace the contours of metropolitan America across the purple cloth of dusk as flight PA 0545 headed for Providence.

'You mind telling me,' Vince Walker asked, making conversation, 'what gives a guy like you the biggest charge: working for Uncle, or robbing banks?'

'Well,' The Bandit drew the word out, 'to be truthful I guess I'd have to say robbing banks.' He popped the ring on a can of Bud. 'And you know when you get the biggest kick? Watching the expression on their face when you show 'em the piece.'

Walker sipped a Seven-Up, concealing his

disgust. The Bandit was a sociopath, over-loaded with delusions of grandeur, and here he was playing partner to this make-believe cowboy.

'Well, sticking up banks is one thing,' he said. 'This job you're going to do now is some-thing else again. You think you can handle it?'

'No sweat,' The Bandit replied, absorbed in the pattern of lights, the highways and the little townships laid out far below. 'Only one way this is going to go down and that's smooth and easy. My man says rip off a truckload of soda, well, that's what I'm going to do.'

'You ever stop to think about it? Maybe get the jitters a little?'

'Why should I?'

'What about the Brits? What if they don't understand the rules?'

The Bandit turned. He looked genuinely sur-prised. 'They're just hired hands, do what they're told. I give 'em a look at the percentage and they're going to do it my way if they want to get paid.' The Bandit drank some Bud and frowned, feeling the explanation of his profes-sional ethics needed more emphasis. 'See, when you've got a reputation, a name in the armed robbery business . . .' He thought about it a minute more. Then he said, 'Like Sundance. When Sundance went back to the Hole in the Wall, all he had to do was show those boys the percentage and they were back robbing the iron horse. Once you know where you stand in the order of things, everything works out plain and simple, nobody goes off getting the wrong ideas. There won't be any problem you need worry about. You and me, we're going to be doing our thing for Uncle.'

Looking into Walker's face, he smiled at the challenge he saw in the cop's eyes. 'You and me, we're on the same side, buddy.'

'For now.'

'I remember someone else like you,' The Bandit reflected, 'same attitude. Now me and him went into Bolivia one time, into the jungle to see if we couldn't smoke out where The Enterprise was processing coca paste, mix the leaves with the gasoline and get the kids to stomp it till they get sores so bad they can't stand up any more, a mean operation. The white knights had some notion of a hearts and minds mission, destabilize the peasants, and if that didn't work napalm the bastards. Well, me and my man went into the green feature to scout out the coordinates, only he was a city boy, liked the feel of sidewalk under his feet, and the jungle is, well, the jungle.'

'You're going to tell me you ended up bosom pals, like a couple of Boy Scouts in the backwoods,' Walker sneered.

'Oh, closer'n that,' The Bandit said seriously. 'I took care of him like he was a baby, taught him how to survive. See, when we were first in there, under the triple canopy, he was dependent on me. I was his life-support system.'

'Oh yeah?'

'Yeah. I showed him how to move down the trails like a ghost, floating on air, watch for the signs. Well, we got in there, torched a plantation to show 'em Uncle meant business, and we got out.'

Walker said, 'So your pal got his woodsman's badge after all.'

The Bandit looked into Walker's face, his eyes blank. 'He learned fast and he was never the same again.'

'He got a name, this mystery man?'

'Butch Cassidy,' The Bandit said.

'You crease me up, you know that?'

Overhead the seat-belt sign flashed on as the shuttle dipped into the descent.

'I never liked these short hops,' The Bandit yawned. 'Get yourself settled, your ears stop popping, you get a drink in your hand and you're ready to enjoy the flight, right away some stewardess is coming around with a bin liner grabbing your drink out of your hand, smiling like she's doing you a big favour, and you're going down and your ears are popping again.'

'You'll get plenty of time to make yourself at home on the transatlantic.'

'Yeah? I still don't see why we couldn't have gone straight out of Kennedy and cut this hassle.'

To fool the computer, Walker thought to himself, but he had no intention of enlightening his travelling companion. Instead he said, 'Because you'd have missed the view.'

He leaned across to squint out of the port side window at the twinkling night-time panorama of downtown Boston.

The shuttle was losing height, turning over the sea on to the approach to Logan Airport.

'Ah, you cops, you got no imagination.' The Bandit shook his head. 'Everything by the book. Some guy with braid around his cap pins a badge on you and right away you're Dick Tracy, roaring around doing good deeds. What d'you do to relax, Walker?'

'Well, I don't rob banks,' Walker replied.

'You ought to give it a whirl,' The Bandit said. 'Nothing like a constructive hobby to keep you on your toes. Look what polishing the badge got you.'

'Yeah, stuck with you.'

The shuttle came in to a flawless landing and The Bandit turned to the window again and watched the runway light flash past. The 727 braked, turned and began to negotiate the taxiway towards the terminal.

'So who was he?' Walker asked, returning to the story.

The Bandit stretched. 'Just a guy like you, out of his depth. All you have to remember is, there's jungle and then there's jungle. City block can be the jungle. We go six thousand kliks to pull a heist, we're still going into the jungle.'

'You want to nursemaid me too?' Walker asked, levering himself out of his seat and reaching for his coat from the overhead bin.

The Bandit smiled. 'Maybe I'm going to have to,' he said.

Seven miles above the North Atlantic, hanging seemingly stationary in clear sky over an endless plateau of cloud, a red-tailed Northwest DC 10 settled into an easygoing night flight routine. In the cabin the plastic debris of dinner had been cleared away, the coffee rounds completed; the movie was over and blankets and pillows had been distributed. The hum of the jets subsided into a low soporific pitch.

In the rear of the economy section the last three rows of seats in the centre block of the wide-bodied airliner had been designed so that the armrests could be folded away, providing space to stretch out. Here in the dim glow of the night lights The Bandit had taken Walker at his word and had made himself comfortable.

'You mind if I ask you a question that's always intrigued me, only every time I ask it the guy I'm asking hightails it for the hills,' The Bandit began.

'Ask away,' Walker replied, lulled by the

steady note of the engines. 'Only don't go expecting an answer that'll make you feel good. We work opposite sides of the street, you and me, so don't go getting any ideas. This truce is just temporary.'

'There you go,' The Bandit said, 'right away you're on the defensive.'

'Ask the question.'

'I want to know where you draw the line, you people behind the badge. You take an oath to uphold the law and when it gets to the point where you can't enforce the law because the rules won't let you, yet you know the guy you've been plugging away at is guilty as hell only you can't touch him, you call me up, the guy who didn't take the oath and is in the line of business for nobody but himself and doesn't have a rule book to follow, and you say to me: "Here's a guy we want set up, and in exchange for setting up this dude we're going to give you immunity for some of the things you've been doing," and I do it and nobody ends up with their ass in a sling.' The Bandit paused. 'So what I want to know is, you, Mulholland, and all the other shakers and movers who want the services of a mercenary when it suits you, where do you draw the line? When do you say, "This can't be done"?'

'What the hell kind of question is that?'

'The kind I never get an answer to,' The Bandit said seriously. 'Like, everybody gets real nervous at the suggestion that an officer

231

of the law could stoop so low as to condone a felony. Closest I ever got . . . I put the same question to Mulholland one time when we were mellow and he told me, "Sometimes you have to forget the oath and consider the greater good." So I pushed him a little further and he got apologetic and said there were times when the word came down from on high that something just had to be taken care of, and there was no way the boss was going to go for a negative attitude. He said it was then that they started to get creative.'

'There's only one problem with that philosophy,' Walker said, his head back and his eyes closed, 'and that's that the trade-off gives guys like you a licence to commit crime. That's where I draw the line. That's where every decent cop draws the line. A snitch I can take, where the commodity is information paid for up front, a straightforward business deal, undercover too, no complaint from me, entrapment I can live with.' Walker opened an eye and gave The Bandit a steady gaze. 'Frankly, if it was up to me, I wouldn't touch it. Not that I have any hang-ups over ethics, you understand, I'm a street cop, always have been and I'll go for the angle if it gets me the job done and I can get it through the courts. Only this thing we're doing is a whole different ballgame, dreamed up not by the flatfoots who toil in the system but by the executives of the structure who don't give a damn what's happening in the streets as long as they're sitting in their air-conditioned offices behind their vice-president status desks filling their quotas and not caring who gets burned in the process.'

Despite himself, Walker became angry. 'I'll tell you something,' he said. 'I've been out there a long time. I've cleared up the mess they've left in the sewers each time some brainwave went down the tubes. There were the street gangs with zip guns tucked in their jeans, looking to rumble over disputed turf. Some genius dipped the stick in the honey and bought 'em off, so instead of wasting each other they upped the ante and started wasting cops. Then the families went on the rampage, blowing each other away in the trattorias and the stick went in the honey again, mention Mafia and you got yourself slapped with a million dollar lawsuit. Now we've got another breed bringing crack down on the streets like a blizzard and the fabric of the city starts falling apart and all of a sudden the honey-pot's empty and City Hall's wringing their hands screaming for action. Only now the cops who could have done the job have been cas-trated. That's where we're at.'

Walker calmed himself and The Bandit watched, a small smile playing on his lips. 'Was probably the same story with the Pink-ertons,' he mused. 'Demarcation problems and everything. Running up against sheriffs and town marshals and regulators and the Cattlemen's Association. Yeah, I can see how it would probably have been the same back then; palms got to be greased all down the line, that's why they got slowed down chasing Sundance into Bolivia. Shelling out to the Federales. I can see how that could happen.'

'The Pinkertons started out as railroad dicks,' Walker said. 'Private enterprise, that's the name of the game. Security guards, magic eye alarms, closed circuit TV on the condos. Ten years' time there won't be a cop on the street, rent-a-badge will have taken over the neighbourhoods. You get mugged in an alley, you're going to have to come up with AMEX before the block watch contract cops will investigate the case. Guy like you could walk into a bank with a sawn-off, you're going to get fried to a crisp by a laser from the security console. When big business takes over law enforcement it's going to be quick, cheap, instant justice. You got any more stupid questions?'

The Bandit eased himself into a more comfortable position across the seats. The aircraft cabin was quiet. 'Guess I'll take a nap,' he said.

Jet-lagged, dehydrated, bleary-eyed and a little disorientated from the six-hour time warp into GMT, Walker and The Bandit shuffled from the DC 10 by the front port exit under the practised smiles of the cabin crew.

'I changed my mind,' The Bandit moaned, sniffing the chill of a misty English winter morning. 'This is bleak!'

'Don't even think it,' Walker hissed a pace behind as they joined the queue for passport and immigration control, 'You're on your own now, Sundance . . . lock and load.'

Leaning against the news-stand, Detective-Sergeant Tony Rowley saw Vince Walker emerge from the Arrivals aisle. The New York detective's raincoat was a crumpled ball under his arm; he had a scarf wrapped around his neck and was carrying a lightweight nylon holdall. His face looked weary and his eyes were deeply shadowed.

'So you finally made it,' Rowley greeted him.

'No thanks to your quaint British fog,' Walker sniffed. 'We had a forty-minute conducted tour of your South Coast waiting for the stuff to clear. Brighton beach looked nice.'

'We lay it on for the turists,' Rowley said. 'You can take it home in a presentation bottle.' He picked up the American's bag. 'This is all you've got, Vince?'

'I travel light.'

'How about our mutual friend?'

'He's coming through. You want to watch?'

'No need,' Rowley said. 'Just as long as he'll be all right, no hitches at this stage in the game.'

They began to walk towards the exit following the black on yellow signs to the car parks. Two PCs, incongruous in bobbies' helmets with pistols on their hips, strolled past, walking in step.

'No problem,' Walker reassured him. 'This guy doesn't have a nerve in his body. DEA pushes the buttons and he goes into his routine.'

Together they walked out of the Gatwick terminal into a blast of jet noise carried on the raw breeze which stirred the low-lying mist. Walker shivered as they headed for the multi-storey car park, Rowley leading the way to the second deck, threading their way between the cars until they came upon a white Sapphire Cosworth squeezed into a slot beside a pillar.

The New Yorker cast an appraising eye over the racing lines of the hot Ford and remarked, 'Fancy wheels you've got here, buddy.'

Rowley opened the passenger's door and heaved Walker's bag into the back seat. 'Only the best for one of the finest.'

'Yours?'

'No, it's a job motor.'

They got into the bucket seats and Walker, still impressed, inquired, 'What'll she do, a hundred and twenty?'

'I'll show you.' Rowley eased out of the slot and headed for the ramp. When they were clear of the airport and on the M23 he pulled out into the fast lane and flattened the accelerator, showing off the sizzling performance with schoolboy bravado, but no sooner had they joined the orbital M25 than they ran into the usual congestion and their speed was abruptly slowed to a snail's pace.

'Welcome to London,' Rowley remarked disparagingly, gesturing at the three clogged lanes.

But the New York detective's head sank back against the seat rest and his eyes closed, 'Jeez, I'm bushed. Hardly got a moment's shut-eye coming over. Our mutual friend started out as the strong silent type and ended up motor-mouth.'

'Maybe that's a signal he's got a problem.'

'Oh, sure he's got a problem. He thinks he's the Sundance Kid, that's his problem. You got any good banks, you'd better tell 'em to put up the shutters until this cowboy rides out of town.'

'We've got enough nutters of our own,' Rowley said. 'What I mean is, you sure he'll go through with it?'

'Relax,' Walker said, 'this guy's learned the script. One thing about the DEA, they provide top-notch tutors. It'll be a breeze.'

Rowley thought about The Twins and felt the palms of his hands moisten. 'I hope you're right, Vince,' he said. 'This is a one-shot job.'

Crawling along in the endless traffic stream, they skirted the southern sprawl of London suburbs and plunged into the hinterland south of the Thames. In the passenger's seat Walker began to take an interest in his surroundings.

They were cruising down streets of beaten-up brick buildings, some of which still exhibited the architecture of another age. There were ornate cupolas of green tarnished copper perched on top of the brick piles, one even had a clock tower. To the Manhattanite the streets seemed like alleys, they were so narrow, and the traffic, even by New York standards was horrific, with cars and trucks, black cabs and ancient-looking red buses jostling for space on the overcrowded roads.

Rowley stopped at a red light and in his mirror caught sight of a motorcycle messenger weaving through the stalled traffic. The Twins' death threat flashed into his mind as the big Kawasaki came alongside and he glanced into the rider's black visor, the sinister bulbous faceless helmet close by his window as he sat trapped in the stationary traffic. He imagined the handgun coming out from under the rider's gaudy tabard. The fusillade of shots, slowed right down so that he could actually see the succession of bullets emerging from the muzzle in a puff of smoke, shattering the side window, driving into his face, his head exploding. Claustrophobia clamped his head in its vice, and in panic Rowley jammed the heel of his hand on the horn, swung out of the jam and roared across the intersection on the wrong side of the bollards.

Headlights blazed and horns screamed as the Cosworth forced opposing traffic to swerve out of the way. Walker looked across, puzzled. 'Say, Tony,' he remarked casually as they regained their correct side of the road, 'last time I saw a burn-off like that was in the Jersey stocks.'

'Sorry, Vince,' Rowley apologized, a little sheepishly, his heartbeat returning to normal.

By the time they entered Dockland, the duel with the traffic had eased. But it wasn't until they reached the comparative safety of Rotherhithe, his own stamping ground, that Rowley stopped flicking his eyes to the mirrors in an involuntary reflex.

All around the wasteland of the derelict docks was in transformation as developers razed the rotting wharves and beavered away on the new riverside encampments of trendy mews, hamlets and apartment blocks, hi-tech hideaways for the new wave of city slickers.

Rowley eased the car around the smooth curves of the newly tarmaced roads running through the developments which were clustered at different angles around central courtyards, creating the impression of villages fortified against attack. The architectural buzzword was defensible space; the purpose, to lock out crime behind the walls. Although it was well into the morning and the mist had cleared, amber lanterns still glowed from their wrought-iron stanchions on driveways where BMWs and Mercedes were parked like toy-town additions to an architect's model.

'Where are we now?' Walker asked, taking an interest in his surroundings. 'On the waterfront?'

'My place is just around the corner,' Rowley explained. 'I thought we'd stop off for a minute, freshen up before I take you over to the Yard.'

'Sounds good to me,' Walker replied. 'Nice neighbourhood . . . looks like somebody threw a lot of money around.'

'Gentrified is the word,' Rowley said. 'You're looking at yuppie heaven.'

He stopped the car opposite a construction site where the steel skeleton of a slender highrise was going up. 'See that? Sentinel Tower. Buy an apartment, you get a Porsche thrown in with the asking price.'

The New York detective raised an eyebrow, 'Yeah?'

'The price of progress,' Rowley said. 'You wouldn't believe it but this was my old neighbourhood when I was a kid. Only you look at it now, you can't picture what it was like in those days. Nobody lived here by choice, just the dockers who worked on the wharves. All the streets around here were rabbit warrens of little back-to-back houses. The men'd spend

240

eight hours humping cargo and then get down to the pub and sink gallons of beer. That was the life: work, booze and a punch-up on a Saturday night while container freight was killing the docks. I'm talking twenty years ago, when life was simple. Coppers walked the beat, shook the door handles, helped old ladies across the street. The Beatles were top of the hit parade.'

Rowley set the car in motion again. Even the street names had been glamourized, he explained.

'This was all poky terraces when I was a kid,' he said. 'You came down here, all you'd see was snotty-nosed kids kicking a ball in the street. We lived in each other's pockets. But it was a real neighbourhood then. Go down the boozer or the chippy those days, you wouldn't even think of locking the door. Leave the rent money on the kitchen table. Nowadays, the sun goes down, you put on the door chains and the five-lever deadlocks, switch on the alarm system, and the only person on foot is the security guard with his trusty hound hired by the residents' association.'

He let the car speed up and a few moments later when they drove into the old quarter of Rotherhithe, the scene actually changed into streets of Victorian terraces, spit-shined and double-glazed, but still tenuously linked to the past.

In Russell Street, Rowley pulled up outside

241

a warehouse, its brickwork blackened with age, its original purpose as a grain repository for the nearby docks long since forgotten. Only the outer shell of the building testified to its former function, for it had been transformed into a warren of apartments by some far-sighted property speculator long before Dockland gained its fashionable cachet with the City set.

Inside, the warehouse had a curious charm, created by a construction technique which had retained much of the sturdy ironwork of the old building. Even Rowley's third-floor bachelor flat had been designed around the latticework of an ornate girder. Walker crossed the room to where the brickwork had been uncovered to form a feature and ran a hand over the rough surface.

'I don't use it a lot,' Rowley said. 'You know how it is in the job, I can lay my head somewhere else, or else I'll doss down in a section house when I'm working.' He looked around and sniffed the slightly musty air, 'Still, it's home.'

Touching the brickwork, imagining the Victorian artisan at work, Walker felt himself communing with history. 'Not bad at all,' he commented. 'You take an old place like this, done up, drop it on the East Side somewhere in the upper Sixties, you'd break the bank.'

Rowley dropped his coat over the arm of a well worn chesterfield and went through into the galley kitchen. Under the glare of the strip light he peered into the fridge and found a couple of stubby bottles of Stella Artois *bière blonde,* flipped off the caps with an opener and returned to the living-room. He handed one to Walker, who was still looking around.

The New Yorker raised the bottle and took a swig. Then he voiced his concern. 'Look, Tony, don't get me wrong. I just get the impression you're kind of jumpy. That stunt with the car just now . . . why'm I getting bad vibes?'

'Probably my horoscope.' Rowley passed off his foreboding lightly. 'Says a strong silent stranger is going to do me harm.'

'Something new come up?' Walker's eyes narrowed.

Rowley told him about the telephone threat and the death of Cindy Miller. 'They hit the girl to remind me, made it look like a traffic accident, only really it's the cat playing with the mouse. So I'm a trifle nervous.'

Walker said seriously, 'I tell you something. If I was looking to get someone whacked, I'd get myself a broad to do the job every time. Right woman's the best assassin in the business, no doubt about it. A woman, knows what she's doing, she's going to catch you when you least expect it, when you're most vulnerable.'

'I doubt The Twins could muster that degree of finesse, Vince,' Rowley replied uneasily as the American's words stirred his fear. 'They're more likely to hit the door with a sledge and come in shooting.'

'You want my opinion, for what it's worth,' Walker said, 'most of the dudes who go running around bragging how they're going to off a cop can usually be persuaded from that course of action.'

'You haven't met The Twins,' Rowley said. 'They don't listen to reason. A couple of East End blaggers with exaggerated ideas of their own importance. They're going to go all the way.' He slumped on to the chesterfield, creaking the hide. 'There's another thing on my mind.'

'The sting?'

Rowley nodded. 'I started to wonder what might happen if this blows up in our faces because the jokers on the other end of the deal are playing a different game.'

'Never happen,' Walker said confidently. 'The whole thing's hooked up to The Bandit. Only people who can screw up this deal now are the DEA and it would not be in their best interests. This is their main man, remember? Their star performer.'

The New York detective stretched out and yawned. 'Besides, our new federal buddies are underwriting the whole shebang. I was talking to Mulholland before I left New York, and he guarantees this thing one hundred per cent. I also touched bases with Deegan, who tells me Snow White wants to handle this end personally, he's so hot for it too. It's all going by the numbers. You've just got to keep your nerve a little longer.'

Rowley sighed. 'Yeah, well, I suppose you're right, I'd be stupid to screw up now we've got this far.'

Walker smiled. 'What about that old partner of yours?'

'Dad Garratt?'

'You think he'd think twice about it?'

'All this ducking and diving. Dad would have been in his oil tot.'

'Then walk in his shoes.'

Rowley laughed. 'Oh, Dad'd' have loved you, Vince. You've got the same swagger. Only rules worth the bother are the ones that're meant to be bent.'

'Aw, come on,' Walker drawled, grinning. 'Me? I'm just an old Broadway hoofer, whistle the tune and I'll dance to it.' He rasped a hand over his stubbled jaw with the realization that he had been in motion for the best part of twenty-two hours and was now close to wilting. He began to lever himself stiffly out of his chair. 'I'll bet you've got a tub in this rinky-dink apartment.'

To the background drumming of the shower Rowley found the dark thought which the New Yorker had planted in his mind had drawn him to the living-room window. He looked down across the central courtyard and his eyes automatically went to a window opposite, a floor below. He stared at the window. It was through that pane that he had seen a girl with smooth olive skin smile up at him as she shed her red dress and danced on the rug. The female of the species. Now his head ached at the prospect. He imagined her coming towards him across the bedroom in the lamplight, himself sated with passion, sprawled on the crumpled duvet. She was smiling as she returned to the bed, and he was dreaming, relaxed, off guard. As she leaned over him, he caught the headiness of her perfume and the merest metallic gleam of the two-inch barrel of the chrome-plated Chief's Special before the bullet shattered his forehead and consigned him to oblivion. Rowley leaned against the cold glass and shuddered, blocking out the memory of Cindy's crumpled, broken body which haunted him. He stared at the window for a long time, but there was nobody there.

CHAPTER 15

Larry Drake sat at his desk in the inner sanctum of the Special Branch at New Scotland Yard, his face contorting rhythmically as he worked his wrist-exerciser first in the left and then the right hand.

The SB Chief was alone in his office, his morning workout observed only by the approving eyes of his senior command course gazing down upon him from the group photograph on the far wall. At his elbow his computer terminal hummed like a contented pet.

Drake used the morning excrcises to relieve the tension which knotted his neck and shoulder muscles and produced a dull ache at the base of his skull. Stress was an important part of his job, he knew that from the management seminars he had attended on the subject, and he would have been mortified if he had not experienced the symptoms which denoted the pressures of his rank. But as each day passed uneventfully his miniaturized iron pumping became more and more frenzied, for it seemed only a matter of time before the faction on the Commissioner's policy group, led by the astringent Deputy, succeeded in ganging up on him to undermine his brilliant concept of a shadowy assassin stalking the streets of London.

Already doubts were beginning to nibble into his resolve and he spent long desperate periods in his office staring at the routine security traffic sliding across his screen, wishing that he could transform the VDU into a crystal ball. As his frustration grew he even began to doubt his newfound confidante at The Box who seemed to have no concern for the urgency required. His strategy was collapsing around him like a house of cards for want of positive action, and with all the intelligence resources not to mention manpower committed to the grand design, he could soon be lighting a rearguard action against his opponents.

As he worked out his frustrations, Drake cursed the injustice of the management system which placed tangible results above the cerebral chess game of national security, ignoring the chirrup of the internal phone on his desk.

In the outer office Joyce Swallow flicked the intercom key with a crimson fingernail, looked up at Detective-Superintendent Donald Bailey and said, 'I told you, when he's got that do-not-disturb light on —' she arched an eyebrow towards the red light glowing over the Commander's door — 'he's not going to answer the phone, not even if the building's falling down.'

'What's he doing in there, Joyce?' Bailey wanted to know.

'Search me,' Joyce Swallow replied, 'but whatever it is, I'll bet it's two-handed.'

Bailey sniggered. Joyce, robbed of her office paramour, had become waspish, a useful ally.

'Oh, by the way, I heard from Ronnie Mason across the water,' Bailey remarked. 'He said to be sure to give you his best.'

Joyce fluttered her lashes. 'Mr Mason would,' she said primly. 'Mr Mason was a gentleman.'

Bailey wandered away from the secretary's desk. Despite his customary dour countenance, he was elated. He had been tipped off that today would be the day and he was determined to be on hand to witness Drake's reaction when it all hit the fan. He turned and looked at the door over which the red eye gleamed on the light box. No, sir, he told himself, he wasn't going to miss this for the world, and for the hundredth time he wished he had X-ray eyes so that he could see inside.

Behind the door, Larry Drake abandoned the task of reviving his flagging confidence and with a sigh verging upon defeat, reached out to the keyboard of his computer terminal and entered his log-on, following up with the security code of the day, thus activating the program which matched the target profile to the deluge of information pouring into the Police National Computer from SB Port Units the length and breadth of the country. From Falmouth to Aberdeen the SB network responded unquestioningly to the command from NSY for information on arrivals at sea and airports, slotting each entry into the vaults of electronic memory.

When it came, the hit registered on the screen in such an unremarkable way that Drake's eyes at first skipped over the slippery green text. But the event he had ached for had registered inside his subconscious, for his scalp began to tingle as he feverishly back-tracked.

And there it was! A routine immigration check by the Sussex Police Ports Unit stationed at Gatwick Airport had positively matched the profile. He pictured a bored DC tapping the details into a terminal, oblivious of the import of his chore, for such was the obsessive secrecy of SB that officers in the field were seldom privy to the reasoning behind an all-ports directive from the mighty Yard.

At first Drake peeked slantwise at the computer screen: in the terse, clinical format required for such communication the message reported the arrival of a passenger on a scheduled transatlantic flight from Boston, Mass. that morning who precisely matched the SB target profile. Out of the blue the phantom assassin had materialized.

The message concluded with the cryptic confirmation that the target would be subjected to close surveillance until such time as further instructions were received. Hardly daring to breathe, Drake fingered the keys causing the printer to chatter out a hard copy which he read over and over, inspecting each word for a trap. Only when he was fully satisfied did he allow himself the luxury of one glorious reflection. This was it! His chance to thwart the enemies of the realm.

Great was the burden which now lay on his shoulders and with all due gravity he unlocked his desk drawer and took out the scrambler phone; tapped in the number engraved on his memory, buzzing the equally secure phone of The Right Honourable Peter Ashworth MP, Junior Minister for the Home Department. When the slightly distorted voice of the Secretary of State came on the line Drake said, 'Peter? Larry Drake . . . can you talk?' He had caught Ashworth during a routine briefing with his civil servants and paused for a moment as the Minister cleared his office. Then, puffing himself up with importance, he said into the phone, 'Peter . . . I wanted you to be the first to know . . . I got a hit this morning. Yes, yes, confirmed. You can whisper in the PM's ear, our man's in town.'

Drake replaced the phone with Ashworth's congratulations ringing in his ear. A sigh of relief escaped him and suddenly invigorated, his mind turned to the next phase of the operation as he strode purposefully across the room. Now that it was happening there was not a moment to lose and when he burst through the door into his outer office he was already deep in concentration. Joyce Swallow was staring at him as though he had gone crazy.

'Get Superintendent Bailey up here on the double!' He rapped out the command in such a masterful way that he was completely thrown when Bailey immediately materialized into his field of vision. Drake blinked and shot his secretary a withering glare. Joyce smiled sweetly. 'Anything else I can do for you?'

'Yes,' Drake snapped, 'get my car to the back hall . . . two minutes.'

He grabbed Bailey's arm and hauled him into his office, slamming the door as behind his back Joyce gave him the finger.

'I was waiting to see you, Guv'nor,' Bailey began, deadpan, but Drake cut him short. 'Never mind that now, Don.' He flourished the printout. 'We've got a hit!'

The Detective-Superintendent, his expression still blank, replied, 'I know. That's what I came to tell you. Sussex SB clocked him at Gatwick.'

'You knew!' Drake was dumbfounded.

'Saw it when I came in, Guv,' Bailey replied.

'I came straight up.'

'Why didn't you tell me, man?'

'You had the do-not-disturb light on.' Bailey peered around the office, relishing the opportunity. 'Joyce buzzed through, but you didn't answer so we naturally assumed you were doing something confidential in here.'

Drake waved the explanation aside. 'Yes, all right, all right. You know what this means, Don?'

'We're in business?'

'Too damned right. This is what I've been waiting for and now we've got a target I don't want any cock-ups. We're going to stick to this character like a second skin until he makes his move.'

'And then we nobble him, Guv'nor?'

Drake nodded, staring into the deadpan face. 'I want this one bang to rights. Understood?'

'Absolutely.'

'Right, get the relief cracking, briefing in one hour, I'll handle it myself. Oh, and we'll keep this in the family. This is our job, SB exclusive, so I don't want those glory-hunters in Thirteen —' he used the numerals of the anti-terrorist squad — 'muscling in on the act. I'm not even going to tell the Old Man until I'm good and ready. So it's need-to-know only, Don, and if so much as a whisper leaks, I'll have somebody's guts for garters.'

Bailey nodded. 'Understood. I'll be sure to

make the point when I muster the troops.'

Drake frowned. The Yard was like a colander with information leaking out in all directions and he contemplated appealing to his subordinate's personal loyalty to keep this one at least sewn up tight, but in his short tenure of office he had been less than generous to his number two and so found himself unable to go much further. All he could manage was a gruff, 'Do this for me, Don, and I won't forget it.'

Bailey gave him a slightly reproachful look and said, 'Don't worry, you can count on me, Guv'nor.'

Drake turned away. He could hardly expect Bailey to share his triumph. After all, the man was just another clone, as locked into the system as the rest of them. No, he told himself, he would have to go somewhere else to savour the moment.

Fifteen minutes later, his black Rover doubleparked in Curzon Street, his driver fending off the wardens, the SB Commander indulged himself in a little ego-massage. In the cramped room at The Box he gazed into Anthea Gibson's freckles and allowed his euphoria to boil over as he recounted news of the hit. Impeccable as ever in his double-breasted pinstripe, he allowed his excitement to spill out at last with a certain boyish charm.

Anthea drank it in, a rapt expression on her

face as her eyes devoured the SB signal which Drake flourished in front of her, both of them unaware of the subtle changes in the target profile. The computer had spoken. The computer was infallible.

'We did it! We actually did it!' she enthused huskily.

'Now just let them try to block my promotion!'

Drake blinked, dimly aware that he had inadvertently touched off explosive behind the sea of freckles as she darted into his arms. 'Oh Larry,' she gasped, testing his biceps, 'you're a real man.'

'What! Hey, Anthea . . . take it easy!' Drake yelped in alarm, but she was all over him and the ferocity of the assault almost lost him his footing. The SB Commander reeled back with the woman, transformed from a frumpy INT-CEL analyst into a fiery animal, clinging to him, her hands everywhere.

'Ohhh . . . ohhh . . . Larry . . . Larry . . . I want you, I want you!' Her voice came urgently.

From somewhere behind the flimsy wall Drake believed he heard a snigger.

'Walker . . . Walker?' Andy Barnes turned the name over a couple of times as Rowley introduced the American detective. They met at the NDIU and Barnes, pleased to have an excuse to escape from the Basingstoke

Bunker, gripped Vince Walker's hand as Rowley said, 'Vince is at Mid-Town South. He held my hand on the Spinelli thing, Guv'nor.'

'Currently on loan to the DEA,' Walker said. 'The Feds are fascinated by NEL and your Snow Man bust. When they knew I was working with Tony here, they sent me across to mind the store, just a watching brief.'

'Well, welcome to Scotland Yard,' Barnes said with a sweep of the hand. 'Famed in fable the world over. Anything we can do for New York's Finest, only too happy to oblige. That's the paid-up benefit of the job, Vince: wherever you go in the world, you're a member of the club. You got somewhere to lay your head?'

'The Embassy'll fix me up,' Walker replied. 'Grosvenor Square's my next port of call, check in with the bureau chief, only Tony thought it would be helpful if I made my number here first.'

'You see there's something else, Guv,' Rowley said.

'Such as?' Barnes paused from the meticulous business of filling his pipe and raised an eyebrow at the serious expression on the Detective-Sergeant's face. Rowley looked at Walker.

'Oh, it's probably nothing,' Walker said. 'Just the DEA's got this bee in its bonnet that some dudes are goin' to hit you.'

'Hi-jack the product we seized on the Snow

256

Man bust,' Rowley put in.

'Grab their investment back to save face,' Walker said.

'Jump us on the way to court for the committal,' Rowley added.

Barnes's eyes flicked from one to the other, then he struck a match and began to work the flame around the bowl of his pipe.

Walker said, 'Probably just hogwash, you know the DEA.'

'Who's supposed to be behind this?' Barnes asked.

'Our old friends The Enterprise,' Rowley said.

'Character called Fabio Rey Blanco,' Walker said. 'Colombian coyote. Troubleshooter for The Enterprise, or so the story goes. DEA call him Snow White.'

Barnes looked at Rowley.

'Probably just a wind-up, Guv'nor.' Rowley shrugged. 'We thought you ought to know, though, just in case.'

Barnes tapped his teeth with the stem of his pipe. 'This strong enough to take upstairs?'

'No. As it's just a whisper we could always handle it at squad level,' Rowley suggested. 'No need to ring any alarm bells.'

'Any bright ideas?'

'We could put a couple of extra teams on the convoy, discreet surveillance.'

Barnes puffed on his pipe. 'We're talking day

after tomorrow, right?'

'Right, Guv.'

'OK,' Barnes agreed, 'let's beef up the escort and watch points.'

'You're the boss, Guv'nor,' Rowley said. 'Probably just a wind-up.'

'Well, you'll be the first to know, Tony,' Barnes said. 'You're the convoy commander.' He turned to Walker. 'And as the DEA's so keen to see how we operate, you have my permission to ride along. If this hi-jack happens, you'll get a ringside seat.'

'You know what they say,' Barnes said over a sandwich in the Feathers that lunch-time, 'there's only three jobs you can throw your weight around in in the police force: chief, divisional commander and detective-sergeant. And God preserve all us lesser mortals from tricky detective sergeants.'

'Problems?' Don Bailey asked, looking pleased with himself.

'Nothing I can't handle,' the drugs chief replied, taking a bite of roast beef. 'Just one of my lads spinning me a yarn.'

'Wouldn't be a certain DS who's been doing a bit for me, would it?'

'Very probably,' Barnes said. 'And he's got a country cousin from the US of A in tow, doing a double act.'

'Working a bit of a flanker?'

'Could very well be,' Barnes said. 'Only

they're going to have to get up early in the morning to put one over on me. What these bright sparks tend to forget is, I was a rip-roaring skipper too, back in the old days. I've pulled all the strokes in the book, so I can see one coming a mile off.'

'You don't look too put out, Andy.'

'Me . . . nah.' Barnes washed down a mouthful of sandwich. 'He's a good lad, learned the wrinkles from Dad Garratt, the old maestro himself, so he's pretty cute. Just needs a word of guidance every now and then.'

'Well, whatever he did for me, he worked the oracle all right,' Bailey confided, leaning forward to ensure a degree of privacy in the crowded bar. 'We got a hit this morning, just like he predicted. Drake came out of his hole rocket-assisted, roared off down The Box to see his girlfriend on the strength, and then came bouncing back all bushy-tailed and started whaling into the troops.' Bailey took another swig of his drink. 'Of course he's stark raving bonkers.'

'So what's new? I thought that was a condition of service in SB.'

'For Christ's sake keep your voice down,' Bailey pleaded, his eyes flicking around the bar.

'Oh I forgot,' Barnes whispered. 'He's got the boozers bugged for enemies of the State.'

'Don't say it, even in jest.'

'So you're up and running eh?' Barnes said.

'A big production, all singing, all dancing.'

'The biggest,' Bailey said happily. 'He's dropped everything else, this is it.'

'With Commander Larry Drake in personal command?'

'Right again.'

'Running it off the computer, sealed orders, read 'em and eat 'em.'

'Not this one,' Bailey said cheerily. 'Far as I can tell, he's going to run the whole cockeyed operation by Zen archery.'

CHAPTER 16

A little after noon on the second Wednesday in December the festive season got off to an early start in a fashionable wedge of London streets.

Into the dull winter day a jovial Father Christmas began ho-hoing the stream of pedestrians emerging from Knightsbridge tube station, thrusting into their hands leaflets extolling the Yuletide virtues of the neighbourhood boutiques. His red cloak swinging as he shook his hand bell and intercepted passers by, the Santa would occasionally pause to mutter into his white beard.

Across the street outside a row of shops a yellow van with a breakdown service logo on the cab door was parked with its nearside wheels on the pavement in front of a red Golf GTI with the bonnet raised. Two men in padded jackets and jeans were running jump leads from the van to the VW while a business type in a sheepskin coat looked on. Each man was wearing what appeared to be a hearing aid and would occasionally incline his head to direct a comment into his lapel.

Among the tide of people in motion on the

pavements, two couples, window-shopping, exhibited the same characteristics as they dawdled in front of the Christmas displays. A man in a tweed overcoat with a yellow scarf around his neck, also sporting an earplug, stood beside a red painted news-stand on which was stencilled *Newsweek* in white lettering. He was flipping through an early edition of the *Standard*, a preoccupied expression on his face, his eyes watchful.

A black cab was parked in a side street with the 'for hire' light on, the cabbie chatting to two men in the rear seats.

Swathed in an army greatcoat, an unshaven busker, his face pinched from the cold, set out a strip of blanket at the kerb, raised a saxophone to his lips and began a rendition of 'I only have eyes for you'. Passers-by threw coins into the blanket.

At 12.20 a Honda Gold Wing eased out of the traffic and came to a halt outside a public house which bore the name Crown and Sceptre in gold signwriting on a green fascia. The rider, a motorcycle courier wearing blue leathers and full-face helmet, leaned the Wing on to its kick-stand, checked his watch and began to take a keen interest in the three lanes of slow-moving vehicles.

A tourist bus with bronzed observation windows momentarily obscured the view of a white Sherpa van carrying the consignment of Colombian cocaine to Bow Street Magistrates Court where it was to be produced as Exhibit A for the prosecution in the Snow Man committal.

'Look at that!' Tony Rowley snorted, working the steering-wheel so that the sports saloon jinked behind the bus like a ferret on the scent. 'Will you look at that!' He gestured through the windscreen at the cliff of sun-dimmed glass as the rear of the bus towered over the Cosworth. 'Why do they have to bring 'em south of the river, snarling up the traffic?' He shot a sideways glance at the winter-bleak landscape of Clapham Common just to check that some miracle had not transformed the district into a tourist mecca overnight and then said, 'It's not as if there's anything to see down here, for Christ's sake.'

Beside him in the passenger seat Walker said, 'Mean street tours, we've got the same thing. Truck the schmucks to Harlem, show 'em how the muggers live on their days off.'

The Ford's skittish race-tuned engine was beginning to protest at the snail's pace when Rowley saw an opening and gunned the motor through to pass the coach and slip back into the covert escort as they swung north crossing Lavender Hill and headed for the river. There were six cars in the block, counting the Ford which was designated the command vehicle, all unremarkable vehicles drawn from the assortment of cars acquired for NEL operations. A silver Toyota Space Cruiser and a black VW Siroco were out in front of the Sherpa, with a yellow Datsun, a blue Cavalier and a brown Renault bunched behind the unmarked white police van. Each vehicle, scarred from earlier dogfights with the traffic, carried a complement of NEL detectives, casually attired in leather jackets, jeans and ankle boots, the working dress of the Drug Squad. In all, Rowley had a total of a dozen ruffians to call on should the need arise, and they talked to each other in laconic asides over the car-to-car cleared through MP on Channel Three. The cars held a bumper to bumper formation with the precision of the Red Arrows.

Rowley slipped the Cosworth into the hang-back slot and reported that he had regained position. The clutch of unmarked cars swept into the hinterland of Battersea on a route calculated to avoid the worst of the congestion which daily paralysed the metropolis.

Inside the car, Walker said, 'I did the sights myself last night, remember? First I had to go running way over to the railroad station, where was that, Paddington, give Mo Deegan his final brush down. Only place he'd agree to see me, where there'd be a few thousand people milling around the concourse so he could make out he's invisible.'

'Do I take it you didn't enjoy your night on the town?'

'Oh, that was just for starters,' Walker replied. 'After I get Deegan settled down, I hop into a cab and chase over to the other place where I have to bring my other prima donna out of orbit.'

'Covent Garden,' Rowley said, his eyes on the van ahead.

'That's the place,' Walker agreed. 'We meet in this bar called Stardust, got a ceiling like a planetarium only the house lights are so dim you can hardly see a hand in front of your face, and m'man is giving me a further ration of bullshit, complaining we're running interference because every move he makes he's got to shake a tail.' He gave Rowley a quizzical glance. 'You wouldn't know anything about these Twins you haven't told me, would you, Sarge?'

'This is a touchy town,' Rowley said as up ahead the Toyota fell back, leaving only the lead car, the black VW, out ahead of the Sherpa. 'Different rules. Be easy for a stranger to let his imagination run away with him.'

'That doesn't exactly answer my question, old buddy.'

'Just hang on to your hat,' Rowley said, remembering how the journey had begun at the Metropolitan Police Forensic Science Laboratory in Lambeth Road where, as the officer in the case, he had accepted two aluminium exhibit boxes packed with the product from a liaison officer whose only interest in a

£20,000,000 consignment of Lab-verified cocaine was Rowley's signature on his clipboard. 'Just hold on tight,' he continued, 'because when we get across the bridge up there you're going to get an eyeful of the Metropolitan Police in action.'

'What the hell's he playing at?'

'Learning to be a bin man, Guv?'

Commander Larry Drake glanced sharply at his companion but could find no guile in Donald Bailey's expression.

'There's got to be more to it.'

'Like what, Guv'nor?' Bailey asked innocently. 'Looks pretty straightforward to me.'

'I've got a feeling . . .'

'What kind of feeling?'

Again Drake shot a suspicious glance at his aide.

'The feeling you get on a big job like this, Don, when you know something's going to happen. Like pins and needles.'

'Maybe you've been cooped up in this tin can too long,' Bailey suggested. 'Could be the cramps next.'

They were crouching uncomfortably in the back of an SB surveillance vehicle, a little Honda florist's van which was parked unobtrusively in Brompton Road, Knightsbridge. Across the six-lane street within their limited field of vision a mammoth ten-wheeler Seddon Atkinson garbage truck, its dark blue flank

266

bearing the legend U-Haul Waste in white stencilled lettering, was standing in the mouth of Brompton Gardens, a crescent of town houses around a little park with brown trees and iron railings. Several men in overalls were busying themselves around the rear opening where hydraulic jaws chewed on the wagon's diet of plastic refuse sacks. Four men could be seen gathered around the rear of the truck. One of them was the SB target.

Drake stared at him, a puzzled frown creasing his forehead. What was the Yank up to? This time he didn't voice the question out loud, but he could feel the spring of anticipation winding up inside him.

As the moments ticked by and no obvious answer came to mind, the more Drake began to convince himself that something momentous was about to happen; that the innocuous-looking truck was some sort of Trojan Horse from which the assassin was about to unleash a terrorist attack. He could hardly contain himself.

Now the crew were manhandling a couple of galvanized rubbish bins on to the back of the wagon. Drake watched them with mounting puzzlement and was tempted to slip out of the van and stroll casually across the street for a closer look, but although he was wearing a borrowed donkey jacket which he fondly believed gave him a certain raffish, undercover appearance, he resisted the urge. He couldn't afford to blow their cover, not now. The timing had to be immaculate.

'You know we don't have to do any of this, Guv'nor,' Bailey broke into his thoughts. 'Plenty of DCs to take care of this and the team leaders'll give us a shout if it starts looking promising.'

Drake took this as a rebuke for his insistence on viewing the target for himself which had led him to join his surveillance teams on the ground. It was practically unheard-of for a Commander to sally forth in such cavalier fashion, but champing at the bit in his office at the Yard, reading the reams of messages coming in as his men plotted the target's movements around London, his patience had finally snapped and he had obliged Bailey to take him out for a look at his shadowy assassin.

The fact that he found the Yank humping garbage in a salubrious quarter of Knightsbridge had further fired his enthusiasm and he had immediately ordered saturation coverage of the area.

'There's a critical stage in every operation when you have to lead from the front,' Drake responded to Bailey's suggestion. 'First rule of man-management. Show the troops even the boss isn't afraid to get his hands dirty.'

Behind Drake's back, Bailey regarded the hunched figure of the SB Commander with amusement. Out loud he said, 'Lead from the front, I'll certainly try to remember that, Guv'nor.'

He was hugely impressed with this bogus terrorist who appeared to be playing the game up to the hilt. Why, the Yank had led them a merry dance around London and had even visited a suspected arms dealer and been clocked consorting with known criminals.

'Pound to a penny those mates of his are CRO,' Drake observed, his attention still riveted on the U-Haul.

'Want me to get the lads to run the smudges back to the Yard?' Bailey asked, referring to the surveillance photographs which charted the target's progress. 'See if we can ID those other faces? Not much prospect though, not with 'em in that fancy dress.'

'I'd give my right arm to know what he's up to,' Drake muttered as the crew heaved the two heavy-looking bins on to hooks on the back of the truck.

'We could always give him a pull on suss, see how he shapes.'

Drake spun around sharply, almost cricking his neck. 'Are you nuts? We show out now and we've lost him! That's not some Paddy out there, this is the genuine article, and I want him nicked bang to rights!' He stabbed the air with a forefinger. 'As of now I'm taking personal command of this operation. You just spread the word and when I give the order to hop to it, I want every man jack out there to jump!'

With no outward expression on his face, Bailey detached the handset from the UHF radio he had with him in the van, switched to secure Channel Six, the SB surveillance net, and issued the order.

CHAPTER 17

Grouped around the police van, the NEL motorcade swept over the blue and red arches of Battersea Bridge and hit a tangle of traffic heading up Beaufort Street towards Fulham Road. Rowley felt the first hint of butterflies in his stomach, reached down and confirmed the reassuring presence of the pump-action shotgun stashed under his seat. The detectives' conversation had been reduced to monosyllables against the background static of the police radio now left open between the cars.

'About two minutes to the off,' Rowley reported.

Walker watched the traffic ahead.

'Shotgun under the seat if we need it.'

But the New Yorker smiled, then reached down and withdrew the Glock automatic from inside the elastic gusset of his boot. Rowley raised an eyebrow, imagining Walker striding through Customs with the plastic pistol in its ankle holster.

'You took a risk, Vince.'

Walker shook his head. 'I'm with the DEA now, remember, the dirty tricks brigade. You

271

think I'd ride with The Bandit without a piece? No way.'

'If you have to use that thing, get rid of it,' Rowley said.

The escort moved rapidly up Fulham Road and swung into Brompton, jockeying for position on the crowded three lanes leading into Knightsbridge. Through a gap in the traffic Rowley caught sight of a blue refuse truck in the distance, tucked into a side-street on the left, and felt a twinge of anticipation.

Beside him Walker slammed the clip of seventeen rounds home, checked the safety and tucked the automatic into his belt. He looked up as Rowley announced, 'Here we go!' Already reaching for the radio handset.

Drake's head bobbed and weaved as he tried to fathom what was happening on the U-Haul, his view constantly interrupted by the stream of vehicles pouring down Brompton Road. The spicy aroma from the Indian restaurant outside which they were parked wafted in through the roof ventilator of the little van and the SB Cornmander was still intent on the big blue U-Haul when the DC up front called back through the partition, 'Yellow peril, Guv'nor!'

Bailey squirmed around in the confined space to take a look and spotted the traffic warden bearing down on them.

'If we don't shake a leg, we're going to get a

ticket,' he told Drake.

'Don't be ridiculous,' Drake said. 'Tell him to clear off. Doesn't he know who I am?'

'Er . . . no, Guv'nor . . . we're undercover, remember? You want me to hop out and tell him we're an SB surveillance unit?'

Drake's head swivelled. 'And blow our cover? Are you crazy?'

'Well, we're going to have to do something.' Bailey squinted at the approaching warden. 'He's got his book out! They're little Hitlers up here, Guv, ticket mad . . . ambulances, fire engines, hearses.'

Distracted by the irritation of how best to deflect the warden, Drake's attention had wandered. Now he shot a glance back across the road and immediately did a double take. The U-Haul truck was on the move.

Grabbing Bailey by the shoulder, he cried out, 'He's moving!' He began shaking the Superintendent's jacket in a state of agitation. 'Get on his tail! Go on, man . . . get after him. We lose him now, heads are going to roll!'

The garbage truck heaved its intimidating bulk across Brompton Road, straddling the two nearside lanes, causing drivers to brake and curse as they huddled right to squeeze past the lumbering wagon. Two of the overalled crewmen were standing on the back step either side of the galvanized rubbish bins which were swaying under the motion of the truck. Smoke belched from the exhaust stack alongside the cab as, with a grating of gears, the giant picked up a little speed. A bronze Jaguar XJ6 eased past the truck and regained the nearside, the orange rear indicators winking a left turn.

Outside the Crown and Sceptre on the corner of Montpelier Street, the bike courier in blue leathers, his features hidden inside his full face helmet, leaned against his Gold Wing, reached over and re-started the engine, then flipped open the lids of his panniers. He looked up Brompton Road and watched the progress of the approaching garbage truck.

The leading NEL unit, the black Sirocco, lengthened the distance in front of the Sherpa and moved to pass the U-Haul. As it overtook, the truck sidled further out, cutting off the van which was about to follow suit, and the men on the back step jerked pins from the hook shackles sending both heavy bins rolling off the back of the truck like depth charges. Spewing rubbish, the first bin caught the Sherpa a glancing blow and the driver swerved instinctively, hitting the second bin square on. The force of the impact sent the police van rearing into the air as it rode over the rolling can with a shriek of tortured metal. Sparks flew as the van canted upwards and skidded to an abrupt halt. Up ahead the refuse truck stopped, blocking the road and the two men on the rear step pulled their woollen caps down into ski masks, reached into the rear of the truck for their weapons and jumped down into the chaos of swerving, colliding cars.

Small wheels screaming through a desperate about turn, the little florist's van heeled over under hard acceleration and in a flash of panic the driver saw the gap he was aiming for suddenly close and with a reflex action stamped on the brakes. Thrown about in the back, Commander Drake and Don Bailey clutched at each other for support.

'You see that!' Bailey yelped in astonishment. Drake could see it, but he couldn't believe it. Up ahead of them the tableau froze, the garbage truck straddling all three lanes, rubbish from the ruptured bins strewn about in a blizzard of waste paper. Somehow a white van had mounted one of the bins and had lurched upwards at a drunken angle. Two hooded figures were running towards the van brandishing —

'Shooters! For Christ's sake, shooters!' Bailey was yelling, seeing it happen before his eyes.

Drake, his own mind thrown out of gear by the suddenness of the ambush, clung grimly to the Superintendent's shoulder, a puzzled frown creasing his face. 'What? What?' was all he could manage.

'Look! Shooters!'

'What?'

'They're doing that van!'

'What?' It was the only word left in Drake's vocabulary as the hooded figures ran to the rear of the Sherpa and with a brisk volley of gunfire shot out the lock and wrenched the rear doors open.

Eyes bulging behind his spectacles like a startled owl, Bailey wailed, 'Look . . . oh Christ, look, they've got . . .'

'What . . . what?' The parrot beside him squawked.

With a plummeting sensation in his bowels, the SB superintendent recognized the distinctive silhouette of the weapons, the gas jacket above the barrel, the crescent shape of the magazine; the terrorist's bride, the world's number one killing machine. He almost sobbed the word, 'Kalashnikovs!'

Even though he knew what to expect, the ambush still startled Tony Rowley and he felt the flash of adrenalin as he swerved on to the pavement. Out of the corner of his eye he saw the two hooded figures snatch the aluminium exhibit cases from the back of the van. Walker released his seat-belt and had the door open even before they had stopped. Rowley picked up the radio mike and gave the order: 'Target teams . . . hit 'em!'

The Toyota Space Cruiser sailed past, doors flying open, men leaping out.

In the florist's van Drake's bewilderment was total. Everything was happening too quickly, slam . . . slam . . . slam . . . too fast for him to make any sense out of it. Automatically he fell back on the only possibility, the sole reason for his elaborate stake-out. They were under terrorist attack!

He snatched the radio and in a voice pitched high with excitement squeaked, 'Sierra Bravo One . . . all units . . . all units . . . go, go go!'

Beside him, Don Bailey, still befuddled by the whirlwind of events, experienced the sensation of being catapulted into a nightmare where terrible things were happening and he was powerless to intervene. 'Christ Almighty,' was all he could mutter. 'I don't believe this . . . not in Knightsbridge.'

On cue, a third man, overalled and masked, swung down from the cab of the stationary U-Haul holding an AK 47 in his right hand. With an economy of movement he covered the other two gunmen as they lugged the aluminium cases to the waiting motorcycle and loaded them into the Wing's open panniers. The bike courier in the blue leathers swung into the saddle, righted the heavy machine and retracted the stand with the toe of his boot.

A short distance away, the turn indicators on the bronze Jaguar stopped winking as the car pulled smoothly from the kerb into the oasis of clear street ahead of the blocking truck. The sequence went like the tick of a stopwatch, all carefully rehearsed. A twenty-second surgical operation under the anesthetic of surprise, but then as the last second ticked on, the scene unfroze and all hell broke loose.

The black Sirocco, reversing back like a bullet, tyres smoking, doors flung open, sent NFL detectives leaping into the fray. Trapped behind the U-Haul, the Space Cruiser disgorged its occupants. The yellow Datsun and the brown Renault, shunted in the tail-back, were locked together, headlamps and rear lights shattered, doors flying open as the detectives aboard jumped out. A dozen men hit the street simultaneously, legs pumping, sprinting through the rubbish strewn across Brompton Road. In haste, some had grabbed truncheons and the armed back-up, one officer to each car, led the charge, drawing short-barrelled .38 revolvers from concealed holsters.

In the same instant the black taxi containing one SB surveillance team shot out of Montpelier Street and smacked into the Jaguar, broadside on, caving in the front passenger's door. Both vehicles slewed to a halt in a shower of wreckage. Four SB men piled out of the taxi and started running towards the

masked trio. On the pavement, the businessman in the sheepskin coat slammed the hood
of the red Golf and leaped in behind the wheel,
gunning the engine. The two mechanics at the
breakdown van reached into the cab and came
out with Remington semi-automatic shotguns
in their hands.

The Gold Wing carrying the spoils of the
ambush moved off rapidly and was under full
throttle when it was clipped by the red Golf
streaking across the road. The big bike went
down, engine screaming, bucked its rider and
spun on its side, showering sparks, spewing
petrol, skidding across the tarmac, panniers
bursting open, flinging the aluminium cases
full of cocaine into the street.

At the news-stand, the man in the tweed
overcoat threw down his newspaper, the plastic button in his ear buzzing like a trapped
bee as he reached under his coat and pulled
out a .38, dropping into a shooter's crouch. But
even as the SB detective-inspector went into
action, one of the charging NEL team, a burly
DC with a red beard, clubbed him down
with his truncheon, then wheeled around to
be confronted by Father Christmas pointing a
shotgun at his head.

Exchanging his saxophone for a walkie-
talkie, the busker stepped back into a door-
way from which he could survey the mêlée in
the street and transformed himself into
the second SB team-leader as he broke into

the general patrol channel, raised MP on the air and called for urgent back-up.

Disbelief was all that registered on Larry Drake's face as he watched the scene unfold from the florist's van. The SB surveillance teams were slugging it out toe to toe with the NEL detectives, each believing the other to be the opposition.

Beside him, Don Bailey watched his men take a pasting and wondered dimly what the hell was going on, the picture confused by the people; people everywhere, the innocent caught up in the ambush, women screaming, dragging kids away, pedestrians running for cover, furious motorists trapped in a mighty tangle of traffic, horns blaring. Chaos prevailed.

'Oh Jesus . . . will you look at that . . .' Bailey wailed. 'We're getting a hammering out there!'

Before their eyes, the masked raiders, seemingly forgotten at the eye of the storm, seeing their escape route cut off retreated to the truck which belched smoke and rumbled into motion.

In the same instant Snow White jumped out of the wrecked Jaguar, a purple bruise from the impact spreading across his right temple. The concussion had a traumatic effect upon the Colombian. As he tried to make some sense out of the whirlwind he was caught up in, his mind snapped back to the streets of Medellin where shoot-outs with the policía were common place and the cartel's firepower inevitably won the day. Blanco was wearing a heavy leather coat buttoned to the throat, his cord trousers tucked into combat boots. He held a stubby Uzi machine-gun in his right hand, braced against his forearm, pointing upwards. His lips were pulled back in a sneer.

Blanco hit the street running. No gringo cops were going to double-cross him, not now the prize on which his reputation depended was lying there in the street. Boots pounded the tarmac as he ran for it, fearless in his single minded purpose. He might have made it but for the police dog-handler who emerged from the back of the breakdown van, spotted the running figure and immediately released his dog.

In a smooth blur of motion the German Shepherd out-stripped the Colombian, seized Blanco by the arm, jaws closing on the leather of the man's coat, knocking him over, sending the Uzi flying. Blanco went down, wrestling the animal, a red mist spreading behind his eyes. He felt the hot breath on his face, but he knew dogs, knew how to exploit their weaknesses. Show no fear. He snarled like a wolf, wrenched his arm free and lunged into the shaggy mane with both hands, finding the throat, pressing the thumbs into the windpipe, expending all his force in one mighty effort, the blood mist drawing a curtain over his vision. Oh yes, in the alleys of

Medellin he would kill a dog with his bare hands just for sport.

Rolling in the road, locked together, the thumbs squeezed relentlessly, the man's lips pulled back in a grin of triumph as he heard the death rattle and the thrashing dog went limp. Blanco tossed the animal aside and scrambled to gain his feet, snatch the prize. But the truck was on top of him, bearing down and the cleated soles of his boots couldn't find a purchase fast enough. The radiator loomed over him and a long scream escaped his lips as he stared into the tread pattern of the wheel the instant before it crushed him.

In an attempt to beat the blockade, the lumbering garbage truck swung across the median into the three lanes of opposing traffic and tried to bludgeon a way through. But the tangle of cars was too tight and within a hundred yards the truck was forced on to the footway, wedged against a shopfront. The masked men made the only move left open to them, abandoning the truck and running down Brompton Road towards a more viable sanctuary.

Watching them go, Drake raised his eyes beyond the fleeing figures to the ornate terracotta superstructure of the flagship of Knightsbridge, stark against the leaden sky. Instantly the SB Commander's forehead cleared and a smile lit up his face. That was it! The solution to the conundrum. Everything he had predicted was suddenly coming true. All this horseshit in the street was just a diversion, a sideshow to smokescreen the real target. Now it came crystal clear and he was consumed with self-congratulation.

He turned to the astonished Bailey and cried, 'You didn't believe it, did you? You didn't believe I could be right! Well, you'd better believe it now! See that? See that! They just hit Harrods!' A triumphant laugh gurgled in his throat.

'Put that on Broadway, you'd play to packed houses,' Walker exclaimed, standing in the open passenger door of the Cosworth, leaning on the roof, watching the mayhem down the street.

Rowley said, 'That's just act one. There's more to come.'

'Who are those guys anyway?'

'That's the cream of Special Branch getting their lights punched out.'

'Cops?'

'You could say that.'

'Looks like they're giving your boys a hard time.'

'They've got thick skulls, nothing they like better'n a punch-up. They'll be all right.'

'Why do I get the feeling you knew this was going to happen?'

Rowley shrugged. 'Why do I get the feeling you knew your country cousin was going into battle with an AK?'

'I said to him baseball bats, right? Only he just naturally had to go for an Oscar.'

'They start using those weapons, we could really take casualties.'

'So what d'you want me to do, huh? Go down there and blow the whistle?'

The two detectives turned at the wail of approaching sirens.

'Here comes the cavalry,' Rowley said.

CHAPTER 18

'I never saw anything like it,' Bailey told Andy Barnes, awe in his voice. 'There we were playing the pantomime which was working out a treat and really getting that soft berk going when all hell broke loose. Those jokers come leaping out of the garbage truck with assault rifles, and just as we made our move a bunch of blokes came rowing in from nowhere and started hammering seven bells out of my lads.'

'That was my bunch of blokes,' Barnes said ruefully. 'I told you we got a whisper the Snow Man exhibit was going to get hijacked on the way to court. They naturally assumed your heavy mob was the enemy.'

'Drake really went ape,' Bailey said. 'Then bugger me if these lunatics with the Beirut shooters didn't leg it straight into Harrods. It had to be Harrods, for God's sake. That's like sacrilege! Now we've got a siege slap in the middle of Knightsbridge.'

The two Detective-Superintendents were at a second-floor window of the colonnaded Barclays Bank on the corner of Hans Road, a side-street which ran down the flank of Harrods from Brompton Road. They were looking down across the narrow street to a set of brass-trimmed swing doors under a scalloped sage-green awning bearing the store logo. Sign-written in gold on the glass doors was the numeral 6.

The bank had been hastily evacuated and commandeered to serve as a police command post and blue plastic screens mounted on scaffolding had been erected across the mouth of Hans Road, throwing an ominous shadow down the cleared and deserted side-street.

The two squad chiefs were wearing Kevlar and nylon body armour with ceramic breast plates over their street clothes.

'Jesus wept, Andy,' Bailey continued, 'those jokers vanished through those doors down there and we came belting up in hot pursuit, only there was nobody going to put a nose inside and see what an AK 47 could do, so the old sphincters were twitching like one o'clock, except for loony Larry of course, who was capering around telling everybody how his Snuffbox fairytale had just come true. We were hollering at MP for back-up when this fellow came trotting around the corner, one of the Harrods doormen, and told us the guys with the guns grabbed hostages and are holed up in the Lovely Legs Boutique. I mean, I was practically banging my head against the wall because I knew I'd got to be dreaming.'

Barnes peered down at the tranquil scene, equally unable to envisage the bizarre sequence of events. He had raced out from the Yard the moment he learned his men had been ambushed and had found Brompton Road ablaze with flashing blue lights. The first police response teams were already there, the blue berets of PT 17 armed with Ruger sniper rifles and Heckler and Koch semi-automatics taking over from the bloodied detectives and the AFOs from Division, who were crouching in doorways and behind police vehicles, their revolvers trained on the famous marble and mahogany display windows of the store as though they feared the mannequins might run amok.

'Drake can't be serious, Don,' Barnes said reasonably. 'The story I'm getting from my people is that this was just a straightforward blagging and we'd've nobbled 'em if you lot hadn't muscled in on the act.' He saw the flare of resentment on Bailey's face and said, 'It wasn't your fault, just a monumental cock-up we're going to have to sort out when this is over. But the fact remains, these characters aren't terrorists, they're just run-of-the-mill villains. Surely to God even Drake can see that?'

'Are you kidding, Andy?' Bailey said. 'He's got this assassin fixation — you know, the thing we talked about? The thing we set up! Only now it's real, the last piece just dropped into the jigsaw, now he can see the target.'

'Harrods?'

Bailey nodded.

'But that's a bunch of villains you've got in there, Don . . . Jesus, I'd better talk some sense into him before this thing gets completely out of hand.'

'Save your breath,' Bailey said despairingly. 'It already has. You know what he's gone and done, this precious leader of ours? He's been on the horn to Ashworth, his mate over at Queen Anne's Gate, who buys the story and gives Number Ten a bell so he can get the Brownie points. Are you getting the picture?'

'Don't tell me,' Barnes groaned.

'So the PM, God bless her, gets her knickers in a right twist at the very idea some sheep's-eyes eater is going to perpetrate an outrage on the streets of London, and she pulls the rip-cord yelling true blue murder. And you know what our lords and masters do then?'

'Don't tell me,' Barnes groaned again. 'I don't think I want to know.'

'They've only opened up COBRA. So what we now have here is a full-blown terrorist incident.'

'Je-sus!'

'Yeah,' Bailey sighed, all the colour draining from his face. 'I tell you something for nothing, Andy. I don't know how this happened and I don't want to know. All I'd like to know is if your lad with the bright ideas has got any more of these purlers tucked up his sleeve.'

Moving cautiously in his body armour and Nato helmet, Detective-Sergeant Tony Rowley picked his way through the gloomy ground floor of Harrods to reach CP 1, the forward command post. No sooner had the store been evacuated than the power supply had been cut, and in the semi-darkness which now prevailed shadowy figures were moving about as specialist police groups in the same bulky garb set up their siege equipment.

Thanks to the efficiency of the store's security system which isolated each section, the gunmen had been pinned down in the Lovely Legs Boutique and technicians were now installing eavesdropping gear and establishing secure communications between the tactics adviser, negotiators and snipers. The blue berets had arrived in force, settling into their routine with an array of weapons including red-eye laser sights and CS gas shells. Screens and lights were being lugged into place and a first aid team had set up inside a display island festooned with Gucci handbags.

Rowley moved carefully through the throng, making for the negotiator's position behind a counter to the left of the barricaded archway where the first line of snipers were in position like a scene from the wartime trenches.

The negotiator was from the Anti-Terrorist Branch, a detective-inspector in shirtsleeves, wearing a telephonist's headset plugged into an open briefcase containing the portable communications pack which was patched into both the comms net and the store's internal telephone system. Inside the lid of the case there was a traffic-light panel of red, amber and green lights through which the incident commander could silently signal the degree of psychological pressure he wished to be exerted at any given moment during the cat-and-mouse game of the siege.

Rowley knew the negotiator reasonably well and struck up a murmured conversation. At the DI's invitation he put his eye to the starlight scope, let his vision adjust to the shimmering image, and took his first peek into the stronghold. Another huddled, whispered conversation followed and then Rowley retraced his steps to where Vince Walker was waiting for him, leaning against one of the pale marble columns trimmed with gold. The classic pillars, the cool bland marble and the burnished brass on the counters put the New Yorker in mind of old-world patronage. 'Swanky joint,' he remarked as Rowley returned. 'Sure ain't no five-and-dime.' He inclined his head in the direction from which the DS had come. 'They got the whole shooting match up there?'

'Yeah,' Rowley said. 'SB have sanitized the area, and they've moved up enough firepower to start a small war.' He eased the weight of the flak jacket.

'So what's the story?'

'They've got hostages, shoppers and staff, got 'em holed up inside the cashpoint island, that's the stronghold. They're lying low, using the hostages as a shield.'

Walker thought about it for a moment and then asked 'What's COBRA?'

Rowley said, 'COBRA? Cobra's the balls-buster. Cabinet Office Briefing Room. It's where the Government get their heads together to lock horns with terrorists.' He took off his blue helmet and held it by the strap. 'Basically there's one procedure, one plan for winkling out armed besieged criminals, and that's to surround 'em, isolate 'em and then keep on talking, talking, talking, until they get so bored they give 'emselves up. Only if it's political, if it's terrorists, the drill's the same except the Government's got the whip hand. At any stage some genius from the Home Office can override the police commander.'

Walker looked astonished. 'They opened up a can of worms for this?'

'They think they've got terrorists in there, an active service unit. They look like terrorists, they act like terrorists, they're armed like terrorists, so they've naturally jumped to that conclusion. Besides, Harrods is a prime target. Any anarchist with a bomb wants to blow up Harrods, get lots of exposure on TV. It's only natural they should believe they've got pukka terrorists holed up in there.'

The New York detective whistled softly. 'Man, that's crazy.'

'You want to tell them what they've really got?' Rowley lowered his voice. 'You want to tell 'em all they've got is a DEA stooge and a couple of nutters?' He watched Walker's face. 'You want to tell 'em this was all a put-up job and all they were supposed to do was rip off twenty million in product which was taking a ride to court at the time? You want to explain how a couple of fine upstanding law enforcement officers happen to know all about this conspiracy to commit a felony?'

Walker said, 'You've got a point.'

Rowley shook his head. 'Here's something else to consider. What if your buddy in there sticks his nose out of the hole and finds himself staring into the muzzles of more guns than he ever saw in his life?'

'That Bandit's got balls like rocks,' Walker said. 'Just loves a challenge.'

'What if he thinks he could end up dead meat and says to himself, "Sod this for a game of soldiers," and comes out of there with his hands high and tells 'em, "Fellows, this must be a mistake, I'm on your side. Ask my partner there, Detective Vincent Walker of the NYPD." '

Poker-faced, Walker said, 'Why me? Can't help you, I'm just a tourist passing by, dropped in to see what all the fuss was about. Never seen this guy before in my life.' Then he said, 'Only that'll never happen. The Bandit thinks he's the Sundance Kid, remember?'

'Think he'll go the distance?'

'You can count on it.'

Commander Larry Drake celebrated victory over his Anti-Terrorist Squad opposite number by slipping the tabard on which was stencilled INCIDENT COMMANDER over his flak jacket, then striding purposefully around Harrods inspecting his troops just to make sure everybody got the message.

No sooner had the alarm sounded than SO 13 came charging out from the Yard determined to ride roughshod over the assortment of police units containing the scene. It was customary at times like this for SB to melt away in favour of the high-profile anti-terrorist branch who always put on a grandstand show and hogged the TV news bulletins. But this time as the prima donnas swaggered in, they ran up against the stubborn might of the SB Commander, already on the scene, refusing to bow the knee. Drake had no intention of surrendering Snuffbox to a bunch of Boy Scouts and he treated the advance guard of SO 13 to a tongue-lashing, refusing point blank to relinquish control.

Now he strode imperiously around inside his cordon sanitaire awaiting the arrival of Ashworth and his entourage. Word had it that the

PM herself was on the end of an open 'phone line eager for news of every development and the international press corps was already gathering outside ready to wing the drama to the world.

Bathed in the glory soon to be his for cornering the latest of terrorism's mercenaries against the backdrop of Harrods itself, Drake walked among his men with the stiff-legged strut of a gladiator, offering a word of advice here, a little encouragement there. At last he was in his element, and in the rehearsal for the moment when he would step out to front the battery of TV cameras he began to adopt a gruff he-man voice, so low and gravelly that the men to whom he spoke were obliged to incline their heads to catch his curiously strangled words.

CHAPTER 19

Oak panelling swept back from an Adam fireplace beside which stood a set of antique brass fire-irons. The mahogany table was polished to a rich lustre around which balloon-back chairs added a touch of old world charm. It was in this room that the luminaries of the banking world gathered to conduct their business, but today as the yellow winter light seeped feebly through the tall windows, the elegant boardroom was obliged to suffer the indignity of a far less civilized meeting as, cursing and squabbling, the police brass huddled over plans of the ground floor of London's most famous store and endeavoured to come up with some tactical ploy which would break the deadlock in the siege.

Twenty men were crammed into the room, some shirt-sleeved, others sweating under the bulk of body armour, each anxious to outshine the others as the siege of Harrods dragged into its third hour. Voices rose and fell as the tide of bright ideas ebbed and flowed, competing with the monotonous drone from a speaker placed in the centre of the table which relayed the desultory conversation between the tactical teams, the negotiator and the hostage-takers.

Two schools of thought dominated the discussion. The hawks were all for storming the stronghold under a hail of gas and covering fire. Jump in from both sides with a fast assault which would catch the bastards off guard. The doves argued equally forcefully for the waiting game, wear the terrorists down by reasonable negotiation, give the Stockholm Syndrome time to work until finally, united by a common bond, the hostages and their captors would link arms and walk out peacefully. In the crush at the foot of the table, Don Bailey muttered in disbelief, 'Tell me it's a bad dream.'

'It's a bad dream,' Andy Barnes told him.

'Then why can't I wake up?'

'Because Superman up there won't let you, he's enjoying himself too much.'

Bailey groaned. 'You locate your man yet, make any sense out of this fiasco?'

'Cast of thousands out there, Don. Be like looking for a needle in a haystack. You know what I see? I see the great mysterious hand of coincidence behind this. Like, how come your soldiers of the Jihad took it into their heads to rip off the Snow Man product before they hit Harrods? Shoot off with twenty million in uncut cocaine on that motorbike which just happened to get side-swiped by one of your tearaways.' He shook his head. 'Then

296

there's your target, this mysterious Yank no-body can put a name to and the dago dog-wres-tler who gets run down by the truck. Makes you think, doesn't it?'

Bailey gave him a haunted look as the voices around them swelled to a new crescendo, then abated as Drake rapped vigorously on the table to call his crisis management team to order.

Another meeting was taking place nearby as Peter Ashworth conferred with his aides in the chairman's office. The Junior Minister had arrived with an entourage of civil servants from F4, the counter-terrorism section at the Home Office, and had slipped inside out of sight of the TV cameras. Now, like their police counterparts, they weighed the options, only the agenda was much more subtle.

When they reached a consensus Ashworth summoned the SB Commander. As he joined them, Drake ached to escape his own chains and float up to this arcane level. He looked around. Apart from F4, The Box was repre-sented and a couple of athletic-looking char-acters in nondescript suits which smacked of a surrogate uniform needed no introduction. Open in front of them were briefcases disport-ing code books, portable phones and lap-top computers. How he longed to be part of their exclusive world.

Ashworth rose lazily from the group, taking

all the time in the world, and placed a paternal hand on Drake's shoulder. 'You're doing a fine job here, Larry.' There were nods and smiles from the group and Drake found himself basking in their praise. Ashworth said, 'That's not just me saying that, Larry. I was just talking to the lady on the phone, the Lady herself, Larry.' His eyes shone. 'And you know what she said? She said make sure the police get the credit for this, she said the police don't get enough kudos for the good work they do and this is the moment to put that right. So you're the man of the moment.' There were smiles and nods of agreement and Drake felt himself grow in stature as Ashworth guided him to one side, out of earshot, leaned forward, his mouth close to Drake's ear and whispered, 'Get them out of there!'

'What?' Drake was stunned.

'Get those anarchists out of there, Larry, right now!'

'But . . . but . . .' Drake stammered. Had he somehow misunderstood, was this some kind of joke? 'How . . . how am I supposed to do that?'

'Do your job, Larry,' Ashworth snapped. 'God's sake, man, negotiate, do whatever it is you have to do. Surely they've got some demands we can meet on the quiet? Pay 'em off, give 'em whatever they want. Just get 'em out of there!'

Drake still couldn't believe his ears. He began to stammer. 'But Peter . . . Peter . . . these are . . . these are terrorists. The Snuffbox threat . . . killer . . . the assassin.'

'I know all that,' Ashworth said. 'What d'you think we've been talking about in here?' His hand tightened on Drake's shoulder. 'Just do what you're told, man.'

'But . . . but . . . what about the Lady? What will she . . . what will she think if they walk out scot free? The Government never bows to terrorists.'

Ashworth barked a short laugh. 'That's just sabre-rattling.' He sighed at Drake's apparent naïvety. 'Grow up, Larry, this isn't some poxy embassy. I've got guiding light on this: do whatever you have to do, only get 'em out of there!'

The SB Commander looked so crestfallen that Ashworth was obliged to shake him roughly. 'Snap out of it, old man, you've done your bit. Time to take a back seat, let someone else clean up the mess. COBRA'll take over, our friends from The Box insist on it. The proper form, you know how it goes?' He took a paper from his pocket. 'It's official, all you have to do is sign this and when you've flushed 'em out, we'll turn the whole thing over to Mr Brown.'

'And if I don't?' Drake muttered.

Ashworth shook his head. 'Larry . . . Larry . . . that would not be wise. Not wise at all.'

Drake's shoulders sagged as the prospect of

a mention in the Honours List faded and the sweet taste of his Snuffbox triumph turned to aloe in his mouth.

The tactics adviser stood in front of the large body of uniformed and CID men gathered in the makeshift briefing area. He wore a blue pullover with the rank insignia of a chief inspector on the epaulettes and carried himself with the ramrod bearing which befitted a senior instructor from PT 17 who had been known to test the mettle of recruits by rolling a live grenade down the classroom aisle.

'Gentlemen,' he informed his audience, 'there's not just three shooters holed up in there, there's four. You can't see old Mikhail, but he's the ideal killer and I know him like my brother. Mikhail Timofeevich Kalashnikov, the Siberian farm boy who invented the world's most efficient killing machine, the Avtomat Kalashnikov, the AK 47 . . .'

At the back of the crowd, Tony Rowley nudged his partner as the briefing went on and indicated a youthful figure who arrived with a bevy of aides and a perplexed expression on his face.

'That's the SB Commander I was telling you about,' Rowley murmured.

'Looks kind of green to me,' Vince Walker observed.

'Yeah,' Rowley agreed. 'Looks like he's lost his bottle.'

Drake appeared deflated, certainly not the bold prince of the Met Rowley recalled from the early days of the Snow Man bust. He had imagined the SB Commander as the same cocky self-assured wheeler-dealer and was astonished to see the man looking so crest-fallen.

The cause of Drake's chagrin soon became apparent, for no sooner had the firearms tac-tician concluded his briefing than the SB chief took the stand. He seemed to be having diffi-culty clearing his throat. When he spoke, a hush fell over the assembled ranks. In a dead voice Drake told them that the hostage-takers were to be turned loose. Then he added the unthinkable: they were to be allowed to keep their hostages and their weapons.

When the SB Commander stopped speaking his voice faded into stunned silence. The Met surrendering to terrorism . . . it didn't bear thinking about!

'Drake's flipped.'

'Hoist with his own petard.'

'Come again?' Bailey shot Barnes an uncom-prehending glance.

'Figure of speech,' Barnes said.

'Anyway, he's shot down in flames.' The SB Superintendent continued to describe his lat-est encounter with the Incident Commander.

'And he's got this cringing note in his voice like somebody just chopped him off at the knees.'

'Now who could do a thing like that, I wonder? One of those cool snakes from Queen Anne's Gate, d'you think?'

'I said to him,' Bailey said, 'I mean, he looked so po-faced I couldn't help jerking him off, so I put this disbelieving look on to my face and I said to him, "Guv'nor, remember the Office of Constable, the Home Office don't have any executive authority, why don't you tell 'em to get stuffed?" And he just looked at me as though I'd trodden in something.'

'None of the authority, but all the power,' Barnes said.

'If he did that, he'd be kissing his QPM goodbye.'

'Be better than squirming on the hook,' Bailey said smugly. 'If he gets hold of the Old Man and tries to pass the buck, there's no way the Commissioner's going to throw in the towel to a bunch of gun-toting nutters, so his pal at the Home Office'd get one right in the eye. And if Drake does as he's told and people do get hurt, then the Old Man's going to nail his hide out in the noonday sun.'

Bailey raised his shoulders and let them fall. The two Superintendents were back in the CP overlooking Harrods from the second floor of the bank.

'If he's got bitten by COBRA, maybe

they've dreamed up a master plan,' Barnes reflected.

'Yeah? I reckon Mr Brown's itchy finger is on the trigger already.'

Barnes pointed down into the street. 'Wish 'em luck, then, Don. Here they go, right now.'

CHAPTER 20

Dragon lights flared, casting stark black shadows. Inside Harrods the ground-floor hostage scene was suddenly, vividly illuminated. The blaze of light flooded the marble hall, winking off the strutting mannequins, the spangled tights and lacy garter belts of the Lovely Legs Boutique.

In the street outside, a green Transit minibus was parked in the sanitized zone in Hans Road. The doors of the minibus were open and PT 17 snipers concealed on the upper floors and rooftops of the surrounding buildings impotently ranged their weapons on the empty Transit despite strict orders to hold their fire.

The bank of glass doors was wedged open, as were the inner doors beyond the threshold. The area was bathed in the white glare.

Faintly, way off, the distinctive rotor thud of a large twin-engined helicopter could be heard as a Bell Triple-Two from TO 26, the Met's Air Support Unit out at Lippetts Hill, began to orbit the capital at a discreet distance.

Suddenly the scene came alive. On to the flootlit stage the three gunmen, faces hidden behind their ski masks, edged cautiously out of the store, hostages bunched tightly around them as they gyrated slowly, AKs at the ready, moving towards the minibus.

The hostages were six women and two men; three obviously store staff, the others shoppers who had happened to be in the wrong place at the wrong time. Their expressions were glazed, sleepwalking.

Beyond the inner cordon, Tony Rowley came back, a little breathless under the bulk of his flak jacket, and told Vince Walker in a whisper, 'I just got it from the negotiator. They turned down the minibus, think it's bugged, booby-trapped or something. They're going for the truck!'

Walker said, 'The truck! Ah, that Bandit, going for the showdown in a garbage truck.'

'Makes sense,' Rowley said. 'You've got a battering ram with that thing, better'n a tank.'

Walker stared at the truck.

'If I was in their shoes, I'd run south of the river,' Rowley said. 'Get lost in the rat-runs. Dump the wagon, switch motors before we can get our act back together. Be dodgy, but it could be done.'

Staring at the big blue refuse wagon with U-Haul Waste on its blue flanks, Walker said, 'You thinking what I'm thinking?'

Rowley narrowed his eyes, gauging the distance, catching Walker's thoughts. Could they really make it? Or would they get cut down in a burst of automatic gunfire, risk blowing the whole operation? He gnawed his lip in concentration.

'Well?' The New York detective's eyes glittered as he threw down the gauntlet.

Rowley made his decision, shrugged out of the clumsy flak jacket and dropped it to the pavement. 'On the count of three,' he said, eyes still fixed on the truck.

The gunmen made the break suddenly. Circling the Transit, checking it out, AKs raised. Suddenly the clutch of hostages fragmented as they made their move dragging just two of the captives with them: a blue rinse in a ranch mink, middle-aged, petrified, one shoe missing; the other a cashier, a black girl without a topcoat, eyes glazed. The rest scattered, screaming. The blur of action created a diversion as the three hooded figures covered the last few yards to the U-Haul truck and in the confusion of the moment gained the cab.

Ready on the blindside.

'One . . .' Two of the bandits grabbed the woman in the fur, threw her bodily into the cab while the third man covered them.

'Two . . .' One and two climbed up and reached down to haul the black girl inside, a dead weight. The sentry raised his AK and jumped up behind them. The cab door began to close.

'Three . . .' Two figures on the blindside made the dash, sprinting, crouching low, and leaped on to the rear step as the engine growled into life, coughing diesel, belching black smoke.

The U-Haul lurched forward in a clumsy jerking motion as the gears engaged in a hasty crash. The truck heeled over in a tight turn, smashed through the shielding screens, carrying away the scaffolding poles. Blue plastic flapping around its snout, the mammoth brushed aside the abandoned news-stand and flower-seller's pitch, and burst out on to the street.

From the surrounding rooftops the blue berets tracked the target in the scopes of their sniper rifles, Drake's voice rasping like a hornet in the plastic earplugs of the command net: 'Hold your fire! Hold your fire!'

The lumbering truck hit Brompton Road, picking up speed. The sound of the helicopter overhead grew louder and over the police radio a calm disembodied voice broke in: 'All Sierra Bravo units from India 99. Blue box is mobile, heading west on Brompton.'

Moving faster now, the U-Haul careened down the clear stretch of tarmac, wheeled left into Fulham Road and then left again into Sydney Street, tyres screaming as it raced between the rows of terraced Georgian townhouses, black iron railings flashing by in a blur of motion. Rowley and Walker, clinging to the tailgate, exchanged glances.

Into Chelsea, past the chain-link fence of a school playground, the black streaked gold of St Luke's. The detectives clung to the handrail, the slipstream threatening to suck them off as they lurched into King's Road and almost immediately swerved into Oakley Street, sideswiping cars stopped at the junction. The truck rattled and shuddered and plunged on.

India 99 was sending hele-tele to the Central Command Complex at New Scotland Yard. Insulated from the outside world in the softly lit control room, the duty shift at the horseshoe consoles watched the TV beaming down from the orbiting helicopter and began to play the war game. Behind them a bevy of senior ranks standing in small groups watched the TV drama unfold from screen to screen.

No sooner had the target made a turn than a wide net cast to head them off was drawn tighter, following the rehearsed plan of an operational order called 'Fast Bowler'. All messages were now relayed on to a secure military radio net and coded 'Hammerhead'.

Arms folded, the command group watched from their electronic capsule, waiting for the moment to pick their ground.

On the radio channels the shift supervisor announced calmly: 'MP to all units, vicinity of Cheyne Walk, Pimlico Road, be advised, blue box is entering your sector. All units be advised, he's heading for the bridge.'

Up ahead the ornate salmon and white superstructure of the Albert Bridge came into view flanked by ochre gatehouses. Victorian lamp-posts marched across the slick of tarmac which straddled the Thames at Chelsea Reach.

The U-Haul hit the bridge without slackening speed, raced under the first pyramid of hawsers. On the far side a car transporter laden with new Volvos had been positioned, blocking the exit. The transporter with its load of gleaming cars floated into view. Even the weight of the garbage truck could not hope to smash through.

In the centre of the bridge the U-Haul skidded to a halt, wheels locked, tyres smoking. The jaws of the trap snapped shut.

The rotor chatter grew deafening as the big Bell swooped low, Night-Sun cutting a swathe through the gloaming, a shaft of blinding light sweeping over the ironwork of the bridge seeking the cab of the U-Haul.

In the same instant dragon lights blazed out from the roadblock, pinning the truck in a concentration of eyeball-searing light.

Protected from the disorientating dazzle by the bulk of the wagon, Rowley and Walker dropped silently from their perch and flattened themselves against the side of the truck where the shadow fell darkest.

Cautiously the hovering police helicopter edged around, inspecting the target, and then a disembodied voice greatly amplified boomed from the Sky-Shout slung under the belly of the machine: 'In the truck! You are surrounded by armed officers. Surrender your weapons! Come out slowly, lie on the road where you can be seen.'

Wordlessly exchanging glances, Rowley and Walker instinctively drew their weapons. Crouching in the shadow, the New York detective thumbed the safety and cranked a round into the breech of the Glock. Rowley stared in dismay at the snub-nosed .38 in his hand. The pistol looked so puny and he wished he could somehow exchange it for the man-stopper of his shotgun.

The echo of the ultimatum was still hanging on the air when the double crack of gunfire came from the distant barricade as marksmen fired two ferret rounds simultaneously. The finned CS gas missiles shattered the windscreen of the U-Haul and burst inside the cab in a cloud of stinging needles.

As if in slow motion, the right-hand cab door flew open and two masked figures tumbled out, trailing white plumes of gas. They hit the tarmac, assault rifles at the ready, mesmerized in the blaze of light.

Without warning, the guns at the road block opened up in a fusillade of automatic fire and, jerking like marionettes, the two figures spun around, hit repeatedly by high-calibre military rounds.

Simultaneously the third hooded figure dived from the left side of the cab, sprinting in a jinking zigzag, firing his Kalashnikov into the lights in short controlled bursts.

The guns ranged on the runner, the crack of sniper fire backfilled with the racket of the automatics.

At the U-Haul Walker muttered: 'This mother's mine . . .' and lunged from the safety of the shadow. Caught off guard, Rowley tried to grab him, yelled, 'No, Vince!' But his hand grabbed air.

Walker running, legs pumping, running through the hail of bullets which richocheted from the ironwork of the bridge. The hooded figure vaulted the chest-high parapet, silhouetted against the skyline for a second as he fired back, emptying his magazine in defiance of the gunners, then took the plunge to the dark waters of the Thames fifty feet below.

Rowley yelled again: 'Vince . . . no!' But Walker made the parapet unscathed, leaped to the rail and dived from sight.

A stillness fell over the kill zone. The helicopter stood off, its ferocious light moving back and forth. The two bodies sprawled on the span lay still, blood seeping into puddles on the greasy roadway. A woman was screaming hysterically from the cab of the garbage truck on which every light was still trained. Wisps of gas drifted down from the cab and stung Rowley's eyes. His vision began to blur and tears streamed down his cheeks. Through the blur he could just make out figures moving in front of the lights, approaching cautiously. Slowly, carefully, Rowley lowered himself to the ground and spreadeagled himself on the road, tossing his pistol away from his out-stretched hand. He pressed his cheek against the tarmac, gritted his teeth and listened to the hammering of his heart compete with the screaming from the cab above his head. As the first of the shadows approached he started to shout: 'Police officer, don't shoot! Police officer, don't shoot!' Yelling the same phrase over and over until his voice became a hoarse croak.

CHAPTER 21

'This fucker took some ordnance,' a lean man in anorak and jeans remarked, a touch of awe in his voice. 'Nice grouping, though. How about yours, Dave?'

A second man, stockier, a combat jacket over his tracksuit, was leaning over the other body, a 9mm Browning Hi-Power automatic hanging from his hand. 'Not bad either,' he replied, apparently satisfied with his examination. 'Ten rounds, upper thorax, through and through. Enough lead to fix the church roof.'

Despite their civilian clothes, both men were wearing black berets bearing the winged dagger emblem of the Special Air Service. A further half-dozen similarly garbed SAS troopers, SLRs cradled in their arms, were standing in a semi-circle around the bodies lying where they had fallen on the span of the Albert Bridge. The soldiers were exchanging professional opinions on the kills.

'Can we get some pictures?' the first one asked.

Don Bailey, his face pinched behind his spectacles, said, 'Long as you don't touch 'em, you can paint 'em in oils for all I care.'

He turned aside to take a call on the portable radio in his hand and then said, 'OK, your commander just handed back to us, so we're going to want statements off you lot, just for the record.'

At his side Andy Barnes was also looking down at the bodies. The drugs chief looked faintly puzzled as he considered the frailty of the human frame. The two Superintendents had arrived with the follow-up group from the Harrods incident and as the most senior police officers present had taken charge of the scene, preserving the continuity of evidence until COBRA handed back jurisdiction to the civil power once assured that the slaughter was complete. Now with a knot of assorted CID and uniformed men hanging around, they waited for a SOCO team to arrive and start work.

A pace behind them, standing with the others, Detective-Sergeant Tony Rowley stared at the bodies, knowing it but not yet fully believing it as Barnes took a thin pair of rubber gloves from his pocket and put them on. 'Might as well see what we've got here, Don,' he told the SB Superintendent 'See what your terrorists look like.'

Bailey turned around as the ambulance carried the catatonic yet physically uninjured hostages away with a soft whirr on the siren. When he looked back Barnes was on one knee beside the first corpse, peeling back the face mask. He moved to the second and repeated the performance. When he looked up his eyes met Rowley's. 'You recognize these characters, Tony?'

Rowley made no reply. They were the faces which had haunted him, slack-jawed, bulbous-eyed, tanned from lazy months in Spain.

'You ought to,' Barnes said, watching Rowley keenly as he straightened up and dusted the knees of his trousers.

Bailey was frowning, his gaze moving from one face to the other, comparing them with the compendium of SB targets recorded in his encyclopedic memory. They meant nothing to him.

'What d'you think, Don?' Barnes asked. 'Abu Nidhal? Black September? Soldiers of the Jihad?'

The SB chief thrust his hands into his coat pockets and shrugged.

'You know who these so-called terrorists really are?'

Bailey lifted his shoulders again, let them drop.

'What you've got here, old son,' Bailey said, 'is nothing more than a brace of cheapjack East End robbers.' He almost laughed at the irony. 'Mr Brown just executed the Pollard twins, isn't that right, Tony?'

He turned, curious to see how Rowley would react, but the DS had gone.

No sooner had the identity of the kills been confirmed than Rowley ran back across the bridge to where patrol cars were parked closing off the approach, their crews waving traffic away, allowing only emergency vehicles through. Roads were jammed in both directions.

The DS ran down the steps to Cadogan Pier, reached the water's edge and, shielding his eyes, scanned the tidal flow of Chelsea Reach. The old muddy river was running faster here, flotsam swirling in eddies around the pier supports. Close up, the choppy brown water chilled him, but it was apprehension which made Rowley shiver as he watched the big twin-engined Bell hovering low out on the river, rotor wash blowing up spray as the cone of the Night-Sun scoured the water.

Two Thames Division launches were circling around and a larger Port of London vessel was stationed upriver near the bobbing string of houseboats moored at the Chelsea Yacht and Boat Company's Old Ferry Wharf, beside the low outline of Battersea Bridge.

A kaleidoscope whirled images inside Rowley's head. Vince Walker, his face set, hurling himself into that crazy kamikaze dash for the parapet; The Twins lying dead in their own congealing gore up there on the bridge; Walker chasing the fleeing figure of The Bandit, diving from the span; the cold, numbing, inscrutable Thames swallowing both of them.

Rowley stared at the expanse of water running under the bridge, but the wily old river simply teased him, offering a plastic drum and a couple of waterlogged crates from its murky locker. Rowley was about to turn away when one of the police launches pulled out of the search pattern, wake churning under a surge of power, and headed for the pier where he was standing. As the boat drew near Rowley could make out the figure of the New York detective huddled in the stern and his heart lifted at once. Below his feet the current chuckled around the pilings.

The blue and white police launch drew alongside, and Walker jumped ashore as the coxswain in the work fatigues of the Thames Division gunned the engine and with a throaty roar headed back to rejoin the search.

'Vince!' Rowley was grinning as he grabbed the New Yorker's arm. 'I thought you were a goner for sure!'

Walker, in an orange police rummage suit which he had exchanged for his sodden clothing, his hair plastered to his head, returned the affectionate grip. 'Could've been . . . if your guys hadn't fished me out.' He shuddered. 'Jesus, it was cold in there.'

'That was a crazy stunt.'

'OK, crazy, yeah, I'll buy that.'

'You should've left him to the Commissioner's Navy.' Rowley waved at the police launch heading back out. 'If he's in there, they'll find him.'

Walker shook his head. 'Man, he's gone . . . that Bandit!' He took a deep breath, sighed and then said, 'Tony, I went over the edge in the red mist, auto-pilot all the way, went down and hit the water, and I went under. Next thing I knew, I came to and somebody's got me. There's a hand under my chin, a swimmer towing me, life-saving, powerful strokes. So I start to thrash around, see who the hell it is, only the grip tightens and he laughs in my ear and he says cool as hell: "Tell 'em they didn't get the Sundance Kid." That's what he said. That was The Bandit.'

'He'll never make it,' Rowley said. 'Don't matter how good he can swim, if he swallows so much as a mouthful of Old Father Thames, he's going to die of typhoid, beriberi and the black plague all rolled into one.'

Walker squinted. 'How'd it end up on the bridge?'

'The Twins got theirs,' Rowley replied flatly. 'There was massive firepower up there and there's nothing our friends with the winged dagger on their hats like better'n to put the enemy away for keeps. The minute The Twins decided to play soldiers they were done for.'

'Instant justice?' Walker was watching Rowley's face.

Commander Larry Drake had been unceremoniously recalled to the Yard. It irked the SB chief that he had been pulled off his own operation, the covert Snuffbox which had preoccupied him since that day when he had received the threat assessment from The Box. The glory of foiling so heinous an enemy of the state as the Snuffbox assassin had been snatched from his grasp at the eleventh hour, and so in peevish ill-humour he could hardly bring himself to be civil to Thomas McKenzie, the Deputy Commissioner, ensconced in his office and spoiling for a fight.

The gravel-voiced Scotsman represented the last vestige of the old guard at the Met with his silver hair and military moustache which bristled when he spoke. McKenzie's fiefdom included the growth industry of CIB, the Complaints and Discipline Branch, which he ruled with the iron hand of a martinet. But the Deputy's fearsome reputation cut no ice with the SB Commander, who felt secure in the belief that he could always count on political patronage to deflect the blunt instruments wielded by such dunderheads. Consequently he regarded McKenzie with haughty disdain.

McKenzie, the Commissioner's hatchet man, regarded Drake with equal distaste. He had no time for whizzkids with fancy ideas who tried to manipulate the system he had spent a lifetime defending from the opportunists who would emasculate the Met. Drake wouldn't have made sergeant in any force commanded by Thomas McKenzie.

Out of deference to the rank alone, the Deputy had decided to visit the charismatic Commander in his own domain rather than summon Drake to the Lubianka of the Complaints Investigation Bureau. McKenzie was a stickler for protocol.

'Let's get something straight. I take the greatest exception to this,' Drake began in his best fluted voice. 'I was engaged in an operation of vital significance to national security when I received your order to come back to the Yard. I need hardly remind you that the security of the Realm is my province.'

'Really,' McKenzie rasped, gimlet eyes fixed on Drake's face.

'Mine and certain Ministers of the Crown,' Drake continued loftily, 'whom I have no doubt will be similarly unimpressed by your attitude.'

'You think so?'

'Most certainly, and they have ways of making their displeasure known.'

McKenzie brushed aside the thinly veiled threat. 'This so-called operation, does it have a name?'

'Snuffbox,' Drake said. 'An assassination threat identified by The Box.'

'Would it surprise you to know that Box 500 know nothing about it?'

Drake smiled condescendingly. 'Don't be ridiculous.'

Eyes still riveted on Drake's face, McKenzie said, 'Just before I sent for you I had a call from a Deputy Director of MI5 wanting to know what the hell was going on. Snuffbox meant nothing to him.'

'It was need-to-know, naturally,' Drake replied, still confident.

'And need-to-know is why you brought half London to a standstill, shot up Harrods and generally caused mayhem on the streets of Knightsbridge?'

'I told you, it was an assassination threat,' Drake said. 'Not a tea-party.'

'You had a hard target, I presume?'

Drake's smile grew bleak. 'What do you take me for? Of course I had a hard target, an exact match of the Snuffbox profile.' A weary sigh escaped the SB Commander's lips as he turned to the computer terminal beside his desk. 'I'll prove it to you, if you insist, as your PV's current.'

'Please do.'

Drake booted the system with a flourish, the technocrat thwarting the Luddite. He entered his log-on and when time and date automatically popped up, the logic virus snoozing in the system awoke and instantly wiped the program. The screen went blank.

Blinking his confusion, Drake tapped the keys but could get nothing more than a livid

321

green hailstorm. He looked perplexed.

Across the desk the Deputy stroked his moustache.

'I don't understand,' Drake blurted, his fingers furiously hammering the keys. 'It was there, a perfect match.'

'MI5 tells me there never was any threat assessment called Snuffbox.'

'But I don't . . . I don't get it!'

'I think you do, Commander,' McKenzie said, the words sounding like the snap of a steel trap. 'This was just a figment of your overheated imagination, wasn't it?'

Flustered, Drake stared at the blizzard on the screen. He couldn't believe it. Somehow the secure system had been breached and his own creation torpedoed.

'You made it all up, didn't you, laddie?' McKenzie pushed him.

'No!' Drake shouted. 'No . . . look . . . look . . . talk to the INTCELL analyst at The Box, Anthea Gibson, she knows, she wrote the Snuffbox threat assessment. Yes, talk to Anthea . . . she'll confirm everything.'

McKenzie's thin lips curled and his moustache twitched at the mention of the name.

'Well, well,' he murmured softly, 'isn't that a coincidence.' He leaned forward. 'You know, you make me want to throw up. You give me that high-falutin' bullshit about security of the state, need-to-know, Snuffbox mumbo-jumbo. Well I tell you something now. My responsibility —' he tapped his chest — 'my responsibility is the reputation of the Metro-politan Police, a bounden statutory duty which I take very seriously indeed.'

'I don't have to take any of this,' Drake broke in.

'I think you do,' McKenzie purred. 'You said you know a Miss Anthea Gibson?'

Drake raised his eyes to the ceiling. 'I just told you, she's the INTCELL analyst who'll confirm the Snuffbox threat.'

'You know this lady well?'

'What?'

'Very well?'

'I already said —'

'Because I've got news for you.' McKenzie moved to the edge of his chair. 'I have received a very serious allegation about your conduct from a senior official of the Security Service.' His eyes were fixed on Drake's face. 'I put it to you that the purpose of your clandestine and quite improper visits to Curzon Street had nothing to do with national security. You went there to seduce the lady in question.'

Seduce! The quaint word hit Drake like a sledgehammer. The colour rose on his face. 'P . . . p . . . preposterous . . .' he began to stam-mer, but McKenzie leaned in to go for the jugular.

'Couldn't keep it in your trousers, could you, laddie? You were observed, *in flagrante de-licto!*'

Before he could stop himself the SB Commander blurted his outrage, 'Ridiculous! We were alone in her office, and besides . . .'

The death's head smile on McKenzie's face so stunned him that he wished he could have bitten out his tongue as it suddenly dawned upon him. He'd been set up!

The Deputy Commissioner's face was only inches from his own. 'Tell me, Commander,' the voice was a contented purr, 'just out of interest, are you going to be a prat all your life?'

CHAPTER 22

'Nothing's changed,' Vince Walker said, leaning on the bridge parapet where yellow chalk marked the bullet scars plotted by the scenes-of-crime team. 'Down in Colombia right now the leaf is coming off the fields under the guns. Next thing you know, it's paste and then it's snow, coming like a winter storm.'

An expression of disgust on his long face, the New Yorker hunched his shoulders under his sports coat, sinking his neck into the scarf around his neck. 'Doesn't matter where you are, you're looking for action, crack cocaine, that's the name of the game.'

Beside him, hands thrust into the pockets of his jacket, Tony Rowley followed the American's gaze down to the Thames glistening like pewter under the hazy winter sun. Behind the two detectives traffic streamed across the Albert Bridge heedless of the chalked-out kill zone. It was just another day.

'Well, we got a bonus,' Rowley said. 'We got Blanco.'

'The Bandit got Blanco,' Walker said, still staring down at the river. 'That was Mulholland's ace. Mulholland and The Bandit went for a hike together in the jungle, they always had their own game plan. We were so busy chasing around we couldn't see it was all a double act.'

'Deegan too?'

'Deegan? Deegan's a New York lawyer, the original chameleon. He set Blanco up for The Bandit, probably got a payoff from Uncle.'

'How would he do that?' Rowley asked, surprised.

'Played on his greed, got him hooked, then told him he couldn't trust a couple of street cops.'

Rowley's breath plumed on the crisp air. 'Well, we hung on to the Snow Man product and we struck a blow for justice.' He felt elated. Drawn back to the bridge, re-running the sequence in his mind, everything had clicked into place. The Twins were dead, judiciously executed by a firing squad. It had been the perfect setup. He'd evened the score, closed the circle. He could breathe again. All that remained of the nightmare was the badger stripe running through his hair and the memory of Cindy Miller's fate. Standing under the ornate ironwork of the Albert Bridge, Rowley smiled.

'Feeling good, huh, Sarge?' Walker said, turning to facc him, hooking his elbows on the parapet. 'A couple of scalps on your belt.'

'I was just thinking,' Rowley said, 'back at the Yard the brass is in a huddle over the morning papers working out how to handle the media. They're going to have to put it all down to a terrorist incident, it's the only way they can come out of it with their reputations intact. They're going to have to rewrite the script. And none of this had anything to do with justice.'

'Now you're getting the picture.' Walker scowled. 'Like The Bandit said, when it comes down to it, when you're between the rock and the hard place, all that matters is survival.' He fished in his pocket and took out the blue and gold shield of a New York detective, polished it on his lapel until the enamel gleamed. 'Survival of the street cop.'

Rowley leaned on the parapet, threw his head back and began to laugh. Dad Garratt's skipper, shedding the weight that had all but crushed the life out of him. He could see Dad looking down on him, lips curling in that cunning smile of his, a wry grin of congratulation. The sun broke through the haze and shone on his upturned face as the realization sank in. The student had graduated.

He pushed himself off from the bullet-scarred ironwork and grasped Walker's shoulder. 'Come on,' he said, 'it's over, let's get out of here.'

But the New York cop was still staring down into the river, reluctant to leave. 'We didn't change a thing,' he said, 'we just played a game.'

'Well, one thing's for certain,' Rowley said, 'your pal the Sundance Kid won't be playing any more. He's feeding the fishes.'

Walker looked at him with something approaching pity in his eyes. 'You want to bet?' he asked, poker-faced.